SHADOWED

Karen E. Olson

severn House

This first world edition published 2016
in Great Britain and the USA by
SEVERN HOUSE PUBLISHERS LTD of
19 Cedar Road, Sutton, Surrey, England, SM2 5DA.
Trade paperback edition first published
in Great Britain and the USA 2016 by
SEVERN HOUSE PUBLISHERS LTD

British Library Cataloguing in Publication Data

Olson, Karen E. author.
  Shadowed.
  1. Hackers–Quebec (Province)–Fiction. 2. Suspense
  fiction.
  I. Title
  813.6-dc23

ISBN-13: 978-0-7278-8599-9 (cased)
ISBN-13: 978-1-84751-701-2 (trade paper)
ISBN-13: 978-1-78010-762-2 (e-book)

Typeset by Palimpsest Book Production Ltd.,
Falkirk, Stirlingshire, Scotland.

ONE

He is looking for me.

I'm not afraid, but I'm uneasy. The messages are cryptic – half in French, half in English – asking to meet, making it sound almost like a date.

Almost.

He doesn't know where I am, doesn't know that I'm online and have seen him there. I'm shrouded by several different identities, by a VPN that keeps my IP address at bay. These are not foolproof, though. Not when it comes to him. If he suspects I'm lurking, if he put some effort into it, he likely could find me.

I could stop going to the site and end it now. Yet every day I scan the conversations, looking for his name, looking for that day's message.

I am doing just that, along with my morning ritual of a cup of coffee and slice of toast, when I spot it, the phrase we'd devised to identify ourselves to each other.

'Le soleil brille aujourd'hui,' I read. *The sun is shining today.* The French is more familiar now that I'm using it every day, even if it's Québécois and not Parisian.

After that, the link to the URL where we could chat privately.

Nothing more.

I wonder for a moment where he is, if the sun really is shining where he is. Here, I see nothing but gray, hear the tap-tap-tap of the rain against the window.

I take a drink of coffee, a bite of toast.

He knows who I am. I'd like to say he's a friend; he's helped me in the past. I have trusted him more than I've ever trusted anyone.

I know him only as Tracker.

I am curious, more than I should be. My fingers itch to respond.

Instead, I pick up my coffee mug and plate and get up from the table. The house has an open layout – a dining area between the living room and kitchen – and it only takes me a few strides before I stick my plate in the sink. I turn and lean against the counter, cupping the coffee mug in my hands.

The wood stove sits cold in the corner across the room, unnecessary now that summer has finally arrived, but very necessary in the dead of winter when the unyielding snow and frigid temperatures wrap themselves around the house.

When I first looked at the house a little over a year ago, I wondered if it wasn't just a little too brown. Wood paneling, a wooden built-in cabinet on the wall that backs up against the staircase that leads to the bedrooms and bathroom upstairs. A beige sofa and a wooden rocking chair. Wide hardwood flooring and a wood table and chairs. But the longer I live here, the cozier it feels, and now I wouldn't change a thing. I've added dashes of color: a locally hand-woven red and gold rug, red and orange ceramic mugs and bowls on the cabinet shelves. And then there are my paintings, which splash the reds and oranges and pinks of the island's sunsets and sunrises across the walls.

I am comfortable here, settled, on Ile-aux-Coudres. The island is small – smaller than Block Island, my previous home – in the middle of the St Lawrence River in Quebec's Charlevoix region, and has two roads: one that circles the island for sixteen miles and one that cuts through it. The mainland is close, two miles, merely a fifteen-minute ferry ride.

I've gleaned some trivia tidbits about the island: how it was discovered by Jacques Cartier in 1535, who named it after the hazelnut trees, and how seamen would stop here to bury people who'd died during voyages. Coastal shipping was a big business at one time, but that gave way to trucking, and now the economy relies on tourism and the island's reputation as a summer resort.

I remind myself that I'm not doing bike tours here, like I did when I lived on Block Island off the coast of Rhode Island, so I don't need to know these small facts, but those years seem to have piqued a curiosity in me that I never knew I had.

I do spend a lot of time on my bike, discovering the island's gems. I frequently visit the two small, processional chapels perched at the side of the road: Saint-Pierre and Saint-Isidore. Their stark interiors are smaller than my kitchen, but there is a peacefulness that I find soothing. I am not a religious person, but I have discovered a spirituality here.

I've learned how to make my own bread, using the flour that's milled at Les Moulins down the road. Kneading the dough is therapeutic, back and forth until it's smooth as stone. As smooth as the stones that Odette uses at the spa at La Roche Pleureuse. I am addicted to them, to the quiet peace that envelops me while she works her magic. Sometimes when she's done I have to remind myself who I am, because I am too relaxed and I worry that I won't answer to the name I've adopted.

I've been Tina Adler and Amelie Renaud and Nicole Jones and now I'm Susan McQueen.

I have painted the chapels and Saint Louis Church and the windmill, filling my canvases with the broad brushstrokes that distinguish my style from other artists here, and the galleries that sell my work find that they are popular among the tourists.

One other thing that is curious: I am not afraid to go to the mainland here, as I was before. It is almost as though stepping off that other island set me free, but I know better than that. Yet I revel in my new life, eager to discover this new place, taking my bike across the river and pedaling as far away as Tadoussac, four-hundred-some-odd years old, where the freshwater Saguenay spills into the saltwater St Lawrence. I've seen beluga and minke whales in the waters there. The Charlevoix region is more like Europe than North America, with tidy houses that sport a bounty of colorful flowers and mountains that rush to the edges of the St Lawrence, with steeples piercing the cobalt sky in small, picturesque villages along the coast.

I have escaped twice now to find refuge in a place that is even more remote than the last one, and I am thankful for my own resourcefulness and the kindness of others. Luck might have more to do with it than any so-called higher power, but regardless of how I got here, I am safely enshrined. Or so I hope.

I might have remade myself yet again, but this time I have kept bits of myself from before: the biking, the painting. And the laptop.

The laptop is a transgression. It is my weakness. I start out with rules: in the morning for only an hour, again in the evening after supper. I set the timer so I can adhere to this, but as they say, rules are made to be broken and there are many days when I lose track of time and hours pass.

It was harder to control my addiction in the winter, the deep snow and chill keeping me indoors, where it's cozy and warm. But once the weather turned, the island lured me outdoors, and I've been able to keep it under control. At least a little bit.

I turn back to the sink and when I finish washing up, glance back toward the laptop on the coffee table. Sometimes it whispers to me, but right now it's shouting.

I pour myself a second cup of coffee and allow myself to be lured back. I touch the keypad and the screen jumps to life. Tracker's message is still there, waiting for me.

When I saw his name and the cryptic French phrase last week, my first thought was to wonder what had taken him so long. My second was, why now? It's been over a year.

The only logical explanation is that something has happened that he means to warn me about. Tracker would not try to reach me merely for the sake of catching up. Our relationship has always been a practical one.

I have been waffling because I don't know if I want to know. But the longer it goes on, the more anxious I get, the more I feel I should find out what's going on so I'm not caught off guard again.

My fingers hover over the keys, and I close my eyes and quickly click on the URL link he's left for me.

My hands are shaking so much that I can barely type.

'Non, le ciel est nuageux.' *No, it's cloudy.*

This is the code that will tell him it's really me and not someone else.

I can't tell if he's here. He is a ghost, and even if I start poking around to try to uncover him, I doubt I will be able to. Tracker is very good at hiding.

No, all I can do is wait to see if he'll come to the chat.

My heart begins to pound, anxious now that I have not covered my tracks sufficiently, that he is, right at this moment, tracing me to this very spot. I double-check my VPN, make sure that it's working properly. I have given myself away in only one way: my screen name, which is no longer Tiny or BikerGirl27, but a jumble of letters and numbers that are meaningless to anyone but me. It's one of five that I've been using for this site as I lurk among the conversations, picking up new tips and getting to know the other hackers here.

I see it without realizing it at first: a blip on the screen that could be a hiccup in the wireless Internet, nothing that's unusual out here.

But I know it's not that innocent.

The button next to the webcam shines a bright green.

I'm being shadowed.

TWO

nstinctively, I put my hand over the webcam and think for a second. Even if I shut the laptop down right now, it doesn't matter. Whoever it is has already seen enough.

I was stupid to click on the link without a second thought. But it was *Tracker*. Wasn't it?

I click to disconnect the VPN. It doesn't disconnect. I try to shut down the Internet, but that doesn't work, either.

Whoever is there has taken control of my laptop with a remote access Trojan – or RAT. He's a rat, all right.

As if reading my mind, a small box appears on the screen, with a message: 'Your computer has been hijacked. All of your files have been encrypted, and in order to get them back, you must follow our instructions and make this deposit as soon as possible.' Below that, there is the figure of one million bitcoins and an account number.

Incredulous, I laugh out loud, the sound echoing in the small room, bouncing off the wood paneling. I can barely believe the irony. I've been hacking since I was fourteen; when I was twenty-five, I stole ten million dollars from bank accounts and because of that, the FBI has been looking for me. I had a close call with them last year, but managed to escape. I ended up here, one of the most isolated places I've ever been.

And now a hacker has hacked me. *Me.*

After this initial reaction, the embarrassment sets in. How could I have been so stupid? I clicked on that link like an amateur; I let my guard down because I thought I was going to talk to Tracker. He would be the first one to chastise me for being careless.

And then there's the worry. Who is it, exactly? Is it Tracker? I really don't want to think so. Maybe it's some hacker, like me – or is it the FBI?

The RAT must have been embedded in the URL that Tracker sent me. Is it possible that Tracker was hacked first? That idea is unfathomable, since Tracker is the best I've ever known. But maybe he's not perfect, either. Maybe he was like me and let his guard down for a second, long enough to let this hacker in.

It's quite possible that this hacker is inserting RATs into URLs all over the chat rooms, just to see whom he can hack, who would be willing to give into his ransom demand. The only way to get any answers is to go to the chat room, see if there's any chatter about someone hacking into accounts. It's a chat room for hackers; it seems like fertile ground for any of us, even though I'd like to think we have a code. A code that says: don't hack your fellow hackers.

Which again makes me wonder if it's not the FBI. It's possible – and more than likely – that they are randomly hacking into hackers' accounts to try to catch any of us at something nefarious. But would the FBI ask for a ransom? And in bitcoins? The virtual currency is more for criminals. The FBI probably would not have made such a demand. They would merely watch.

I am in denial that it could be Tracker. It doesn't seem in character. But I am suspicious of everyone and everything; that's what being a fugitive for sixteen years will do.

I realize that I've taken my hand away from the webcam, exposing myself.

Without waiting for another message from the hacker, I finally manage to disconnect the Internet. I need to find the port that the shadow has opened and shut it down. I can't go into safe mode, because then the RAT could load into the memory, and I'll never get rid of it. I make sure that every program that can connect to the Internet – email, messages – is closed.

I should be on autopilot. I should be scanning the ports, seeing what's open, looking for anything unexpected. I need to search the source code to make sure my shadow hasn't inserted a back door, somewhere he can get inside even if I think I've gotten rid of him. Instead, I stare at the laptop as it sits on the table and another emotion overcomes me. I feel betrayed. Ridiculous, really, but nevertheless, that's how I feel.

A sudden, awful, sinister thought startles me. I could do the same thing as this hacker. I could hack into computers and hold files for ransom, too. It wouldn't be that difficult. Not with my skills.

RATs are easy enough to get; I've seen the other hackers talking about it in the chat rooms. Forty dollars and anyone can buy the code, insert it into a URL, and email it to unsuspecting victims who click on it only to find themselves with a locked computer and a shadow who is able to access all their passwords and usernames and information.

What am I thinking? I get up and walk over to the front window. The rain has stopped, and the clouds are beginning to clear. A small sliver of sunlight pierces the sky and illuminates the river below.

I begin to wonder how hard it would be to hack the hacker. Granted, whoever it is will see me if I log back into the laptop, but would I be able to shroud myself in some way in order to trap him, to turn the tables on him? I'd have to keep that port open for him, give him a false sense of security. And then if I got another computer, one that is not compromised, I could go into the chat room and poke around a little. Everyone there is leaving a footprint. I could follow those prints and see if they end up in my laptop.

I am always up for a challenge, and this one intrigues me. But I need to think it through, and the best place is on my bike. The laptop is no longer connected to the Internet, so I can leave it alone for now. I go upstairs and change into a pair of leggings and slip on a T-shirt with a fleece over it. Even though it's July, it's been raining and is cool outside. Welcome to Canada. I pull on my sneakers and make my way back downstairs. I grab my daypack and helmet as I head out.

My bike is leaning against the side of the house. There is no need to lock anything up here. I climb on the bike, and soon I am flying down the road, my legs pumping the pedals, my head reeling with thoughts about my shadow and the ransom demand. A million bitcoins seems excessive. Does he really think that someone he hacks has that kind of cash? I couldn't access that much money, either in real or virtual currency. To get bitcoins, you need to have an actual bank account, and I don't have one of those, so even if I wanted to play along, I can't.

The road curves; I can smell fresh bread in the air. I am distracted by the delicious scent, but just for a moment.

I am curious about my shadow. Is he an amateur, a script kiddie, who is using the RAT designed by someone else? Or is he a black hat and did he code the virus himself? I have no way of knowing.

Even though I was careless and clicked on that link, I have no bank account numbers to compromise, no credit card numbers to steal. There is something, however, that I do want to protect. While I use a VPN, someone inside my laptop will see that I have been hiding behind it and he will see what I've been trying to keep secret: my IP address.

He will be able to find out where I am – or at least the general vicinity. While the island is remote, it is still accessible. There's no way he can know who I am, though. I've seen postings online about ransom requests like the one I received and news stories about hackers taking pictures through webcams and then demanding payment or the pictures go public. The moment he got into my laptop, he must have realized I have nothing to steal, no files to encrypt and hold hostage. If he saw me through my webcam for that moment, he would have seen a nondescript middle-aged woman.

If he is so inclined to track me down despite that, he can ask anyone here about me and they will tell him my name is Susan McQueen and that I am an artist, an American expat who decided to leave the States for a more peaceful life.

No one knows that I came through Vermont on foot with a backpack and a laptop. I am living here as I lived on Block Island, under the radar, selling my paintings and paying my bills with cash. While I became complacent there, being able to hide for so long, I am not as relaxed here. It's only been a little over a year. I am constantly looking over my shoulder. I was found once, I could be found again. This time it might be as easy as through my own laptop.

Again I am distracted. The bread oven is perched on the edge of the parking lot, its aroma stronger now that I'm here. My stomach growls, despite my breakfast. It is hard to resist the scent of freshly baked bread. There are no cars here this morning; the rain and gray skies probably have kept the tourists away. I turn into the lot and climb off the bike, leaning it against the wooden post fence. I take the steps two at a time and enter the shop.

Danielle is behind the counter, and she greets me in French. I ask for a loaf of bread, and she slips one into a paper bag and hands it to me. I take a couple of bills from the small daypack and put the bread inside. It fits perfectly.

I hear the gristmill working hard, and the sun is starting to move out from behind the clouds. The day may be salvaged after all.

I bid Danielle adieu and head back out.

I pass a surrey with a family of four pedaling hard under the bright yellow canopy. The little boy is laughing, and it's nice to see that the weather has not deterred everyone. The road runs alongside the coast, and the water is choppy, a deep, dark eggplant color that would be easy to capture on canvas.

But thoughts of my shadow and what I can do about him push everything else aside. I decide to circle the island, work my legs until I can feel the muscles burn to take the edge off my anger.

By the time I arrive home, I know what I want to do.

THREE

I take my time with putting my bike and helmet away. I shed my sneakers in the mudroom and push open the door that leads into my kitchen. My house is quiet; the sun is casting beams through the trees into a pattern on the floor. The laptop is where I left it: on the table.

I pick it up and go into the living room. I sink down into the couch cushions, my feet up on the coffee table, the laptop resting on my knees. I open it; I can see my reflection in the dark screen. I turn it on, and the screen jumps to life. I do not turn on the Internet connection. First I have to find that port that shouldn't be open.

It's not too difficult. I see it almost immediately. But that's because I'm a hacker and I'm used to finding ports that shouldn't be open. I seek them out. The difference nowadays is that I don't do anything with them. It's merely a challenge to see if I could. I used to hack into my father's business accounts when I was a teenager, to show him up. This shadow, since he's holding my laptop for ransom, clearly has more nefarious reasons for creating a back door. He also could use my laptop to hack illegally into a system, send emails with my address, and message people using my identity.

Yet I don't want to close the port. I want him to come back in. I want to see where this goes, see if I can't catch him.

Just to see if I can.

I admit I have an addiction, a sickness. I spent fifteen years without a computer because I knew what I was capable of and I can't back down from a dare. I stole ten million dollars by transferring money from bank accounts to offshore accounts all over the world because the man I loved asked me to.

I don't pretend that I'm above doing that now. I don't pretend that I wouldn't do it all over again. Because I probably would. I can't help myself. This shadow has no idea who he's up against.

Before I turn the Internet connection back on, however, I find a piece of tape and put it over the webcam. He's already seen me, but I don't want to make it that easy for him again.

A normal person would have gotten an anti-virus program and installed it right about now. A program that *might* make the shadow disappear. Not necessarily. The risk would always be there that the program didn't work, and the shadow would remain. This is my justification for not even bothering.

Out of curiosity, when I'm back on the Internet, I check the history of my online page views. I didn't clear the queue before shutting down the laptop earlier, but the shadow was already there so it wouldn't have done any good. I see the chat room where I found Tracker's message, but the next site reminds me what I had been doing before the chat room.

I'd visited the website for Dominique's art gallery, to see which of my paintings she'd added to the site. I'd also gone to the website for Veronica's gallery on Block Island to see if she'd sold the last of my paintings that she'd been advertising.

I barely have enough time to register this when I see the webcam light go on.

He's back. I'm glad I taped over the camera.

He's also probably watching everything I'm doing, so it's no use to try to hide my actions, although I tell myself that he most likely had already seen my page view history before I noticed he was there. It's the first thing I would have looked at, and I can't underestimate him.

I go back to the chat room and scan the names to see if Tracker is here. I still have doubts about him; I wonder if he is my shadow but I don't want to believe it. He's never had to hide from me before. He is as guilty as I am, too, since he helped me with the bank job. If it weren't for him, I might not have even gotten into the accounts, and it would have been a lot harder for me to transfer the money. He was there, every step of the way. We were partners, and I trusted him.

I want desperately to trust him now.

The webcam light is still on, distracting me. I have no idea what he's doing beyond watching me. I go into the source code to see if I can't find him, and I spot something that doesn't look right. But before I can investigate it further, the screen goes black.

I stop breathing for a second as my muscles tense.

The box from earlier pops back up on my screen, but this time, there is a new message: 'We are waiting for your deposit of one million bitcoins. Until we get it, we will have total control over your computer.' The account number is added at the end, and this time it includes the site where I need to make the deposit. Perhaps the shadow realized that he had failed to tell me that the first time. Not that it will make a difference. I still don't have a bank account; I still can't get bitcoins to pay even if I wanted to.

I see the message icon at the bottom of the screen. I have never written a message to anyone, so when I call up the program, it is blank, with no contacts listed. But maybe it's possible to write something directed to the shadow and he'll see it, because he's watching everything.

So I do just that.

'I have received your message, but I am unable to meet your demand because I do not have a bank account.'

I leave the program open, the message on the screen. I have no idea if he sees it or if he will acknowledge it.

I sit, my stomach in knots as I wait. Finally, I can't stand it anymore. I am still sweaty from my bike ride, so I go up the stairs, taking them two at a time, and pull off my clothes as I reach the bathroom. I turn on the shower, the water as hot as I can stand it, and climb in. I close my eyes and put my face up into the stream, then turn around and let it pulsate against my back. I wait to relax, but I can't. I can still see the message on the screen in my head. After a quick shampoo and rinse, I get out and dry myself off, wrapping the towel underneath my armpits and securing it against my chest. I go downstairs in my bare feet and around to the laptop that's still sitting on the coffee table.

It has gone dark with inactivity, so I brush my fingers against the pad and it springs to life.

My message is still there, but there's another one, too, now:

'Maybe you should tap into that bank account that the FBI never found. And if you even think about not paying, your friends will pay in a different way.'

I don't understand what he's talking about until the pictures pop up on the screen. It's Steve, leaning against the side of his SUV in Old Harbor on Block Island, waiting for the next ferry to come in. And then there's Jeanine, looking flushed as she approaches the spa, the early morning pinks and oranges of the sky behind her.

I catch my breath as I first think how wonderful it is to see their faces again, but then the reality of the situation creeps in. He has pictures of them. He knows about them, where they are, what they do, what their lives are like. He has access to them, and he is telling me with these two photographs that he is in control.

He is also telling me that he knows exactly who I am.

FOUR

A ll of a sudden the pictures disappear; the message program shuts down. I sit, stunned. *He knows who I am.* This is not a random hack.

I reach over and turn off the Internet connection. My hands are shaking, my fear palpable. I am not thinking so much about myself, but his threat against Steve and Jeanine. If I don't pay, they will pay. He is right that there was a bank account, one that the FBI never found. Ian Cartwright, my former partner and lover, came to Block Island last year looking for me, demanding what he felt I still owed him, angry that the feds had frozen all the accounts so he couldn't get any of the money, sure that I'd set up a private account that was still accessible, that I was still drawing money from. He was half right. He didn't believe me when I told him that I couldn't access it. That I didn't even know if it still existed.

Tracker had access to the private account. I set it up specifically so he could pay everyone who'd helped. I hadn't hacked into the bank alone. I have no idea how many people Tracker enlisted; that was the idea. I begin to see my shadow in a completely new light. Is he someone who helped all those years ago with the job and that's how he knows about the bank account? Whoever it is must know about Tracker, because he knows how Tracker was trying to reach me with the French phrases. That wasn't common knowledge, but if the shadow is on the chat site, it wouldn't be hard to figure out.

The knowledge of the French phrases makes me pause and consider Tracker again. Neither Tracker nor the other hackers on the chat room site know about Steve and Jeanine.

Who does?

The only ones I know for sure are those who found me last year on Block Island: Ian, his boss and my father's former associate Tony DeMarco, and the FBI.

I think about Ian, but then I dismiss him. He knows nothing about computers, about hacking. Even if he could figure out how to invade

my laptop with a forty-dollar remote access Trojan, I'm not sure
he would ever have the skills to send a ransom note, much less set
up a bitcoin account. Even I have a hard time understanding exactly
what a bitcoin is and how it works, but then again, I choose to live
my life without any currency except cash. But Ian was angry last
year, and it's possible he got someone to do this for him if he
couldn't do it himself. Still, he never knew about the chat site or
Tracker, which makes me think he is an unlikely culprit.

Tony DeMarco has reason to hate me. I stole from him, although
not on purpose. I had account numbers, no names attached to those
accounts, so I didn't know whom I was stealing from. Ian knew,
though, and Tony's been making him pay it back all these years. I
did transfer money from Ian's account to Tony right before I left
Block Island, hoping to make it right. It's possible that it wasn't
enough. Tony is not someone anyone should cross, and the threat
would be in character for him.

Or it could be the FBI, as I suspected earlier. I wouldn't be
surprised if they weren't still trying to figure out where that money
disappeared to. The FBI agents who followed Ian to Block Island
in order to find me certainly were still interested. I might see them
demanding a ransom to see if they could find out where the money
comes from, but why would the FBI threaten Steve and Jeanine?
Unless it's just another ploy to find me. I wouldn't put it past them.

Whoever it is, I have to figure out how to get him his money and
keep my friends safe. In the meantime, my IP address has been
compromised, and he knows about my paintings in the gallery in
Baie-Saint-Paul. My hiding place is no longer a safe haven.

I spend the rest of the day preparing. The laptop sits, closed, on the
table, taunting me. My fingers itch to get inside, to confront my
shadow, but I can't. I have devised a plan and I have to stick to it.
I can't keep my friends safe until I'm safe.

I make a ham and cheese and tomato sandwich on the bread I've
brought home and wash it down with a glass of milk. Once I've
cleaned up, I go upstairs and sift through the few clothes I've got
hanging in the closet and folded in the drawers. I can't take everything with me, only what can fit in the backpack. I've got to sacrifice
some things because of the cash that I need to bring.

I lay everything out on the bed, the pile of cash in one corner, essential undergarments in another, toiletries in the center. It's a decent-sized backpack, and I have to be smart about how to pack to fit everything.

When I left Block Island, I had very little in the pack besides cash. I'd had to leave quickly, and I hadn't had access to my house at the end. I don't feel like I've got a lot of time now, either, but so far no one has come knocking. This escape is all about getting away before that happens and being one step ahead instead of one step behind.

I decide what I'm going to wear tomorrow and then pack one pair of jeans, two T-shirts and one sweater. I want to bring my sneakers, but they take up too much room, so I'll have to make do with the sandals I'll be wearing.

When I've fit everything I'll need, I slide the laptop inside and zipper the pack shut. I stare at it on the bed. My life is reduced to this again. I had hoped that I could be here a while, maybe forever. But I have to assume that my shadow is already on my trail, maybe even leading the FBI to me again if he's not FBI himself.

I think about Zeke, that FBI agent, the one who found me in Paris and ended up dead. I have tried to convince myself it wasn't my fault, but I cannot erase the guilt.

I make my way downstairs and out the back door to the yard that overlooks the river. It's low tide, and the scent wafts up the shore, a little fishy with a touch of wet dirt, but it's not unpleasant. A boat is passing by in the distance; I settle in the Adirondack chair that sits at the edge of the lawn and watch it move slowly past. I may look like I'm relaxed, but my heart is beating too fast, every muscle taut. I am ready to run, but I have to wait.

I debate going out to one of the pubs, but choose to stay home in the end. I don't think I can act normal, and I don't want to raise any suspicions. For supper, I have another sandwich, but this time I wash it down with a glass of wine. I turn the small television on and watch the local news. Apparently there is confusion about house numbers that are out of order.

I pull on an oversized T-shirt and crawl into bed by ten, but I merely stare at the ceiling while fine-tuning my plan. At some point I fall into a fitful sleep, and I find myself looking at the clock every hour.

*   *   *

The sun splashes light across the room when I open my eyes and see it's finally an acceptable hour to get up. I climb out of bed and take a hot shower. I have yet another slice of the bread, buttered, with my morning coffee. The backpack is now on the sofa. I pour more coffee into a travel mug, then put the kitchen right. By the time I hear Dominique's car outside, everything is in its place, so tidy that it is hard to imagine anyone has been living here.

Dominique knocks on the door, and I grab a white cotton sweater and shrug it on, winding a bright blue scarf around my neck and stepping into a pair of sandals before I let her in.

Dominique laughs when she sees my attire. It is the beginning of July, but I am never without a sweater. The scarf is more of an affectation, something I wear to make myself look more artsy than I feel.

'It's not that cool,' she teases, but she is used to me by now and doesn't say anything more about it. 'Are you ready?'

I indicate the two bags next to the door that I also packed last night. They are full of paintings.

'Is that all you've got?'

'You'd be surprised how much I could fit,' I say, and she reaches for one of the bags and we take them out to her car. She's left the back hatch open, and we load up.

'All ready?' she asks.

'No, I need to get my backpack,' I say, going back into the house.

I shrug the pack on my shoulder as I grab the travel mug full of coffee that's sitting on the counter, then go back out, not bothering to lock up behind me. If anyone wants to poke around my house, they will find nothing that will lead to me. Only my paintings on the walls have my name on them, and it's not even my real name.

When I climb into the passenger seat, I put my mug next to Dominique's in the console between us and shove the backpack on the floor at my feet. I can't dwell on the things that I wish I could have packed; I've got all the essentials. I hate using Dominique like this, but I have no choice. This is the best plan – the only plan – I could come up with quickly.

'You've got everything?' She frowns at the backpack but says nothing else, not realizing I've been taking inventory in my head.

'Yes.' I think about my bike tucked inside the back mudroom, my biggest regret.

'Then we're off.'

We drive in silence along the edge of the island, the river spreading out beside us, until she turns and we are on the Chemin de la Traverse, cutting through the middle of the island. Things here are much closer than I'm used to, and even closer when I'm in a car and not on my bike.

Again I think about my bike, and it reminds me of where I was a year ago. Another island, another lifetime. I'm feeling a huge sense of déjà vu.

My thoughts turn to my shadow, his threat against Steve and Jeanine. He said I have to pay, but he didn't say when. If I have a deadline. This makes me even more anxious, but there's nothing I can do about it right now. I have to hope that he'll be patient. At least within reason.

'Susan?' Dominique is saying something, but I am not paying attention.

'I'm sorry, what?'

She smiles. 'You seem very far away today, Susan. Is everything all right?'

'It's fine,' I say, but in English, not French, and she frowns. It's not as though she doesn't speak English, it's just that I always speak French here, despite my English name.

Dominique politely ignores my faux pas. 'We are almost at the ferry,' she says, and I see it as we turn the corner. There is a long line of cars waiting to board, so Dominique puts the car in neutral and cuts the engine so we don't waste gas.

Once we dock on the other side of the river in Saint-Joseph-de-la-Rive, we will drive the thirty-one miles to Quebec City.

Dominique and I have been making this trek every weekend since the end of May to sell my work at the rue du Trésor alongside all the other artists. Dominique owns the gallery where I show my work in Baie-Saint-Paul on the mainland and proposed the idea of expanding my exposure in the city when a friend of hers offered a booth for rent on Saturdays for two months. So far, it's been a success.

I nudge the bag at my feet; it gives me a sense of security to have the laptop with me, even though it has a ghost living in it. Dominique wouldn't understand. The only technology she thinks is necessary for our day is the wireless credit card machine. I resisted the idea at first, but she swears by it. I know it's not safe, that anyone could hack into it.

I hacked into it within minutes.

I am so aware of the backpack at my feet that I pick up my mug and take a drink of coffee to give myself something to do.

I almost feel bad that I can't tell Dominique, but lying has been second nature to me for so long that any guilt I might feel doesn't make a difference.

She doesn't need to know that I won't be coming back with her.

FIVE

I t is still very early when we unpack the car and bring the bags and two step stools out to the spot that Dominique has secured for us. The road is more a cobblestoned alleyway lined with built-in black booths. Dominique unlocks ours, opening it up, lifting the awning on its metal bars to uncover the display space. The hooks are still in place, so we unload the paintings, and Dominique points to where I should hang them so they will have the most pleasing presentation. I like watching her as she directs me, her movements graceful in the long skirt and gauzy blouse. She is older than I am, but I have never been sure by exactly how much because the bright highlights in her hair make her look younger. She has tried to get me to color my hair, but I like my salt and pepper. I've let it grow, though, and I style it so the curls aren't quite so out of control.

When we are done with the paintings – we slide the extras in a hidden cupboard behind the display – I hear:

'Dominique!'

Jean Bessette comes over and gives her a kiss on each cheek before turning to me. 'Susan. You're looking well.'

I suppress a smile. Jean has a crush on Dominique, but he has little use for me. His work is displayed next to mine, and while there are plenty of tourists who gravitate toward his abstracts, more of them tend to buy my colorful landscapes that allow them to bring home a piece of where they've been. Jean thinks my work is too pedestrian, that the tourists who buy my paintings have no taste.

He has not actually said that to me, but he doesn't hide it very well. Because of his crush, we maintain a polite distance.

I turn away and busy myself with organizing the pile of unframed paintings that customers can flip through. The cobblestones are hard beneath my sandals; I am completely surrounded by art. My display seamlessly moves into Jean's on one side and into one featuring tiny watercolors of flowers on the other. I glance up to my left and see the castle-like Château Frontenac looming in the distance. Quebec City is a European city in North America, but it does not

remind me of Paris – or any other city, in fact. It has its own person-
ality, the only walled city in North America, Old Quebec transforming
into Modern Quebec beyond the walls.

I hear the clop-clop-clop of one of the horse-drawn tourist
carriages, its scent faint in the air. I never understood the appeal,
but then, I was never one of those girls obsessed with horses. I had
a very different obsession.

'Susan?' Dominique touches my elbow. Her frown tells me that
she is still concerned about my lack of concentration today.

The display is ready for business, and already a couple is admiring
one of my chapel paintings. I am not good at this part of it, at
having to make small talk with customers to make them feel that
their purchase is personal in every way. Today is even harder; my
mind is on the laptop and the shadow. But I force a smile, nodding
at Dominique, ready to make a sale.

The morning quickly turns to midday. The sun is bright now, and the
temperature has risen. I shed my sweater, tying it around my waist,
my eye on the backpack tucked behind the stool at the edge of the
display.

Five framed paintings and two unframed ones have sold, and
Dominique is glowing. Jean is glowering, however, because he has
not sold one. The brightly colored abstracts look harsh next to my
soft palettes. I have often wondered if he arranged this seemingly
serendipitous display rental so he can chat up Dominique.

He is doing just that, preening as he runs his hand through his white
hair. His ruddy complexion complements his high cheekbones and long
nose. His stance belies his height, making him seem taller somehow.

Every once in a while, he glances at me, and it makes me
uncomfortable, but I can't explain exactly why.

I reach under the stool and pull out the backpack, slinging it over
my shoulder.

'I'm going to get something to eat,' I tell Dominique, purposely
not looking at Jean.

'Don't take too long,' she says. 'I'll go when you get back.' We
always stagger our breaks. Jean hardly ever leaves; Dominique usually
brings him something.

I take off without saying goodbye, walking briskly between the
walls of artwork, not bothering to pay attention to any of it.

I head in the direction of Rue Saint-Jean, a long pedestrian road lined with shops and restaurants. Tourists crowd the thoroughfare, pausing to look in shop windows and at menus posted for their perusal in the hopes of luring them in for a meal. I weave between them; I don't have time to linger and I have a mission. Finally, I reach my destination, next door to the French bookstore.

'Atelier de réparation des ordinateurs,' the sign in the window reads, and I push the door open, a small bell jingling. No tourists in here looking for local treasures and art. Instead, the wall to the left is neatly filled with cases for smartphones; the one to the right sports shelves holding a variety of Bluetooth speakers and laptop cases and various other computer accoutrements. Philippe is behind the counter that is teeming with laptops, the only disheveled thing about the store. He grins when he sees me.

'Susan!' he exclaims, coming around the counter and taking me by the shoulders, kissing me lightly on each cheek. 'What can I do for you today?' he asks in French. We speak French, even though he knows I'm an American. I think he does speak English, but I can't be one hundred percent sure.

I discovered Philippe's shop while wandering the first day I came to Old Quebec. I was surprised to see the modern technology inside the weatherworn stone building that is clearly from an era more than four hundred years ago. I couldn't believe my luck in such a find, and I immediately bought a power cord. On my second visit, I purchased a neoprene case. Philippe's jovial manner was at odds with my reluctance to get close to anyone when I first arrived, but he won me over with the best cup of coffee I've ever had and his confession that he is an amateur hacker.

I have never told him about my past, pretending instead to be ignorant and willing to learn anything he can teach me. So far he has taught me nothing, but I have a friend who makes great coffee.

Speaking of which, he is pouring me a cup from a large silver Thermos he keeps under the counter. His hands are thin, with long fingers that are nimble like a piano player's. The rest of him is thin, too, and his face is a jumble of angles, his hair cropped short on the sides with a long piece that hangs over his eyes. My father would have called him a beatnik. I'd say he's in his early thirties, a bit younger than me.

I take the coffee and sip. Delicious, as usual.

'What brings you here, Susan?' he asks.

'I need another laptop.'

His face darkens. 'What happened to yours?'

'Virus,' I say simply.

He nods. 'It's so easy to get one these days. Do you want me to look at it?'

'Thanks, but I think it's best to get a new one.'

'I can take it off your hands for you.'

I think quickly, taking another drink of coffee to stall. 'I appreciate that, but I'm going to hold onto it for now because I need to see if I can't get some stuff off it first.'

Philippe frowns. He glances at my backpack. 'Do you have it there? Can I see?'

I shrug off his concern. 'It's not a big deal.'

'I might be able to help.'

I am not so sure about that.

'I really think I should take a look at it.'

I can tell that he's not going to take no for an answer, and it will look odd if I don't show him, so I pull the laptop out of the backpack. I open it and power it up, but I'm careful not to let him see the screen. I want to make sure the messages are gone. And they are. The screen is dark, so I set it in front of him, facing him.

'You say it's a virus?' He frowns at the tape on the webcam, and before I can say anything, he takes it off.

He starts hitting keys, and I worry that my shadow is going to send another message; however, with the tape off the webcam, he will be able to see that it's not me at the keyboard, but a stranger. I eye the laptops piled on the counter. Some have repair tags on them, but others don't, and I wonder if these are the ones he has for sale. In addition to the cash in the backpack, I also have access to a bank account that Dominique set up for me through the gallery. The money from my painting sales go directly into that account, and she takes out her commission. The rest is for me, but it's in her name, not mine. I suggested the idea for the account, and she didn't question it. It's surprising sometimes how little people question.

'Um, Susan?' Philippe's tone concerns me, and I move closer to him. 'There's something wrong here.'

Uh-oh. My shadow must have put up another message. I reach for the laptop, but he's already turned it around so it's facing me. And I see what he sees.

The screen is filled with a close-up image of someone's eyes and a message below: 'Three days.'

SIX

I t's the deadline I was wondering about, and I shiver. 'I told you I had a virus,' I try to say flippantly, but the irises of the eyes are bright red and even though whoever is inside my laptop isn't physically here, my heart begins to pound.

I reach out my hand, aware that it is shaking, and close the laptop cover, putting it to sleep.

Philippe is staring at me. He sees my fear. 'That's more than a virus, Susan. What's going on? What does this mean: three days?'

I try to keep my expression neutral, despite the pounding inside my chest. 'Someone hacked me. He wants money, and that's the deadline.'

'How did this happen?'

'I don't know. I clicked on a link and got a message saying that my laptop had been hijacked. But I didn't see this until you did. These eyes, I mean. This is new.'

'You should call the police. They have special units now that deal with things like this.'

I force a small smile. 'It's nothing, Philippe. Not to worry. Hackers get into computers all the time, but they don't actually physically harm anyone.'

'But he wants money. To let you back into your laptop?'

'That's right.'

He reaches over and touches my arm, as though it will comfort me. 'I've heard about this. You really should call the police.'

I can't tell him that I can't do that, that I can probably find out more than the police could. That I am a fugitive and am in this country illegally, without a passport or an identity. I have to distract him from this idea.

'Maybe you can help,' I suggest.

Philippe's eyes widen.

'Maybe you can help me figure out how to fix this,' I go even further. 'I mean, you're pretty good at this sort of thing.' I doubt this, considering our conversations, but I have tapped into his ego and he is smiling.

'Really?'

'Maybe an anti-malware program?' I'll need to get rid of the virus before I dump the laptop anyway, so no one else will be able to track me in case they can get back inside.

'Yes, yes, of course. The best thing to do is download one into a flash drive on another computer and then install it on this one.' He indicates the compromised laptop. 'You might not need a new laptop, then.'

'I think I still want a new one. I don't know if I'll be able to trust this one again. It's like having a ghost in the house. Is it ever really gone?' I give him a sheepish smile, and he smiles back as if I've said something that makes sense.

'I understand. But first things first. We still need a computer that's not compromised in order to do the purge.' Philippe turns his attention to the laptops on the counter. He picks up one from the end and waves it at me. 'This is the same one you've got. Someone brought it in because he bought a new one, but it's as good as new. I need to clear the hard drive. If you want, I can do that now.'

I make a show of looking at my watch. 'I have somewhere I have to be.'

'Can you come back in a little bit, and I'll have it ready for you? Say, an hour or so?'

I don't really like the idea of having to come back, and I could clear the hard drive myself, but he looks so eager to please I don't want to disappoint him. 'Two hours, probably.'

Philippe grins. 'It will definitely be done by then. I'll download the malware program, too. If you leave your laptop, I can run it for you.'

I hesitate. I don't want to run that program now. I need to keep the lines of communication open with the shadow; I need to get him the bitcoins – I haven't yet figured out how I'm going to do that – and make sure that Steve and Jeanine are all right before I get rid of the machine altogether. If Philippe runs the program, it could wipe the system clean and the shadow could make good on his threat.

I don't feel like I can reject his idea outright, though, because to Philippe – and anyone not in the know – this is a good plan. So I think fast.

'Why don't we wait on the program? I'd like to see how it's done, in case I have to run it again for some reason.'

Philippe nods thoughtfully. 'OK. I'll wait until you get back and we can do it together.'

'How much are you charging for the new laptop?'

He names a price that is fair, then he apologizes. 'I know we are friends—' he starts.

'I don't expect special treatment. You have a business to run. I respect that.' I open my backpack and try to count out bills without him seeing how much I have.

He puts his hand up. 'You can pay me later.'

'No, no, let's do this now.' I don't want to waste time later. When I have enough cash, I hold it out for him, using my elbow to keep the backpack's contents hidden.

Philippe takes the money, but peels off two bills and tries to hand them back to me. 'Family rate,' he says simply.

'I'm not family.'

'Friend rate, then. Whatever. Susan, I can't take this much from you. It's all right. My business is fine.'

The store has been empty every time I've come by, although the pile of laptops on the counter has not dwindled. Maybe he does know something about fixing them, and perhaps he has a loyal clientele. If I don't take his refund it will insult him, so I pocket the cash and touch his arm.

'Thank you,' I say, and I see I have made him happy. I slip my laptop back into my backpack and give him a kiss on the cheek before leaving the shop.

I stop to pick up a takeout salad, and as I walk back, my thoughts drift to the eyes and message on my laptop. I glance at the people surrounding me. There are too many of them, too many tourists, too many strangers. I know that whoever has infected my laptop could be on the other side of the globe, but he feels so close that I am claustrophobic with fear.

As I approach rue du Trésor, I am struck with a sense that I am being watched. Perhaps it's the eyes inside my laptop, but even if it's just paranoia, I peel away from the crowd and go toward Dufferin Terrace, the site of Fort Saint-Louis, built in 1620, where a statue of Champlain stands. A street performer juggling fire torches is surrounded by a crowd right before the entrance to the funicular that goes down to the Quartier du Petit Champlain. The crowd shouts as the juggler successfully catches all four torches and the fire is extinguished.

The Château Frontenac, its green towers majestically stretching up toward the blue sky, is directly in front of me. I should turn around, go back to Dominique, act as normal as possible until I can do what I need to, but I still cannot shake the feeling that someone is watching me.

It's silly, I know. Even if whoever was in my laptop discovered my IP address, traced it to Quebec, to the island, and actually decided to come find me, it could take a day or more for him to actually show up.

Unless he is already here.

I can get into the Château through the Starbucks, so I sidestep the outside tables and push the door in. The scent of coffee hits my nose, but I ignore it and find the door into the hotel. An elaborately designed blue carpet runs between square columns. This floor houses conference rooms, so I find stairs and go up, stepping into luxury. A trilogy of silver vases containing brightly colored flowers adorns a sleek wooden table. To the left of it, a hallway is lined with upscale shops; the lobby is to the right. Its lush elegance in blues and golds – glittering chandeliers, wood inlaid ceilings and satin drapes – settles my nerves a little. I almost feel invisible.

I wonder what it would be like if I took a room here. I am already creating another identity, one of a woman who is merely here on vacation to see the sights. I could wander the Plains of Abraham and admire the flowers, maybe take one of those horse and carriage rides, a tour of the Citadel. Je me souviens. *I remember.* The official motto of Quebec.

I am caught up in my daydream, but then I see him.

SEVEN

Jean frowns as he comes toward me. 'Dominique has been waiting for you,' he chides.

'I'm sorry. I've been coming here for weeks but I've never been in here before,' I say, 'and I wanted to take a look.'

He doesn't believe me, but he leaves it be. 'I saw you come in here.'

So it was Jean who was watching me. I wasn't imagining things. 'Were you looking for me?'

He peers at me out of the corner of his eye. 'I saw you outside.'

'You followed me?' I challenge him, and he cannot lie.

'Yes,' he says, standing up a little straighter, proud of it. 'You have been gone a long time, and Dominique needs a break.'

'Who's watching your booth?'

'She is. She knows I went looking for you.'

I don't try to hide my distress. Even though it won't matter in a few hours, I don't want Dominique upset with me. She has been good to me, helped me when I knew no one here, became my friend when I felt I would never have another friend again because of the things I've done.

But this is not the only thing I'm worried about. Jean never leaves his booth. Even though his search for me is most likely another ploy for Dominique's affections, something about this doesn't seem quite right.

'Let's go, then. I'm sorry I was gone so long.' I don't really know why I'm apologizing to Jean; it just feels like the thing to say at the moment.

I begin walking toward the lobby doors, and when I'm outside, I have to get my bearings, because this is not the way I came in. The valet's gold stand shines as the sunlight hits it.

'This way,' Jean indicates, and now I'm following him, trying to keep up as he moves swiftly down the sidewalk and through a stone archway. I follow him across Place d'Armes, a small park with a gothic-style fountain in the center that serves as a traffic circle.

Dominique does not look put out when we arrive back at the booth. She smiles at me, and it is genuine. She picks up her bag from behind the stool and gives me the credit card reader. 'Sell a lot of paintings,' she instructs with a wink, and she heads off, not saying anything to Jean. He sulks back to his chair and paintings, clearly annoyed that she has not rewarded him for bringing me back.

I settle onto Dominique's stool and absently watch the tourists who are shopping for something to bring home with them. I study their faces, wondering yet again if I could ever paint a portrait. I never put people in my paintings, which are all landscapes illustrating the small world I live in. My thoughts wander back to those paintings in the gallery on Block Island; has Veronica kept them, sold them? What does she think about when she looks at them? My friendship – or my betrayal of that friendship?

I try not to remember, because it's been too hard to stay away, to keep myself from making that phone call to say I'm all right, don't worry about me, how is Steve, does he still go to Club Soda on Fridays, does he go alone or has he found another friend to go with him?

The hardest thing I ever did was leave that life, which is why I keep my distance here.

I do consider that the threat against Steve and Jeanine could be an empty one, that the ultimate goal is to locate me. But I cannot take that chance and not go through with the demand.

'Miss?'

I am not paying attention. An elderly couple is standing in front of me, holding one of my paintings of Chapelle Saint-Isidore. I shake my thoughts away and give them a smile.

After Dominique gets back from lunch, the afternoon moves slowly. We make small talk, but the more time that passes, the more I am thinking about my shadow and trying to figure out whom he might be. Jean has been watching me closely, as though he knows I'm up to something, and perhaps he does. He is still wary after finding me loitering in the Château lobby, and his wariness makes me uncomfortable but I cannot pinpoint exactly why.

Finally, I stand up. 'I need to stretch my legs,' I tell Dominique. It is not unusual for either of us to want another break before we start taking down the booth to head back home, so she does not share Jean's suspicions. I feel his eyes on me as I sling the backpack around my shoulder and walk away. Even though I want to look back to see if he is still watching me, I resist.

Philippe is not behind the counter when I enter his shop. The sound of the bells bounces off the back wall. I pause just inside the door, letting it close slowly behind me, but something is off here and I have a sudden urge to flee.

It's the counter. The pile of laptops that adorned it earlier is no longer there. Philippe could have taken them to the back room as a bit of housekeeping, but every time I've been to the shop, the pile has remained consistent.

I hold my breath and strain to hear anything, but the silence is loud.

Again I want to turn and run, and I actually am facing the door with my hand on the handle – to hell with the laptop, I can always get another one somewhere – when I see him coming down the sidewalk across the street, his head moving from side to side as his eyes dart around, watchful.

It's Jean, and I wonder if he is again looking for me.

I decide that it's safer to stay in the shop, and as I pull my hand away, I hear her voice.

'Can I help you?'

She is young, perhaps in her mid to late twenties, with a bright pink pixie haircut and a long, thin, very pale face with the largest blue eyes I've ever seen. She is tall and extremely thin. She is wearing skinny jeans and a tight-fitting T-shirt that doesn't hide the colorful tattoo that crawls around her upper arm.

'Hello,' I say. 'I'm looking for Philippe.'

'You must be Susan,' she says matter-of-factly.

The comment takes me aback. How does she know this? She notices the confusion on my face, and she grins.

'Philippe has told me about his older woman friend.' She doesn't wait for me to come to her; she walks across the room and holds out her hand. 'I'm Alice.' She is speaking English, and I listen for a trace of a French accent, but I can't detect one. She's definitely Canadian, though; Americans have an attitude about them. I have tried to shed my American identity as much as possible, but I know the natives can tell where I'm from.

I take her hand. She has a firm grip. 'Where is Philippe?' I ask, in English. I don't want to have to wait too long. I just want my laptop so I can leave.

Alice goes to the counter and runs her hand along the edge. 'He stepped out for a moment. He should be back soon.'

'And you are who, exactly?'

She grins. 'I'm Alice,' she says, and clearly that's all I'm going to get out of her.

'I didn't realize he had anyone working for him,' I say, trying to prompt her, but she says nothing, so I indicate the empty counter. 'What happened to the laptops?' I can't help but ask.

She circles around, before facing me and shrugging. 'I don't know.' She studies my face for a few seconds, then crooks her finger. 'Come on,' she says, disappearing around the corner.

I hesitate. I'm not in the mood for games. But when she peeks around the corner and says firmly, 'Come *on*,' I take one glance out the front, see Jean moving past the door, and decide to do what she wants.

I brush down my skirt and straighten my scarf, smooth my hair with my hands. I walk around to the back room.

This is Philippe's workshop where he repairs the computers. I've never been back here, and if I had thought the pile of laptops on the counter was messy, it was nothing compared to this. Old and new desktops are stacked on top of each other, creating little towers around the room. Laptops are everywhere, too, although if they are the same ones from the front, I can't tell. Some laptops are sleek and silver, some black. Some are larger than others, but it would be easy to pick up any one at random, pretend it's mine, and walk out and never return.

Alice huddles over her phone, her fingers flying. I've never seen anyone text so fast. 'Look for your name,' she instructs without looking up. 'See? He's got those notes stuck to them.'

She's right: the laptops have sticky notes with names on them. I do a cursory search, but I don't see one that has my name on it. I turn and shrug. 'I don't know where it is.'

The bell on the front door jingles. Alice disappears around the corner, and I am close on her heels. Philippe has come back, and he's carrying a cup of coffee and gives me a smile.

This reminds me of the island, how everyone there is so much more relaxed than in the city. My anxiety about him not being here when I arrived isn't about him – it is about me and how it has thrown me off schedule. I smile back.

'Did she give you your laptop?' he asks, indicating Alice.

I shake my head, and he disappears around the corner to the back room. Suddenly he is back, like a magic trick, holding out a laptop. I take it from him. 'Mine?'

He nods, then glances toward Alice, who is standing between us and the front of the shop. They exchange a look that I can't read, and he says, 'I downloaded the malware program.' He hands me a flash drive.

'Thanks.'

'That's for the virus?' Alice stares at the flash drive.

'That's right,' Philippe says.

'He tells me it's a RAT.' Alice is talking to me, and the switch from English to French back to English is throwing me off a little.

'Yes.' I pause, then look at Philippe. 'Who is she?' I ask, indicating Alice.

A sheepish expression crosses his face. 'Now, you told me you didn't want to—'

Alice interrupts. 'Susan, I'm with the cybercrime police unit.'

EIGHT

I feel like someone has punched me in the stomach. I cannot speak for a few seconds, and Alice takes this as an invitation to continue.

'Philippe told me about the shadow, and how you clicked on a link. You really can't do that sort of thing these days.'

No kidding.

'Why did you call her?' I ask Philippe, trying to keep my tone as normal as possible.

'She's here as a friend. She isn't a police officer; she helps out the cybercrime unit. But she's here as a favor, not anything official. I know you were embarrassed and didn't want me to, but that image on the screen was pretty scary, and I knew it was a bad virus.' He cocks his head at Alice. 'She can help.'

While I'm sure that she can, I don't want anyone else poking around in my laptop, much less someone who helps the police. Even if she's here 'unofficially'.

'Why don't you show me what's going on?' Alice asks. She wants the laptop. She wants to see inside it. I can't tell her no, because then she'll get suspicious. But if I hand it over, she'll see – well, what will she see? I think fast. She'll see what the shadow is seeing, which is precious little. Except that I did not clear my recent history, which shows that I've been in the chat room. But I might be able to talk my way out of that one.

I pull the laptop out of the backpack and hand it to Alice. While she opens it and boots it up, I tell her, 'I was in a chat room. I have a couple of friends there, they've been explaining some computer stuff to me, and one of them's the one who I got the virus from.'

'I don't think he's a friend, then, is he?' Alice's tone is definitely frosty. 'And why are you on this chat room? It's for hackers.' She's looking at the site now, scanning it. 'I know this site. What exactly were you looking for?' She is watching me intently. Her gaze is unnerving. 'Are you a hacker?' she asks without waiting for me to answer.

'Seriously? You think I'm a hacker?' I make every effort to keep my tone light, teasing, to show her that her question is a ridiculous one. Even though I have not answered her question.

I am pretty sure I am not remotely what she associates with a hacker: a middle-aged woman wearing a long skirt and scarf, with salt and pepper curls and thin, tortoiseshell glasses.

'So let's see,' she says.

'See what?'

'What's going on inside your laptop.'

'You seem very young to be working with the police,' I tell her. She winks at me. 'They hired me because I was a hacker.'

If Zeke had come to me and asked me to work for the FBI instead of lurking around my house, spying on me and my father, would I have done it? Probably not. I was already a criminal; I was more than a hacker at that point. I still am, in their eyes – at least it seems that way, from the way they were after me last year on Block Island.

I wonder if the police know all of Alice's secrets, if she had to tell them for the job. Or did she keep anything to herself at all? Is she familiar with this chat room because she's been there, like me? Or does she know about it because she keeps an eye on it 'unofficially'?

Her fingers move across the keyboard, but because I'm looking at the back of the laptop, I have no idea what she's doing. It feels as though she has taken my child away. I force myself not to reach out to take it back. She bites her lower lip as she concentrates. It strikes me that there's something familiar about Alice right now. She reminds me of me. When I was Tina Adler. I recognize the concentration, the complete disconnection from her surroundings as she focuses solely on the screen in front of her.

She really is a hacker.

She might think that she isn't anymore, because she's with this cybercrime police unit, but a hacker is always a hacker. She's just hacking now for the police instead of herself.

I was maybe a little younger than Alice when I had to leave.

I move around to her side, but she quickly moves the laptop so I can't see what she's doing. It's reflex for her and so familiar that I can't help but smile at her. I reach over and turn the laptop toward me so I can watch her. She does not stop me.

She is in the source code for the chat room, scanning it, looking for – what, I'm not sure. I'm not sure how I feel about someone else poking around inside my laptop. My competitiveness begins to rise.

'You might want to change your password,' she advises with a straight face, but I can see the amusement in her eyes. She knows that isn't going to make any difference now. I am screaming inside, wanting to tell her everything, who I really am. But it would merely be reckless bragging.

There is no sign of the ransom demand, the pictures of my friends or the watchful eyes; I am relieved that none of them pop up on the screen, even though they're still there somewhere.

'What did you first notice?' Alice is asking. 'I mean, when you noticed the shadow. How did you discover it?'

'The webcam light came on, and then I got a message. It said that my computer was hijacked, and if I wanted it back, I had to pay.'

Alice's fingers fly across the keyboard. 'This message?'

There it is. I admire what she can do. I begin to worry that Alice is going to find the other messages and the images.

And then Alice asks, 'So who exactly is Tracker?'

I tense up when I hear his name. 'I told you, a friend.'

'If he's giving you a RAT, he's not a friend,' she says again.

I need to pack everything up and walk out of their lives right now, before there are any more discoveries. I reach for the laptop, shutting the cover and sliding it out from under Alice's fingers. She frowns.

'I can help.'

'I have to be someplace.'

'Where?'

She is bold, challenging me. As if she knows.

I have never told Philippe where I live; I have never told him that I show my paintings on rue du Trésor every weekend. He knows I am an American, but he thinks I am from Kansas City, a city he knows even less about than I do, and that I came here to live after getting laid off from a job at a bank. These are little white lies that I have fed him over several months, little white lies that if anyone ever asked him about Susan McQueen, no one would be able to connect her to Tina Adler. Or Nicole Jones.

But the longer Alice keeps poking around inside my laptop, the more likely that she might be able to unearth my secrets, and I cannot risk that.

'I really do have to go.' I hold up the flash drive, which I have been clutching in my palm. 'I've got the anti-virus program, so I'll run that as soon as I get home. Hopefully that's all I need to do.'

Alice looks at me warily. 'Hopefully,' she says dubiously.

Philippe frowns. 'Will you be back next weekend?' I only visit the shop on the weekends when I'm in town, so it's natural he would ask.

I force myself to smile. 'Yes, of course. I'll come in and show you how I've done with the program.' I shove the old laptop into my backpack. I'm going to have to shift everything around if I want to put the new one in there, too, and I can't do that here, so I merely hold it. I stick the flash drive in the front pocket of the backpack.

Philippe walks me to the door. Alice watches us but doesn't even say goodbye.

I give Philippe a short wave as I go to the door and step out onto the sidewalk, clutching the laptop to my chest, the backpack slung over my shoulder, bouncing against my side. The door closes behind me, and I don't look back so I don't know if he's watching me walk away.

I duck inside the bookstore, the French titles taunting me. I begin to shake. I grip the side of a shelf and take some deep breaths to try to get it under control. Even if Alice was off duty and only doing Philippe a favor, she is still working with the police – and more than that, with the cyber unit. She is a hacker, and she now knows enough about my time in the chat rooms so she might be able to follow my tracks. She already found Tracker. He could lead her right to me. It was a mistake letting her look at the laptop, but I don't know how I would have been able to get out of it without raising alarms. And leaving the way I did was probably not a good idea, either.

I finally allow myself to look through the window at the street. I scan the passersby, but I don't see Alice. That's not to say she's not there, it's just that she might be good at hiding in plain sight.

Like me.

NINE

When I approach rue du Trésor, I begin to feel this was a mistake, coming back to see Dominique. But I owe her an explanation. I also need access to the bank account, and I can't risk her blocking me yet.

I wish I could go back with her, but I knew the moment I found the shadow that I couldn't.

Jean's eyebrows rise when he sees me. Dominique's back is to me, but she must see Jean's expression because then she turns. Her jaw is set, and she does not smile. I don't let my gaze linger on Jean. I take Dominique by the elbow and steer her a few feet away, where he might not be able to overhear.

'I'm sorry,' I say quickly, 'but there was something I needed to do.' I hold out the laptop. 'I've got a virus in my computer.' I am not proud of what I'm about to say, because it is merely for effect, despite being the truth. 'I got hacked. Someone is watching me through my computer.'

Her expression changes quickly to one of concern. Before she can say anything, I add, 'I went to a computer shop, and it took longer than I thought it would. I should have told you, but—'

Before I can finish, Dominique puts her hand up to stop me. 'Don't. It's fine. I do wish you'd told me, but it's fine. Has the problem been fixed?'

I shake my head. 'No. It's not. I need to go back and have them do a little more work on it. I'd like to stay here; I'll find a place to stay overnight.'

'How will you get back?'

'Train. Le Massif.' Even though this is spur of the moment today, I have been researching trains to and from the Charlevoix region and know that there is a tourist train that stops in Baie-Saint-Paul. I could conceivably get off there and not take the rest of the tour. If I were, in fact, planning such a trip.

Dominique is buying it, though. 'When you get in, you call me and I'll have someone pick you up and take you to the ferry if I can't fetch you myself.'

I am able to be genuine when I thank her, and then add, 'I'll help you with loading up.'

She does not discourage me, and we go back to the booth. Jean openly glowers at me. Dominique, to her credit, pretends not to notice, and together we begin to take down the paintings that have not sold. It does not take too long, as we have a system for this as we have one for setting up. Dominique's arrangement for the booth rental is on Saturdays. Another artist will be in this spot tomorrow.

Dominique pulls the car around to the side street and together we carry the bag of paintings, the step stools, and the box with the credit card machine and other various items.

Jean has not said anything to either of us, but when we are done, he comes over to the car, where I am saying goodbye to Dominique.

'You're not going back?' he asks.

'No. I'm staying here tonight.' I try to sound as though this is something that has been planned. Dominique does not let on about my laptop, knowing that Jean is not someone I want to share anything with. She has been amused by our dislike of each other, but says little about it and will not speak ill of either of us to the other.

She is one of the more genuine people I've known in my life, and I will miss her. But not enough to tell her any more than I already have. She doesn't know about Philippe or to which shop I'm taking my laptop.

'Where are you staying?' Jean is asking.

'I might try the Château Frontenac.' I say it before thinking.

His expression changes, but I can't read it. 'Is that why you were there earlier?'

'Yes.' The lies are tying nicely together. 'I'll be a tourist for a night.'

'You must make a lot of money with these.' Jean waves his hand in the direction of the car, where my paintings are packed.

Dominique gives me a wink, then turns to him. 'Don't worry your head about how successful Susan is. You'll do better next week.' She quickly kisses him on the cheek to let him know she's teasing, before giving me a kiss first on one cheek and then on the other. 'Call me when you get back,' she whispers in my ear, squeezing my arm.

I squeeze back. 'Thank you for understanding.'

Dominique pulls away and gives a wave to no one in particular. 'See you soon,' she says, and it could be to either me or Jean. She climbs into the car, and I watch until it moves around the next corner.

As I turn, I realize Jean is still standing here. I begin to pass him, but he holds out his hand to stop me.

'How can you lie to her like that?' he demands.

TEN

In the days before I was Susan McQueen, or even Nicole Jones or Amelie Renaud, I was Tina Adler and I learned how to hide. I hid behind a computer screen and got past firewalls and into portals and stared into strangers' lives and secrets. They weren't all strangers, though. My father, the famous financial adviser Daniel Adler who died while serving a twenty-five-year sentence for conning millions out of his clients, had more secrets than most, and I hacked my way right into them.

Lying was second nature to him – and I learned from the best.

So when Jean accuses me of lying to Dominique, I am a little surprised. So he found me wandering the Château Frontenac. Why doubt it was for any other reason than what I'd told Dominique?

'Why were you following me around?' I demand.

Jean gives me shrug. 'Why do you think I'd spend my time following you?'

'I have no idea, but you've made it your business to know where I've been all day. Why?' I genuinely want to know, but I doubt he's going to tell me.

His eyes flicker to somewhere over my head as he scratches the side of his nose. I anticipate the lie.

But he surprises me. He looks back at me and says, 'I don't trust you.'

It takes me aback, his honesty. He sees this and laughs. 'What, has everyone your whole life trusted you?'

It's almost as if he knows. But he can't possibly. I give him a smile. 'There has never been any love lost between us, Jean. Perhaps we should agree to always disagree.'

'I don't like that you lie to Dominique.'

'I don't know why you think I'm lying to her.'

He narrows his eyes at me, studies me in a way that perhaps is supposed to make me uncomfortable – and it does. I try not to show it, force my expression to stay neutral. I reach over and touch his arm. 'I'm glad you're such a good friend to her.' It is possibly the most honest I have ever been with Jean, and he can see my sincerity. It throws him off, and he forgets that he meant to unnerve me.

'I have an appointment,' I say, backing up. 'I really have to get going. See you next week.' I turn away from him. I don't look back to see if he's watching me; I know that he is. I push the conversation out of my head. It won't do any good to dwell on it. I will never see Jean Bessette – or Dominique – again, so I have to let it go. I turn my thoughts to what I need to do now. My best planning happens on my bike, but that's not an option today, so I have to do it on foot.

I find myself on the Promenade des Gouverneurs, a boardwalk that begins at Dufferin Terrace and ends up along the Citadel walls, leading to the Plains of Abraham, the battlefield where the French and the English fought in 1759 that has been turned into a beautiful park. I'm not going that far, though. I am just past the Château, and there are a lot of tourists. I stop at a small shop along the perimeter that sells gelato. I get a cup of strawberry and sit on a bench overlooking the river. Behind me is a line of cannons, and children are climbing all over them. A woman has set up a portable microphone and is singing in French for passersby a few feet away. The sky is beginning to darken slightly with the late afternoon. Instinctively, I think about painting it, capturing it in this one moment, but then realize that I have not only left my bicycle behind, but my paints and easel.

I have become a creature of habit over the years, enjoying a quiet life. Leaving Block Island last year threw me a bit. I'd had no idea how addicted to routine I had become, and when my life was thrown into chaos, I had a very hard time adjusting. I chose Ile-aux-Coudres because I felt it would restore that stability to my life, and it did. To a point. But I let the Internet back into my life and that in itself is disrupting. I should have known I would have to leave sooner rather than later. It was inevitable.

I finish my gelato and take stock of what needs to be done. First, I have to get out of Quebec City, but leave some breadcrumbs so no one can find me right away. Second, I have to figure out how I'm going to pay the shadow. I don't know too much about bitcoins, except that I don't have any and I don't have any money for an exchange. Which means that I need to find out exactly how they work and how I might be able to get my hands on some, because

I have to keep Steve and Jeanine safe. While I do want to find out who my shadow is, right now my safety and the safety of my friends is critical.

In order to do any of this, I need wireless Internet. I get up, throw away my cup, brushing past a couple taking pictures of themselves with the cannons in the background, and head back to the Château Frontenac. Instead of going in through Starbucks this time, I make my way around to the front, where I came out with Jean, and go through one of the rotating doors. I find an empty plush armchair in the lobby and open the laptop that I got from Philippe. He has left it to me to set up, so I do that, creating an identity for it much like I've created identities for myself.

I make a reservation on Le Massif with the debit card that I have through the gallery. In case Dominique checks, she will believe I have every intention of returning to the island. Second, even though I am but feet away from the main desk, I make a one-night reservation at the Château. The price makes me pause for only a second.

In the days when I was Tina Adler, luxury accommodations were the norm. I slept on soft mattresses, my head resting on down pillows, a soft European comforter keeping me warm in the cool central air that circulated throughout the Spanish-style mansion on the sea that I called home.

I pretend I have not been living in a small brown house in the middle of nowhere, using firewood for heat and reusing teabags.

I turn my attention back to the laptop. There is no free Wi-Fi here; I need to enter a name and a room number. Since I now have a reservation, I go over to the front desk and check in. The woman behind the counter doesn't question when I tell her I will use the same credit card that I made the reservation with. She hands me a card key and tells me to go around the corner to the bank of elevators to get to my room on the eleventh floor.

I would have more privacy there, but I don't really need it, and I'd rather not be tempted by a luxurious hotel room, so I go back to my seat in the lobby, armed with the information I need to get onto the wireless Internet. Once I'm online, I go to the chat room. Here, I am now a stranger. I am sorry for that, because I have fostered relationships with people on this site in the past months and now I will have to prove myself all over again as someone who can be trusted. I create yet another alias and begin to search for

Tracker. I am still suspicious of him, but he is the one person I can turn to about the bitcoins. However, I cannot find him in the chat. Angel is here, and Phreak, one of the other regulars. I trace their footsteps, but I see nothing out of the ordinary, no sign that they're doing anything other than sharing some source code information for a site that Phreak is doing some paid work on.

I need to get behind the chats. I need to see what's going on in the private rooms, see if Tracker is there.

This is not going to be easy. There are more firewalls here than on the FBI site. The hackers have set them up, to protect themselves against the FBI, against people like me who want to unearth the secrets here.

The screaming startles me, and I look up to see a little girl throwing a temper tantrum near the front desk, her mother trying to reason with her, her father shaking his head as if disbelieving that a small child could behave so badly in such a beautiful place. The porters and front desk workers are acting as though nothing is wrong.

I turn my attention back to the screen, where I had been scanning the source code for the FAQ page before being distracted.

And that's when I see it: a place within the code where I can slip inside and try to find Tracker.

I am vaguely aware that the screaming has not stopped. That people are passing me, wheeling their luggage on the soft carpeting. All the sounds dissipate and I hear nothing, see nothing except the code in front of me.

My fingers fly on the keyboard. I manage to get inside several private chats – it is a lot easier than I thought it would be – but they don't interest me because I don't recognize any of the names. But then I see him. Tracker. I am invisible, although if he really wanted to see me, he could.

He is here with someone named Z.

And they are talking about me.

ELEVEN

'She was gone a long time,' Z writes, 'and she came back but then disappeared again. Why do you think she'll show up again?'

'Because she can't stay away. I wouldn't be surprised if she's here somewhere and we just don't know it,' Tracker responds.

'You couldn't find out?'

'I'm trying. But so far, nothing.'

It's possible that they're talking about someone else, but who else was gone a long time, came back, and then left again? I don't feel as though I'm being narcissistic.

I do wish I knew why Z is asking about me. Who is he, and what does he want?

'Keep me posted,' Z writes, and then he's gone, out of the chat.

Tracker is still here. It would take only a keystroke and he would know I am here, too. But his exchange with Z has made me uneasy. Why is he looking for me, and why does Z care? I'm not ready to have a conversation; I need to think about this a little. And I can't do it here, in the lobby at the Château Frontenac. I consider again going up to my room, but I would rather not leave any signs of myself there. My fingerprints are undoubtedly on file somewhere; if Dominique declares me missing, they will find out that Susan McQueen is really Tina Adler.

I don't want to make it that easy for them.

I scoop up the laptop and sling the backpack around my shoulder, then ask for directions to the ladies' room. The concierge is pleasant and tells me it's downstairs. I make my way there, past a shop with an elegant evening gown in the window and another with a large, old-fashioned world globe and a telescope. I wonder about the people who buy these things, whether anyone buys them at all.

Once in the ladies' room, I lock myself in a stall to take stock of what I've got with me. The front pockets of the backpack hold an extra pair of glasses, some make-up, a hairbrush, a face cloth in a plastic bag, some hand cream, and deodorant. Inside the larger compartment is the stash of cash at the bottom, a pair of jeans, two T-shirts, and a sweater.

Quickly, I shed the clothes I'm wearing and put on the jeans and T-shirt. By taking those things out of the backpack, there's room for both laptops inside. When I leave the stall, I shove the skirt, blouse, and scarf into the trashcan beneath the paper towel dispenser. I turn and look into the mirror.

My hair is the salt and pepper it's been for the last couple of years, but I've let it grow out and had it styled. My glasses are distinctive: round, plastic tortoiseshell. I bought them because they screamed 'artist' at me. I take them off and squint. I haven't worn contacts in years, but maybe it's time again. I turn the water on and cup my hands, wetting my hair down. It does what I expect: the curls bounce to life. I pull the dangly earrings out of my ears and wash my face next, the make-up coming off, all except for the mascara. I take the extra pair of glasses out of the backpack, the metal frames I wear when I bike, and exchange them for the plastic ones.

When I look again at myself, I no longer see Susan McQueen. Except for the longer hair, I have transformed back into Nicole Jones, the woman who ran bike tours on Block Island and ate hamburgers and onion rings at Club Soda every Friday night. Somehow, this transformation comforts me. I am comfortable being Nicole.

As I head outside and down the sidewalk, the backpack slapping against my side with the weight of the laptops inside, I wonder why I am not more nostalgic about this place I have called home for the past year. Perhaps it's because I've kept my distance emotionally, knowing this day was inevitable.

I buy a ticket for the funicular across Dufferin Terrace. The ride is slow, but smooth, and soon we are at the bottom. I scramble out. The pedestrian streets are so full of tourists that it's hard to maneuver around them. The shop doors are open, inviting everyone in to browse and buy. I can go either to my right or straight ahead, and I choose the latter, making my way down the slight incline to the Place Royale, a cobblestone square housing Notre-Dame-des-Victoires, the oldest stone church in North America, built in the sixteen-hundreds. I head inside the church to see the replica of a French regiment ship hanging from the ceiling. I've always liked the oddity of it, and I sit down in one of the back pews.

I close my eyes and lean back, breathing deeply as I learned to do in yoga classes. I have a plan, and I have to stay focused. But I need to slow my heartbeat, relax a little. I have changed my looks somewhat, and despite the reservation at the Château Frontenac, no one will find me there. I almost feel safe. Almost.

It's time to leave.

I find the bus stop on rue Dalhousie, not far from here. I have a schedule, something I researched last night, and I know this bus is one transfer away from the train station that will take me to Montreal.

As the bus approaches, I feel no emotion except relief. I climb on, pay my fare, and I'm on another leg of a journey that seems to have no end.

The train is fairly comfortable; I am able to buy a sandwich and a bottle of water, and it has free Internet. I think I could live on this train forever.

It is not crowded, so I have a row to myself. I spread out a little and take the new laptop out of the backpack.

I go back to the chat rooms and scan them. I'm feeling a little obsessive compulsive, but my heart stops for a second when I see another message for me from Tracker. It's the same as before, same as the one that gave me the shadow. I want to be able to open it, see the source code, to see if there's another RAT hiding inside, but I can't do that. One compromised computer is enough.

The date and time on this message is today. An hour ago. Maybe Tracker realized that I caught him and thinks he can trick me again.

I don't know why I'm thinking like this. I eliminated Tracker from the list of suspects, due to his ignorance about Steve and Jeanine, but there is still a little twinge of doubt. Tracker is resourceful; he's smart. It's possible that he found out about them somehow. But would he threaten them to get me to pay him a million bitcoins? That's not the Tracker I know. Granted, I have never met him face to face, but in many ways we are like kindred spirits. When we worked together before, we were always in sync, each able to predict the other's actions simultaneously. Anyway, if Tracker wanted a million bitcoins, he'd have ways of getting them – and not through me.

I lean back and eat a little bit of my sandwich and drink some water. The more I think about it, the more ridiculous it seems that I'm even suspecting Tracker, yet his conversation with Z still raises questions.

With a few keystrokes, I am looking at Tracker's profile, which is logically scant. Not even a nationality, although there is a birthdate, since allegedly we must all be over eighteen to be on the site. Nineteen hundred fifteen, it reads. The site is not smart enough to realize that someone who is over a hundred years old would not be on a hacker chat. He would be dead. But the site's algorithms see that he is over eighteen, and thus, eligible to participate.

When I first saw Tracker's birth year – the year I was seventeen but told the site I was thirty – I made a crack about it.

'You're an old man.'

'Who says I'm a man?'

That made me think twice. I was a girl hacker, why couldn't Tracker be a girl, too?

'OK, so you're a girl.'

'Maybe.'

'You're so coy.'

'You're easy to tease.'

'Seriously, maybe we should meet.'

'We can never meet, Tiny. That will be the biggest regret of my life, never meeting you. But it wouldn't be a good idea.'

'Why not?'

'Someday you'll figure it out.'

I remember the conversation so vividly that it could be happening right now. I find myself desperately wanting to click on that link, to go to the chat where Tracker is waiting. Instead, I finish my sandwich, staring out the window but not paying attention to the passing landscape. I have never been to Montreal. When I crossed the border, I made my way through the sparsely populated countryside into Quebec City. It was there that I learned about the island, and, being partial to islands after fifteen years living on one, I decided to head there, the opposite direction of Montreal.

Since it's a city I don't know at all, I have no idea where this train will drop me. But I have the Internet, so I quickly find the city's tourism site and a map. To my surprise, I see that Montreal is an island, and I smile to myself. Granted, this one will be far different than the two I've inhabited recently, but it does seem like a sign. If I believed in that sort of thing.

According to the map, the train will drop me in the center of downtown, and I see the Fairmont Queen Elizabeth hotel nearby. It is luxurious and expensive – and quite possibly too visible. I search the tourism site for other hotels and inns. The city has a subway system that seems easy enough, and I find a smallish hotel that is more nondescript just a short ride from the metro stop that is closest to the train station. The price is also more reasonable; since I'm not sure how I'm going to replenish my cash, I need to put myself on a budget.

I close the laptop and think about soft cotton sheets and goose down pillows. There is still an hour before we reach Montreal, so I consider a nap. But I need to find the rest room first, and as I get up and look down the aisle, my heart stops.

Jean Bessette is sitting in the car ahead.

TWELVE

J ean is not facing me, but I can see his profile. It is definitely him. What is he doing on this train?

Immediately, I drop back down into my seat and move to the one closer to the window to hide myself completely from Jean. Why is he here? Has he been following me since I left him? I'm sure he wasn't on the bus I took to the station; I would have seen him. Maybe he was in a car, but the route I took to the bus stop is mostly pedestrian and he would have to be psychic to know exactly where I'd end up.

I feel paranoid; maybe it's not about me. But it's too much of a coincidence that he's on the same train.

My head is spinning, yet I have a moment of clarity. I pull the laptop open again and after signing on, do a quick search for Jean Bessette, Quebec City. Why I have never done this before, I don't know, but better late than never.

I don't like what I find.

Jean is a retired police detective.

This has never come up in conversation, and Dominique certainly has never mentioned it. I would remember if she had. When I've seen Jean, he has spent most of the time flirting with Dominique and glaring at me. He's never followed me around before, or at least I've never noticed if he did. What is so special about today? And what on earth is he doing on this train? Does he know who I am? Is that what his comments about not trusting me were all about? If he followed me to Philippe's shop, then it's possible he knows. Isn't it?

I try to keep my paranoia at bay so I can think rationally, but there is nothing rational about this situation.

I think about Alice – I realize now I never got her last name – and wonder if she is part of this. Maybe she alerted Jean about me for some reason and that's why he's on the train now.

I am seeing conspiracy at every turn.

Since I don't know Montreal or its train station, I don't know if

I'll be able to slip off the train without Jean noticing me. I lean over and look down the aisle at the car behind this one. I am in the middle of the train; there are at least a couple more cars back there. Quickly, I gather up my things, shoving the laptop into the backpack and shifting it over my shoulder. I glance at the car where Jean is sitting, and he is talking with someone across the aisle from him. If I move now, it's possible the motion will register in the corner of his eye and he'll see me.

My entire body is tense as I ponder what to do. As I think, a large man two rows up gets out of his seat and lurches into the aisle. He is heading for the rest room in the direction of Jean's car. I take this chance and slide out of my seat, hunched over so the man is blocking anyone's view of me. When I reach the door to the next car, I hit the button and it slides open; I rush through and down into the next car.

I glance back, but the large man is standing in front of the door, and no one ahead of him can see anything that's going on back here. I pass quickly through this car and move into the next one, putting even more space between me and Jean.

It doesn't solve the problem of how I'm going to avoid him when we get off the train, but it gives me a little more peace of mind, a little more room in which to think.

More time to do some research online.

There is a story in the local newspaper about Jean's retirement. While I've had a little adjusting to do with speaking Québécois French – the dialect threw me off at first, and sometimes I still have trouble understanding some people – reading it is not a problem, since written French is the same. Jean was with the Royal Canadian Mounted Police's national and border security division, working with immigration. He was on a team responsible for cracking down on illegal immigrants.

Like me.

I lean back in my seat and contemplate this. Does Jean know that I'm here illegally? Has he had his colleagues check their records for a Susan McQueen? Is he aware that she does not exist? That she never came over the border through customs? That there is no passport for such a person?

From what I've seen of Jean, though, these past couple of months, I would have thought he would have confronted me. Or at least spoken to Dominique about me. He wasn't shy about telling me earlier today that he doesn't trust me. If he knew the truth, wouldn't he have said something? More likely, he'd probably have already put me in handcuffs and hauled me off to prison or handed me over to the feds.

I can't take the risk that he doesn't know. I have to assume he does, and that his journey on this train is to catch me.

I need a new identity.

A year ago, documents were waiting for me in Chinatown, in New York City. I never showed up for them. I'm regretting that decision now, even though at the time, I couldn't go. I couldn't risk getting caught. Tracker arranged everything, like he had before the bank job. His help got me to Paris as Amelie Renaud. And while I'd trusted him, I didn't trust that no one else knew. It could have been a trap. Much like the shadow that's been set loose in my laptop.

For a quick second I think that I could hack into the State Department site and get myself a passport. But that would be a lot more difficult than hacking into the chat rooms. I need a Social Security number, photographs. And I'm out of the country. I wonder if I could get a Canadian passport, pass myself off as a citizen. Right now I have no country. I could choose any one I'd like.

My fingers tap the top of the laptop. My connections are within it; my way out is here in front of me.

I don't want to do anything illegal, but I'm afraid I might have to.

I peer around the seat in front of me toward the car where Jean is sitting, but I can't see him from here. I touch my curls, the edge of my glasses. Jean Bessette has never seen me like this; he's never been to the island, never seen me on my bike. He's never met Nicole Jones. As far as I know, he doesn't know she even existed.

I'm not even sure that he is on this train for me, but if he is, I doubt that I am disguised enough so I can slip past him once the train stops in Montreal. I look at the backpack, the one I've been carrying around with me all day. Even on the off chance that he doesn't recognize me, he has seen the backpack and could make the connection between it and me. I try to push my paranoia aside. The backpack is neutral enough so anyone could be carrying one like it.

I settle back into the seat and watch the landscape move past the window, every once in a while checking to make sure Jean isn't coming back here.

I don't want to go back online now and get distracted. I have to stay on alert.

When the train stops and I disembark, I see Jean get off the train up ahead. He looks around, and I duck behind a large man – I think it's the same one who blocked his view earlier – and when the man begins to walk away, I see Jean going in the other direction, away from me. He has not seen me. He is talking to someone, though, a tall man with dark hair wearing a dark blazer and jeans. Something about the man's stance seems familiar, but it's impossible. I know no one else here. He is walking stiffly, his arms at his side. When he shifts a little to the side, that's when I see it. The jacket bunches a little at the armpit, and the outline of the holster is evident. He's a cop. He could even be FBI.

The FBI came after me before, and as far as I know, they're still looking for me. It has to do with the bank job, but it also has to do with Zeke. I left him to die in Paris after he came looking for me. I wonder if the FBI knows that one of their agents was going to defect and disappear with me. If I would have had him.

I shake off the thoughts about Zeke. I don't have time to reflect. I ignore my growling stomach – the sandwich was two hours ago – and ask directions to the metro. There is a whole underground city here in Montreal, and I could navigate its avenues far away from Jean if I liked. Instead, I buy a metro ticket, find the stop I need for the hotel on the map, and when I finally emerge, I am at the Saint-Laurent station. I glance around to get my bearings and after walking a block or two, I spot the auberge, or small hotel.

The man at the desk doesn't even blink when I hand over cash to pay for the room. He doesn't ask if I'm going to stay more than one night. He merely takes the money and puts it in a drawer and gives me a key – an actual key, not one of those card keys – and points to the stairwell. I thank him in French and make my way upstairs. The room is small, dark, straight out of IKEA, but it is cheap and fairly clean.

I have decided that I cannot speak English here; I have to use the French I've learned over the past year and pretend that I am francophone, or a French-speaking Québécoise. While it was clear

I was an American in Charlevoix, perhaps it won't be as noticeable in Montreal, a large city, especially if I put all my effort into being Québécois. I was Amelie Renaud in Paris, but I've decided to be Hélène Leblanc here. I will soon need a notebook to mark down all the names I've had so I won't forget them.

THIRTEEN

I hadn't even asked about wireless, but I turn on my uncompromised laptop to discover that the signal is strong and it's free when I enter my room number, just like at the Château Frontenac. I find myself back in the chat room, looking for Tracker. It's time for me to reach out to him. While I am still a little suspicious about whether he is my shadow and put that RAT into the URL himself, the other suspects are more likely, so I decide to take this chance. I need some help with the bitcoins, and regardless of my uncertainty, he is the only one I can turn to. I'll feel him out first, though.

I find a site to chat privately; I copy the URL. For a moment, I wonder about those RATs, buying one myself, embedding it inside and tracking Tracker. It would be easy – if I had a bank account. If I had a credit card. I can't use Dominique's card; it would raise a red flag if I used it to buy a remote access Trojan. So I am at a distinct disadvantage.

I write a short note, asking Tracker to meet me. I don't use any French phrases – I don't want to tip anyone else off as to my identity – merely a simple request for help with a source code: 'I've heard that you might be able to help.'

I sign it Elizabeth. Elizabeth McKnight. The name on the documents he arranged that I never picked up in Chinatown.

I find my way to the private chat room URL that I've given him. I have no idea if he'll be here, if he even remembers the name Elizabeth McKnight.

But I don't have to wait too long before he shows up.

'Hey, Tracker,' I write.

'Tiny? Is it you?'

My fingers hover over the keyboard for a few seconds, then I type: 'Yes.'

'I've been looking for you. I saw your message, but you weren't there.'

That's right. I'd left my message in French to indicate I was willing

to meet, but the shadow got in the way. 'There was a problem.' I
hesitate again; should I tell him?

'The RAT.' He writes it before I can say anything. 'When you
disappeared, I wanted to make sure the URL link hadn't broken. I
found the RAT. Is he inside your computer?'

My hands are shaking, my head spinning. He knows.

'Tiny?'

I put my fingers on the keys. 'Yes. He's inside.'

'Now?'

'I have a different one. A new laptop. We're OK now.'

'You thought it was me.'

Tracker and I have always been in sync.

'Yes.'

'It's not. Do you believe me?'

I want to, I really want to. 'He wants a million bitcoins.' I don't
even give him time to respond before typing: 'He knows. About the
bank account. He knows who I am.'

It feels like an hour, but only a few seconds later: 'How?'

'I don't know. There's nothing in the laptop that would lead
anyone to me. I've been very careful.'

'You've always been careful. But I've been afraid of this.'

'Afraid of what? What's going on?'

'Someone's been in the chat rooms asking about you, wanting
to know if anyone's heard from you, if you've been in contact with
anyone.'

That must be Z, the other person in the private chat room with
him. I can't ask him directly about Z, though, because then he'll
know I've been lurking. Maybe Z is my shadow, whoever he is.
'Someone told my shadow about you. About you and me,' I write.
'So he found you and managed to use you to find me.'

'Whoever he is knows about your French. Somehow figured out
that a message in French was directed to you.'

'So he was waiting for me to answer you.'

'Do you have any idea of who he might be?'

'I thought it was you. Who else knew about the bank account?'

'I didn't tell anyone, but I don't blame you for thinking it was
me. I can't expect you to believe me when I say it wasn't me, but
I hope you can.'

I do want to believe him, I really do.

'I've spent a lot of time trying to find out who he is, Tiny, but he's smart. He's getting in through back doors I didn't even know existed on the site. I've closed several, but I don't know that I've found them all.'

I am about to tell him that he hasn't, that I've been able to get through, but his next question makes me pause.

'Did you tell Ian Cartwright about the bank account?'

'He suspected, but he never knew for sure. But I don't think he has the skills to get through the source code and find an open portal or use a RAT.'

'You don't need skills for a RAT.'

I've already thought about this, though, and I tell him so. 'He never knew about the chat room. He never knew about that part of it. No, I don't think it was Ian. Is there anyone on the chat who helped out, you know, back then?' Even now I am afraid to spell it out, to incriminate myself in writing.

'No. Everyone's gone.'

Something still nags at me. 'But how would anyone now know that you and I are connected? Someone is poking around the chats, asking about me, but they're talking to you about where to find me, so someone has connected us.'

The moment I hit 'send' I realize what I've done. I've shown my hand. He had said that someone was looking for me, not that someone had been asking him specifically about me. Before he can respond, I type: 'You haven't closed all the back doors.'

After about five minutes, he finally responds. 'Nice to hear you haven't lost your touch.'

'I only went in after I got the shadow. It seemed necessary.'

'And what was your conclusion?'

I sit back against the pillows for a second, thinking about this before typing: 'Who is Z?'

'He's not the one, Tiny, although I can see why you'd be suspicious. But I know Z. I've known him a long time.' I get the impression that he knows Z personally, that it's not just an online relationship. I don't know if that is a reason to believe that Z isn't my shadow, but I don't have much choice.

'OK, but besides Z, I didn't find out anything that was helpful.' I am not about to tell him that I only visited the chats he was involved in himself.

'Did you ever tell anyone about me?' Tracker asks.

I am about to type 'no,' truly believing it, but then the memory comes back, slams into my head, and I realize that's wrong. There were two other people who knew about Tracker, about the chat site, two people whom I could trust. The two people I am trying to keep safe now. I remember: Steve, looking over my shoulder, as I talked to Tracker in the chat room. Jeanine, noticing that I was having a conversation with someone named Tracker. I never completely explained who he was to Jeanine, but Steve knows and he may have told her after I disappeared.

Did the shadow do anything beyond get their photographs? Did he go to them? Ask about me? Would either of them tell anyone what I was doing last year? Did they tell the shadow about me inadvertently? Or did the shadow threaten them to get information?

I think Tracker believes my silence confirms that I have told no one, because before I can answer him, he asks, 'Has anything else happened lately that you've noticed?'

'Only the shadow.' But then I remember Jean – and Alice. 'Well, I might have gotten the attention of a retired detective. But I'm not sure exactly what he knows, if he knows anything.'

'How, exactly, have you gotten his attention?'

'He doesn't like me. I don't know if he actually knows anything, but he's suspicious for some reason.' I pause, and then continue. 'I met him a month or so ago through someone else, but I didn't know he was a retired detective. We've had a—' I consider how to describe my relationship with Jean '—cordial relationship, although he's made it clear he doesn't like me too much.'

'LOL. How could he not love you, Tiny?'

I smile to myself, then continue. 'I can't really say much more about it, but he started following me around today. I saw him a few places, I confronted him, and he told me he didn't trust me. But I didn't think too much of it. But then he showed up on the train I was on. Going to the same place.'

Have I said too much? I re-read my message and think not. There is no clue here to where I am or what I've been doing exactly.

'How did you find out he was a retired detective?'

It's a logical question. 'I did an online search on the train.'

'You didn't think to do a search before then?'

'I didn't have a reason to. He was more of an annoyance, and I didn't see him all the time.'

'You don't think this retired detective is your shadow, do you?' Tracker is asking.

'No,' I type quickly. But Alice is a different story. 'There's someone else, a young woman who had access to my laptop. Although it was after I got the shadow, so I'm not sure she's responsible.'

'How did she end up with your laptop?'

'I went to a computer repair shop that I've been to before. I know the owner. I told him I got a virus, and he downloaded an anti-malware program for me to use. But—' I stop typing, thinking about Alice.

'But?'

I wonder if I should tell him, and finally decide it's best. 'He thought I should call the cybercrime police unit. When I went back to his shop to get the program, he had brought in a young woman who works with the police. She's a hacker. I couldn't keep her from looking at the laptop without raising suspicion.' I stop writing, realizing how stupid that was.

Tracker, to his credit, doesn't point it out, but I know he's thinking it as his next message pops up.

'Does she know about the chat room where you got the RAT?'

'Yes. And she knows about you. That I got the RAT through your link.'

'Well, that might explain it.'

'Explain what?'

'I had to switch laptops earlier today.' I know what he's going to tell me next, but even knowing doesn't make it any less upsetting. 'I got a RAT, too.'

FOURTEEN

'Can you tell me who she is?' Tracker is asking.

I can't tell him without revealing where I am. I'm caught between wanting to say and being unable to for fear of being found. So, instead I write, 'We don't know that she was the one who gave you the RAT. It could have been *my* shadow. Clearly he knows who you are and your connection to me. Maybe he's trying to get to me through you.' But Alice is not above suspicion. She could have inserted the code when she was on my laptop, although she did say she was familiar with the chat room so it might have been later. 'Did you get a message?' I ask. 'Is your shadow asking for a million bitcoins, too?'

'No.'

'How do you know you've got a shadow?'

'My cursor moved, and I wasn't doing it.'

'Then I guess whoever it is isn't all that careful about it. I wonder if he wants you to know.'

'Did it seem like this hacker knew what she was doing?'

If it *is* Alice, she managed to hack Tracker, which is pretty impressive, but I don't want to throw that in his face. I remember, too, her expression as she concentrated on the screen in front of her. That told me more about her than anything else.

'Yes. I think she knows what she's doing.'

'Let's say she's the one who did it. Why do you think she picked me?'

I think about this for a few seconds, then write, 'Maybe because I got the RAT from you. Maybe she was trying to catch you. Maybe she thinks you're somehow involved with something like Blackshades.' Blackshades was a remote access Trojan at the center of an FBI sting in which almost a hundred people were arrested all over the world.

'And she thinks that if she catches me, then it will elevate her in the eyes of the police?'

'It's possible, I guess, but she didn't seem like that type.'

'Then what type is she?'

'She seems like a loner. She wouldn't do it to impress anyone, just to prove something to herself.'

'Dangerous and arrogant.'

The way Alice physically took control of my laptop makes me think my theory is more on target than Tracker's. But wasn't I dangerous and arrogant, too?

'You were different,' Tracker writes, again reading my mind.

'How?' I really want to know what his perception of me was back then, back when I was in my so-called heyday.

'You were thoughtful about your hacks.'

'But I still wanted to catch my father.' Tracker is wrong about me being thoughtful. I began hacking my father's business accounts when I was fourteen. I hacked to prove to my father that I was smarter than he was. Because I got away with it, I became arrogant. I paraded myself in front of him, showed him up. And then, after the bank job, when Zeke started coming around, I convinced myself that he didn't know anything, that I'd fooled him, I'd fooled the FBI. Even when I caught Zeke looking at my laptop after he'd spent the afternoon in my bed, I ignored all the clues that he knew. He knew what I'd done. But I was unwilling to admit that I'd laid myself open to anyone, convincing myself that I couldn't be caught because I was too good.

This is why I spent fifteen years without a computer, why I resisted any temptation to hack again. Until then, all my 'friends' had been online, friends with no faces, no voices. Ian could argue that he was my friend, but he was merely my lover who manipulated me into using my computer skills to steal ten million dollars for him. Zeke had never been my friend, either, only the lover I used to try to get back at Ian.

Running away changed everything.

Suddenly there was Steve and our Friday night hamburgers at Club Soda; Jeanine and our wine and spa treatments and long conversations about men; Veronica and the gallery and the realization that I truly was an artist, not just some hacker.

I miss them every day. And now, even though I didn't give up my laptop again, I don't really hack. I'm more of a lurker, someone who gets past the firewalls, sees the portals and sneaks inside but does nothing once I'm there except observe. I can't help myself from doing that, but I can stop myself from doing anything to show my hand. My father's death last year made me realize that none of what I did made a bit of difference. He still went to prison; I'm still a fugitive.

I try to tell myself I don't need it anymore – I just like it – but I'm lying to myself. And even though the laptop is an extension of myself, like an extra limb I can't live without, Tracker doesn't really know me; he only knows my online persona. He knows Tiny. He doesn't have a clue about Tina.

'I need to know who she is, Tiny.' He is still talking about Alice.

'I can't.'

'You have to trust me.'

I want to. I really want to. But if I do, I'm laying myself wide open. 'You know what you're asking,' I write.

'I know.'

'If you've got a new computer, then why is it important who she is? She can't find out anything. Can she?'

'You know me better than that, Tiny. But she might not have just hacked me. She might be hacking other people on the chat, and I need to warn them. I need to know if she's lurking.'

'She wouldn't use her real name.'

'Why are you resisting?'

'Because I'm a fugitive. Because I don't want anyone to know where I am.' I pause. 'Even you.'

Is this our first fight? I've never argued with Tracker about anything before, but then again, he's never asked me to reveal where I am, like he wants me to now.

He is gone so long, I think he has logged off, but then: 'Are you in a safe place?'

I am relieved he has switched gears and let go of the idea that I give him Alice's identity, but I hope this isn't another ploy to find out where I am. 'Yes.'

'Do you have a good connection?'

I know he means Internet. 'Yes.'

'I think we need to catch this shadow. Mine might be this girl hacker, but what if they're the same person?'

The same person trying to catch both of us.

'He wrote me through the laptop's message program,' I type. 'I was going to try to find his IP address through the program, but it threw me off when he—' I haven't decided whether to tell him about the photos of Steve and Jeanine and catch myself just in time '—mentioned the bank account. So I lost the opportunity.'

'You have to engage him again, then,' Tracker says. 'That IP address is there. He's watching. Be careful, because he'll know what you're doing and he might be able to reroute the address even while you're looking.'

'He wants the money. The bitcoins. I have to get it to him.'

'Why?'

Can I tell him? If he helps me, I have to give him a reason. It wouldn't be fair not to. 'He's made a threat.'

He doesn't respond right away, but finally: 'Against you?'

By threatening Steve and Jeanine, he's indirectly threatened me, too, so I simply say, 'Yes.'

'Do you have access to bitcoins?'

'No.'

'What do you want to do?'

'Same thing as before.' There. I've written it. I'm willing to go black hat to make sure my friends are safe.

'It's not easy.'

'I know.'

'You've got a wallet to transfer to, right?' He's talking about an account, the one where the shadow wants me to transfer the bitcoins.

'Yes. How hard will it be?'

He knows what I'm asking. 'You need a key.' Bitcoin isn't real. It's cyber currency, bought and sold, and can be cashed in for real money. People who own bitcoin actually own a private cryptographic key that includes a long string of numbers and letters that will unlock an address to release the bitcoin. What I need to do is get a key and transfer the bitcoin to what is called the wallet at the address the shadow has given me.

It sounds easy enough, but there is a catch. 'There aren't that many bitcoins, though, in one place.'

'Right.'

'And he wants a million of them. So I need more than one key to get access to enough.'

'It's been done before. There are databases that contain hundreds of keys. And remember, you can see the blockchain. It's public. So you'll know how many bitcoins are where. And people can see where it's going once you make the transfer.'

Which means that the bitcoins might be traced to whoever is taking them. 'That's the idea.' So maybe I'm not so black hat after all. Maybe I'm more of a gray hat. I can't be held responsible for anything that happens once I transfer the bitcoins. I will have done what I've been asked to do, and I can only hope that the shadow will keep his promise and leave Steve and Jeanine alone afterward.

'Let me see what I can find out.' Tracker is going to hunt down a key for me. He thinks I'm doing it to find the shadow by tracing the bitcoins. That's enough for him to think.

'And I'll do the same on my end.' I pause, then add, 'I've got three days.'

'That's tight, but we can probably do it. When I find out something, I'll send a message to Elizabeth McKnight. If you want me, sign the message EMK, and I'll meet you. Be careful.'

'You, too,' I reply before signing off, but then wonder what he has to be careful about. No one has been looking for him for sixteen years. He doesn't have a retired immigration detective on his tail. And he doesn't have a shadow demanding a million bitcoins and threatening his friends.

At least I don't think so.

FIFTEEN

I know I should begin work immediately on the bitcoins, but I'm hungry. I set out for something to eat after I've thrown some water on my face. The sandals are not very comfortable after wearing them all day, and I'm getting a couple of blisters. I'll have to find a pair of sneakers tomorrow.

The man at the desk points in the direction of Chinatown when I ask for an inexpensive meal. The towering gate leads me into a brightly lit street, the smell of exotic food hanging in the air. I'm too tired to be picky, so I go into the first restaurant I see.

The hostess makes a fuss over me, and soon I am drinking green tea and digging into delicious dumplings filled with lamb, chicken, and shrimp. I find myself making a mental note of the name of the place, as though I plan to be here longer than a day or two, and while that might be a fantasy, I still take a business card from the hostess when I leave.

It's chilly, and I'm glad I wore my sweater as I make my way back to the hotel. I pass a couple of people on the way; it's late, and now that I've eaten, the fatigue has set in.

I let myself into my room and sit and stare out the window at the red brake lights of the cars passing below, the streetlamp illuminating the shop fronts along the sidewalk. If I were home, in my little house on the island, I would have a glass of cognac and settle in on my sofa and listen to the wind rush past. Have I made a mistake running away from that? Would anyone really ever find me there? Now I'm in an unknown city, with no means of escape.

Again I think about how I need a passport, a driver's license, to make any travel feasible. I don't have enough money for those things now, though, despite what my shadow thinks. That bank account he thinks I have such ready access to was set up so long ago, and I gave Tracker free rein. I can't imagine that there's any money left.

Is there?

I eye the new laptop.

What am I thinking? I can't put myself out there like that. The minute I tried to get inside would be the minute they'd catch me.

I do go online, though, to check the chat room. There is no message from Tracker. I wonder if the three days includes today or if I have three more days. I have to assume that I only have a couple more.

I do some research about bitcoins and explore the marketplaces where the blockchains of keys live. I read a couple of news reports about how the marketplaces can be compromised; hackers have gotten into them and stolen bitcoins before. I'm not quite sure where to start with this, though, and the thought of trying to get inside now exhausts me. I have to be on top of my game when I do this, so I pull the power cord out of the backpack and plug in the new laptop before grabbing the large T-shirt I brought to sleep in. Once changed, I go into the small bathroom and wash my face. I stare at the lines around my eyes in the mirror; I'm not getting any younger. How long can I keep running?

After brushing my teeth, I shut out the light and climb into bed. The mattress is soft. I pull the blanket up around my neck and close my eyes. Despite everything, the fatigue takes over, and I am asleep.

I pull the curtain over in the morning to let in the sunlight. I peer outside and see a bright blue sky. It's a beautiful day, and I wish I could ride my bike and enjoy it. Instead, I am hiding in this nondescript hotel. I eye the laptop, which is completely powered up now, on the bedside table. As much as I want to get back to work, I've got other things to do. The clock is ticking, but I still need to keep myself safe first. I head in to take a shower, and afterward, I slip into my jeans and T-shirt again. I'll have to find some new clothes soon – or a Laundromat.

I have checked online for local hair salons, and there is one open in Chinatown – even today, on a Sunday – near the restaurant where I had dinner last night. I pack up my backpack and check out of the hotel; a woman is manning the desk this morning and she barely gives me a glance as I hand over the key. Once outside, I find a patisserie and buy myself a café au lait and a croissant. I pick up a newspaper that's been left on a chair at a small table in the corner, and I absently translate the French as I nibble on the croissant. I don't care about world events right now, but I do need to look as though I'm engaged so as not to arouse any suspicion. I keep looking up at the door out of the corner of my eye, wondering if Jean Bessette is going to come in for a coffee.

My breakfast proves uneventful, however, and I head to Chinatown on Boulevard Saint-Laurent. I walk under the elaborate gate and enter the bustling neighborhood. A group of old men smoke cigarettes on the corner; shops display red Chinese dresses, cheap painted umbrellas, bronze Buddhas, and a variety of teas; cooked, skinny ducks hang inside restaurant windows, hoping to lure the hungry. I finally spy the hair salon on the corner. They have just opened, and they take walk-ins. The fact that everyone in here is Asian does not bother me, as long as they can take care of my hair.

They don't speak much French, so I begin to worry when they don't quite understand what I'm looking for. I glance around the salon and find a station with hair color tubes and point to them and then at my head. The woman standing closest to me suddenly grins and nods. She scurries over to the tubes and picks one out. I see from the package that it's a dark brown, and I shake my head. That color would be too much like Tina Adler. But the salt and pepper of Nicole and Susan has to go. The woman touches my hair and frowns. She exchanges the tube for another one, and after a few seconds, I agree.

Turns out, I don't look half bad with auburn hair. She cuts it shorter than it's ever been, but leaves it longer on the top; it makes my face look narrower. She shows me how to style it, and I don't even attempt to tell her that I don't own a blow dryer. It will work even without straightening it. And when I see my reflection, it takes me aback a little. I don't look like myself at all, which is the idea, but instead of relishing it, I am a bit wistful.

I have to find another hotel for tonight. It's a risk, staying a second night, but I am not yet ready to leave without a plan. Even though I left Quebec City abruptly, I had had a plan in place for some time, in case the time came. I need the same security – so I don't make a mistake.

I leave the salon and a block away I see a small hotel tucked between an Asian grocery and a shop selling tchotchkes. I push the door in and it's even darker here than the hotel I stayed in last night.

No one is at the desk, but I see a bell on the counter and I hit it. The sound echoes through the darkness. I hear rustling somewhere to my left, and suddenly a small, elderly Asian woman is coming toward me, smiling and nodding. Again, language is a little bit of a barrier, but she finally understands I need a room for the night. I pay in cash again, and she gives me a key, pointing me down a hallway. The sconces on the walls throw off a lot more light here than in the lobby, as though they realized their guests might need to see where they're going, and when the tiny elevator arrives, I slip into it and go to the third floor.

I have no complaints about the room. I sit on the bed and gauge how comfortable it is and determine that it will be fine. An inspection of the bathroom tells me that it's bright and clean.

I push the curtains aside to let some more light in, and I can see outside that the sun is high in the sky. I keep thinking about what I *should* do – begin looking for bitcoins I can compromise, go back to the chat room to see if Tracker has left me a message – but it's as though the enormity of what I'm about to do again has paralyzed me. While bitcoins could be considered make-believe by some people, the cash they generate is all too real. It is not unlike the bank job sixteen years ago, and I swore I would never do that again.

I think about Steve and Jeanine, and while I will be doing it for them, I have to be OK with it, too, and right now I am not OK. Maybe some more fresh air will clear my head. It might not hurt to see if I can't get another pair of jeans and another T-shirt, too. I unpack my toiletries and put them in the bathroom, then slide the new laptop into the backpack, leaving the old one powering up on the small night table. If anyone wants to break in and steal it, they're welcome to it. I smile to myself, thinking how that would throw off my shadow.

The tourist map that I pick up in the hotel lobby shows that Vieux Montréal – or Old Montreal – is not too far away by foot.

The boundaries of Chinatown are small here, and within a block, I am heading up a hill along Boulevard Saint-Laurent. I can see Notre-Dame Basilica up ahead and I am taken aback by the similarities to its sister cathedral in Paris, although the closer I get, the fewer those similarities are beyond the façade. I find myself in Place d'Armes, the statue of someone called Maisonneuve dated 1642 holding sentry over the square. There is a line to get into

Notre-Dame, and I forget about anything else and take my place
in it, handing over five dollars to gain entry and only mildly annoyed
at the cost.

Once inside, I am no longer annoyed. This is worth seeing: the
spectacular wooden altar ahead is illuminated by the skylight, blues
and golds shining as though God himself has touched this place. I
turn and look up behind me to see the gigantic pipe organ; to my
right is an elaborate wooden pulpit with two levels. The sun lights
up the stained glass. I slip into a back pew, the extravagance and
beauty overwhelming me.

I never once stepped into a church on Block Island, but I know
Steve did go every Sunday. I conjure an image of him, coming into
my house with his familiar 'Hello, hello!' greeting, and it's as though
someone has taken hold of my heart and twisted it. I have to do
this for him, I have to keep him safe.

It's time to go back and begin.

I reach over and shrug on the backpack as I get up from the pew.
I take a couple of steps toward the doors when I see him.

Jean Bessette is lighting a candle in the back.

Instinctively, I touch my hair, the corner of my glasses. I glance
down at my jeans and T-shirt. Do I dare pass him? If I keep going
in this direction, I will have to walk right by him, close enough so
I might even be able to hear him breathe. But if I turn now, I might
force him to notice me as the woman who is avoiding him. I take
a deep breath, move the backpack to my other shoulder, and continue.

Jean does not look up as I pass by. He is concentrating on the
candle, his eyes half shut as if in prayer.

I don't let myself relax until I am outside and moving quickly
down the sidewalk. I am walking along rue Notre-Dame, but I have
no idea which direction I'm heading or where I'm actually going.
I am a little breathless because I am walking so fast. I have not
looked behind me to see if Jean is following; I am pretending that
I am late for an appointment and every once in a while look at my
watch for effect. I'm feeling a little crazy, but I can't afford to get
caught.

The street becomes more Paris-like, and a majestic building soars
over me. In front of it is a long pedestrian walkway dotted with
artisan kiosks and street performers. When I get down to the next
cross street, it is rue Saint-Paul, and I realize I have stumbled into

Old Montreal. Restaurants and shops and small auberges line the streets. I am regretting my sandals, but Susan the artist wouldn't wear sneakers. I am not sure what my style should be now, as Hélène, but I am pretty certain that fashion sandals will have to go.

I duck into a restaurant. The whole front of the restaurant is open, with tables and chairs on the sidewalk, but I ask to be seated in the back, facing the front, in order to see anyone walking by.

I am compelled to order, as I sit here hiding in the back; however, the thought of Jean discovering me distracts me from the club sandwich and frites. I manage to eat half the sandwich and a few fries, and when I am done, I feel better and ready to move on. I have not seen Jean, and logic tells me that I am being silly. There is no way he could possibly know where I am staying, and now, with my new look, he may not even recognize me. I only saw him on weekends for the past four weeks, and he had eyes only for Dominique.

Except for yesterday.

This is why I can't let my guard down. Why I allow myself to worry.

SIXTEEN

People are walking along the sidewalks, enjoying a Sunday stroll. They're laughing, talking, some are holding hands. I had friends before, real friends. People I spent time with, had dinner with, laughed with. I have not had friends like that since I left Block Island. Dominique and I have a business relationship, but I have never been to her house for dinner, nor she to mine. I've shared drinks and meals with a couple of people on the island, but not frequently enough that they will even miss me all that much. They will notice that my house is closed; my landlord will be looking for me. But I have been holding back so much this past year, afraid to let anyone in. I haven't wanted to get close again, because it hurts too much when I have to leave.

I miss the quiet of the island, but at the same time savor the city sounds and smells. I am not quite ready to go back to the hotel. I am worried that Jean is lying in wait for me and will follow me. While it's a gorgeous day, with the sun high in the sky, I feel as though I'm better off staying underground and out of sight. Blisters are forming on my feet from the sandals, so I decide it's time to go shopping for a pair of comfortable shoes and another pair of jeans.

I make my way to the Place d'Armes metro station and am told at the information booth that I can take the subway to Bonaventure and I will be able to access the underground city from there.

The underground city is truly a city under ground. I am stunned by the number of stores and restaurants. I wander aimlessly, constantly looking around me to see if Jean is following me, certain that since I have not brought breadcrumbs to drop I will never find my way home again.

I easily find a store that sells sneakers – not running shoes, but canvas shoes with rubber soles – and peds, and the sales clerk allows me to wear them while taking my sandals off my hands. She seems hesitant about the latter, but I tell her that they are useless to me and I am just going to throw them out anyway.

The new shoes cushion my feet, and I wonder why I would ever wear anything else.

Jeans are next, although I don't want to get rid of the ones I'm wearing, so I take a bag. I also buy another sweater and two more T-shirts. I have not had access to this much shopping since I left Miami and Paris. I feel almost giddy with the possibilities, but I rein myself in. I can't afford to have too much, otherwise my things will not fit in the backpack.

The backpack. I sit with a cup of coffee and run my fingers along the straps. It's old and beginning to show its age. Do I need a new one? Or should I buy a larger duffel? No, that's not practical. But maybe a backpack that's a bit larger?

I throw away my paper coffee cup and find a map of the underground. Even though it's marked to show where I'm standing, I'm still confused about direction. That's what happens when you're underground, you're like a blind mole. Still, I manage to find a store that sells all sorts of outdoors equipment, and the selection of backpacks is impressive. I don't need a hiking backpack – although if I decide to hike back through Quebec into Vermont, it's not a bad idea – but I do choose one that is a little larger than the one I've been carrying since Block Island. I should be able to fit everything in here: both laptops and my clothes and toiletries and my stash of cash.

I have almost – almost – forgotten about Jean and my shadow while I navigate my shopping excursion, losing myself in something that's so *normal*. I am feeling much more relaxed. The tightness in my shoulders has dissipated, and I wonder about trying to find a spa for a massage. It would soothe my brain as much as my body.

But the feeling doesn't last too long because as I turn a corner, there he is again: Jean – waiting in line at a coffee shop. He holds a newspaper, turning the pages as though he is reading, but I can tell he is not. His head is bowed, yet his eyes are everywhere except the paper.

I smooth out my hair, adjust my glasses on my nose. My glasses. I should find a place to get contact lenses. Even with my new hair-style and color and clothes, he might still be able to see me behind these frames. I glance from side to side, ducking into a bookshop and making my way to the back. I grab a book off the shelf and begin leafing through its pages, but all the while I am keeping an eye on the doorway.

He comes by then, no coffee in hand, the newspaper folded under his arm. He scans the store, and as he does, I slip behind a display of books. He possibly can see the top of my head, but it's a redhead he'll see, not Susan McQueen.

How did he end up on that train anyway? Was it a chance encounter in the church or has he been following me the whole time I've been here?

That thought makes me pause. If he's managed to follow me, then he knows about the new clothes, the new hair, the hotel. He knows everything I've been doing. Then why doesn't he confront me? He had no problem doing that in Quebec City. He had no problem telling me outright that he didn't trust me.

I peer around the corner of the display. He hasn't left. He's now inside the shop, too, looking at a book. I'm trapped back here; I can't leave the shop without passing right next to him. I exchange the book I'm holding for another one, as though I am truly interested in the most recent bestselling young adult novels.

Part of me wants to go over to him and say hello, get it over with, see if he's really here for me. But if on the off chance he isn't, then I'll be throwing myself wide open and showing him my new look, which might actually work if he *hasn't* been following me around. The problem is, I have no way of knowing anything, and that makes me more anxious.

Although not as anxious as when I see who has come into the store and greets him.

SEVENTEEN

t's Alice. Alice from the computer shop. Now I am almost certain that this is not a coincidence, that Jean has been tracking me ever since Quebec City. He had been outside Philippe's shop; Alice works for the police. These two have not gotten together by chance. I am the common denominator.

My disguise is a sham. I might as well come out from hiding and turn myself in.

Except . . .

Alice is gesturing, pointing outside, toward the escalators that make their way upstairs. Jean absently puts the book he's been holding down on a shelf. They are saying something to each other, but I cannot read lips, so I don't know what's going on beside the fact that they are leaving the shop. They are moving in the direction Alice has been indicating. Suddenly they are out of sight, around the corner.

I have to make my move now. I put the book back in between the others and move around the display, making sure I don't see them, that they can't see me. I slip out the door, spot them near the escalator, and quickly walk in the opposite direction, trying not to run, because that could draw even more attention to myself, but walking at a steady clip. I am happy that I've been riding the bike so much, so I am in good shape and am not winded as I manage to catch the elevator just before the doors close. I shimmy in between a large woman and another woman with a stroller. The little girl in the stroller is sleeping. My heart is pounding so hard I'm surprised she doesn't wake up.

The doors open and I maneuver myself around the stroller and out into the mall again. I have no idea where Jean and Alice have gone. As far as I know, they could be around the next turn. I need to get out of here. I'm glad I've switched the sandals for the canvas shoes, because I feel a lot more comfortable, more steady, despite carrying the bags with the new clothes and backpack, the old pack still hanging on my back.

A sign to the restroom beckons, and I go inside, find an open stall and lock myself in. I eye the new backpack, which should be able to hold everything. I pull out the laptop and the money and begin to organize the new pack, which does seem to have quite a bit more space in it than the old one, even though it doesn't look that much bigger. Soon, I am re-packed, the old backpack lying empty and looking forlorn on the floor. Someone has come in and is at the sink. I shove the backpack behind the toilet; if Alice comes in here looking for me, she'll find it, but if she's really looking for me, she'll find it even if I put it in the trash, and I don't want to show my hand to whoever is at the sink.

Whoever is at the sink. What if it's Alice? I shrink back against the wall, around the toilet. I realize then that I can catch a glimpse through the crack in the door jamb, and the woman at the sink is older, with white hair and glasses not unlike mine. I begin breathing again, suddenly aware that I have been holding my breath.

I swing the backpack around and settle it on my shoulders, against my back, and exit the stall. The woman doesn't even look up as I wash my hands and dry them under the electric dryer. I stroll out of the washroom as though I am not being hunted, as though I am just another shopper.

I look both ways but do not see Jean or Alice anywhere. I don't let my guard down, however, and manage to find my way to an exit. When I finally get outside, the sun shines in my face so brightly that I squint, wishing I had sunglasses. I feel as though I've run a marathon, but the race isn't over yet. I want to go back to the hotel, but I can't be guaranteed that they won't show up there, either. I have no idea where they are. Maybe I should have tried to follow *them*. Then I could have a better idea of what they're up to, how much they know about my time here.

I kick myself thinking about it. I had a chance to do that when they left the bookshop, but it hadn't even crossed my mind until now.

The best thing I can do is go back toward the hotel and see if they're lurking anywhere. Again I wish for sunglasses, contact lenses, something more than different clothes and a new hair color and style. The backpack might have been a bad idea, too, because Jean knows I always have one. I don't carry a purse or a small bag like most women. Not that he's ever commented on it, but he's a detective. These are things that a detective would notice. At least I think he would.

I could find another hotel for the night, but the old laptop and my things are still in the room I've paid for. I need to hold onto that old laptop for the time being; it's the only way to communicate with my shadow, not to mention that the bitcoin address is in there, too, for the transfer, when I actually manage to figure out how to do that.

I linger about a block up from the hotel and keep watch. I don't see Jean or Alice, but an elderly man who has been sweeping his stoop notices that I'm here, and I think that perhaps I need to switch it up a bit otherwise he might call the police on me. He's got that look about him.

I walk around the block and peer into windows, pretending to check out restaurant menus but all the while making sure that no one familiar is nearby. I wander into Chinatown, beneath the elaborate and ornate gate, and go into a shop, where I scan the Asian novelties and souvenirs. I finger the silk scarves, admire the orchids and bamboo. I like the teapots, dark earthenware that looks as though it's come from somewhere within the belly of China, where people work the land, plowing the fields with oxen. For a moment, I forget and think that I'd like to bring one home with me. It probably makes delicious tea.

But then my surroundings come back into focus, and my daydream dissipates. I no longer have a home. I am on the run again, and a sadness rushes through me.

I have been in this shop so long, I feel obligated to buy something. I spot a glass case with some necklaces inside it, so I move closer. The shop owner has begun to follow me and sees what I am looking at. She smiles, opens the case and pulls out a jade pendant in the shape of a dragon. She points at it and then at me and nods.

It's beautiful, and I reach out and take it from her, my fingers moving over its surface. I don't care what it costs; I want this. I ask how much. She takes a pad and writes a figure down. It seems like a lot, so when I hesitate, she crosses it out and replaces it with another figure, one that's much more reasonable.

'Yes, please,' I tell her in French.

A grin spreads across her face, and she takes it back, holding up a hand as she turns her back to me. I see her with a long strand of thick, red thread and within minutes, she's created a necklace for me. I take it and slip it over my head. The pendant nestles against my chest, heavy yet light at the same time. I reach into my backpack and pull out the cash to pay for it, and she takes it, smiling the entire time.

I leave the shop feeling better, a little less anxious, although I still keep my wits about me, aware of every passerby. Every once in a while, I touch the jade dragon and it seems to center me.

Because I have not seen Jean and Alice since the underground, I am beginning to think that I should go back to my hotel and settle into my room. I have to start working on the bitcoins. I have to see if Tracker has had any luck with them.

The Chinese woman at the desk at the hotel starts to give me a nod when I come in, but then she notices the jade dragon. She cocks her head at it and a smile tugs at the corners of her mouth. It is the most emotion I have seen in her so far. 'Do you know what it means?' she asks me in her heavily accented French. She points at the pendant to make sure I know what she's talking about.

I shake my head.

'The dragon in China is strong. It is a protector. You will find good luck.'

I feel as though I've stepped into a fortune cookie, but I like what I hear. I could do with a little good luck right about now.

I take all of my new things out of the backpack. I am feeling slightly nostalgic about the old backpack and its unfortunate fate in the toilet. I take the tags off my new clothes and put them in the drawers. It all feels so normal.

Yet I am far from living a normal life. I begin to think again how I need a passport and how I might go about getting one. I'm not sure I want to ask Tracker to arrange documents for me again. I don't want him to know exactly where I am. They would have to be delivered here, and if Jean and his border patrol people are watching, that isn't possible. I could tell Tracker I'm in Toronto, but he knows about my French and would be able to figure out that I might be comfortable and find it easier to hide in Quebec. Tracker is anything but stupid.

Although as I think this, I am not convinced that I am *not* stupid.

Just as I had never done an online search for Jean until yesterday, I have not searched for Alice. Granted, I don't know her last name, but how hard could it be to find her? I power up the laptop and search for 'Alice Quebec City cybercrime'.

The results pop up on the screen almost immediately, and I stare at them, unbelieving.

Alice's last name is Bessette. The same as Jean's.

EIGHTEEN

Alice Bessette is an administrative assistant with the cyber-crime unit, so she and Philippe may have exaggerated her position. And she is the daughter of retired detective Jean Bessette. So there might not be anything suspicious at all about seeing them together today. Maybe they were only meeting for lunch or coffee, a father-daughter get-together. It seems as though it could be all so innocent, and I feel foolish for even thinking that they had teamed up to find me.

But at the same time, why, if they are both living in Quebec City, are they in Montreal? They didn't travel here together.

This is my paranoia again. There might be a very logical reason for them to travel separately and meet here. Maybe there is other family in Montreal that they are visiting. Maybe it's a day outing, since it's merely a three-hour train ride.

I have to get my mind off this. I log back onto the laptop and go to the chat room. I still don't see a message from Tracker. What's going on? What's he doing?

I know I should be more proactive. I have to stop relying on him so much. I think again about Steve and Jeanine, how they knew about me and Tracker and wonder how someone could get them to tell him about Tracker. How someone could have put pressure on them to tell. This is the only explanation for what my shadow knows about me, and it could answer questions about Tracker's shadow, too. So instead of focusing on Alice and Jean and the bitcoins right now, I try to think of a way to contact my old friends without putting them in any more danger – or risking my own freedom.

I could send an email, which wouldn't indicate where I am. But if they are involved in some way, then their computers might be compromised, too. I wonder about a disposable phone, how it would work, and if I could somehow mask my location. So I go online and do a search, finding out that while I can pre-pay a phone with cash at a local petrol station, I can also indicate where my calls will be listed as originating from. I could easily say British Columbia, on the opposite end of the country, and if anyone figures it out, I will be long gone from here. I won't even have to hack.

On my way out, the Chinese woman at the desk stops me and smiles warmly, pointing to her chest and says, 'Xu.' It sounds like 'shoo'. I'm not sure what she's saying, and she repeats it, adding, 'Madame Xu.' It's an odd mixture of French and Chinese, but I now understand that's her name and we are becoming acquainted.

I smile and nod, and she nods back before turning her attention to something below the counter. I head back outside; the sun a little lower in the sky now. It's warm today, warmer than usual, and I am regretting the jeans and the fact that I got rid of my skirt. I don't want to buy any more new clothes, though, because I don't have room for them in the backpack and I can't have any more baggage, so I have to live with a little discomfort. If I do manage to get back to the States, I will need a pair of shorts, at least, but this warm weather probably will not last too long.

I have checked the locations of the petrol stations that sell the disposable phones, and I make my way to the closest one. I walk slowly, window shopping, knowing that I am stalling, and I know the reason. The purpose for this phone is to call Steve. Steve, my best friend, the most important man in my life for fifteen years. The man I lied to the entire time I knew him, except for those last couple of days when I told him everything. He was willing to help me escape – he did help me escape – but over a year of silence could have hardened him against me. He might have willingly told the FBI about me and Tracker because he feels so betrayed by me.

Finally I reach the station, and I buy a phone without incident. In fact, the clerk barely registers my presence except to take my cash to cover a month's fees. He hands me the phone, which is packaged tightly between clear plastic, and I stuff it in my backpack and leave, my hands shaking so much that I grip the strap tightly to stop it.

Madame Xu gives me another nod when I come back into the lobby. I can feel her eyes on me as I pass her and wait for the elevator, but I don't turn around. I don't want to engage; I have to stay focused or I will be a coward and not go through with it.

Once back in my room, I activate the phone and indicate that the calls will seem as though they are originating in Ontario. I decide against British Columbia, because I am afraid the phone might not work if it thinks it's so far away. Ontario is the next province over and could still mask my location enough. I also figure out how to block the number from appearing on the other person's caller ID.

I am pre-paid, so I know the call to the States will be covered, but I procrastinate and spend more time than I need reading the frequently asked questions on the website.

Finally, I tell myself I can't delay this any further. Steve is probably be waiting with his taxi at the ferry dock for the afternoon tourists to come in. Perhaps if he is distracted enough, he won't be angry, he will have to be polite.

So I dial the number that comes back into my head as though a year has not passed.

I almost end the call when I hear the first ring. My heart pounds so loudly that I am afraid he will be able to hear it.

'Hello?' His tone is tentative, because the call is from an unknown number.

'Hello? Steve? It's Nicole.' The words spill out so fast; I don't want him to hang up.

'Nicole?' I can hear his disbelief.

'Please don't hang up. Yes, it's Nicole. It's really me.'

'Oh my God, Nicole, it really *is* you. Where are you? What are you doing? Where have you been?'

His voice wraps itself around me and comforts me. Tears spring into my eyes as I realize how much I've missed him, how much I've wanted to hear his voice again.

'I can't tell you where I am, Steve. But I can tell you I'm OK. I've been OK, so you don't have to worry about me.'

'Why is your number blocked?'

'Don't worry about it.'

'So even if I try to trace you, it won't lead to you? You've hacked it or something?'

'Or something. How are you? How is Jeanine, Veronica? How is the season going?'

He lets out a short laugh. 'It would be better if you were here. We all miss you, Nicole.'

'I miss you all so much. So much more than you can even imagine.' The tears are sliding down my cheeks now, and I wipe them away with the back of my hand. I am grinning, even though he can't see it.

'Why has it taken you so long to call?'

'I don't know,' I say, but I do know, and he knows, too.

'You found out,' he says flatly.

'You told someone about me and Tracker, didn't you, Steve?'

He is quiet a few seconds, then, 'Not me. Jeanine. She came to the spa. She said she was your sister.'

'I don't have a sister, Steve.'

He is quiet for a second, then, 'She knew all about you, Nicole, that you lived in Miami, about your father, Ian Cartwright, even that FBI agent Zeke Chapman. Jeanine didn't mean to say anything about what you'd done the last days you were here, but she ended up telling that woman everything, about the laptops in the spa, how you were on that chat room, that you were talking to Tracker. This woman told her that she was worried, that you'd been gone so long and she just wanted to see you again. Like we do.'

With each sentence, I feel as though I have been hit in the gut. 'Who was it, Steve? What was her name?'

'She said her name was Patricia Hale. Who is she, Nicole? Do you know? What did she do?'

I try not to gasp when I hear her name and force myself to concentrate on the conversation. 'She – or someone – put a virus in a link that Tracker sent me that took over my laptop. There's been a ransom demand for money.'

'I don't know that I'm going to tell Jeanine.'

'No, please don't. She'll blame herself.'

'She already does. This woman made it sound like she knew where you were, that she would get you to call, and Jeanine was happy about that. And then when she left, and some time passed, she realized it might not be on the up and up. Who is Patricia Hale?'

'I don't know,' I say, but I do.

Patricia Hale was my mother's name, but my mother has been dead for twenty years.

NINETEEN

'**A**re you coming back?' Steve is asking.

'No. I can't.' But as I say this, I close my eyes and picture the island: the majestic Mohegan Bluffs, Rodman's Hollow where the shad dances along its branches, the North Light, the stone walls. I imagine riding my bike up and down the hilly roads, the scent of sunscreen hanging in the air near the beaches.

'Can I meet you somewhere? I'll be discreet.' His voice distracts me from my daydream.

'It's not a good idea. Maybe someday, but not now.'

'If I call this number back, will you answer?'

'I'm going to get rid of the phone, Steve,' I say softly. 'I can't hold onto it. Can you please understand?'

'So you only called to find out if one of us ratted you out?' He is starting to get annoyed now, which is a good thing. It will be easier for him to be angry with me when I say goodbye for the second time.

'I'm sorry, Steve.' I want to hang up, but I am physically unable to. I want to keep talking; I want to pretend I am just up the road from him and he can come by for a sandwich and a game of Scrabble. I close my eyes, remembering.

'I miss you, Nicole.'

'I miss you, too. So, so much.' And then I do it. I hang up and turn the phone off before he tries to call me back, before I lose my nerve.

I need to get out of here. I can't stay cooped up in this room right now. I grab the backpack and go downstairs, exchange another nod with Madame Xu – she might be curious why I keep coming and going – and find myself on the sidewalk, speed walking as though someone is chasing me.

It's my past, catching up with me again.

I don't think about Jean or Alice or whether they are waiting for me to emerge. Instead, I still hear Steve's voice in my head. I almost forgot how he sounded, the timbre in his tone. I know now how he felt when his wife Dotty died, how much he missed her, because that's how much I'm missing him. How much I have been missing him all this time.

I push away those thoughts and try to concentrate. Who would use my mother's name? Ian had used Zeke's name last year to smoke me out, and I can't help but think this is another ploy in the same vein. Someone used my mother's name on the off chance that I will find out. But who?

Patricia Hale became Patricia Adler when she married my father. I was an only child. My mother suffered severe post-partum depression, according to my father, and that's when she became addicted to the drugs: Xanax, Valium, and later, morphine. She didn't have a chance. I was raised by my father and housekeepers who 'protected' me from my mother. I don't know when she started cutting herself.

I could have blamed my father for what happened to her, but he truly loved her and tried to get her the help she needed. Nothing worked, though, despite the parade of nurses and psychiatrists through the years. It felt as though a ghost was living among us; she was there, but she wasn't.

The summers with my grandmother in France saved my childhood; and then there were my computers. I didn't have friends in Miami – I couldn't have any, not anyone I could invite over – and when I was fourteen I discovered a whole new world online.

She came into my room one night when I was in the chat room. She was beautiful even in her illness, her long dark hair framing her face, emerald green eyes, full red lips. I could see why my father had fallen in love with her, still loved her enough to try to bring her back, but those green eyes were vacant, her lips moving in a silent prayer. I was in mid-sentence, mid-conversation with someone, I can't remember who, and my mother and I stared at each other for a few minutes.

'Are you OK?' I asked softly, in the tone we used when she was around.

She shook her head, reached over and put her hand to my cheek, stroking it for a second before letting her hand drop back down to her side. And then she turned and went out the door, her satin dressing gown billowing around her legs.

I wonder who is using her name. It has to be someone who knew her, or knew of her. Most people who know me wouldn't use her maiden name, so this is a clue, even though I'm not quite sure to what.

I fumble in the front pocket of the backpack, where I have stashed the disposable phone. As much as I want to dump it, I do need to make another call, so I punch in another familiar number.

'Sunswept Spa.'

I can almost feel the heat from the stones soaking into my skin. 'Is Jeanine there?' I ask.

'Hold on a sec. Can I ask who's calling?'

I hesitate for a second. 'Tell her it's Nicole.'

'Nicole? Um, sure, OK. Hold on.'

I wait about a minute before I hear: 'Nicole? Is that really you?'

Her voice washes over me, and it is the same feeling I had when I spoke to Steve, and again tears spring into my eyes. I am still walking, but I slow down now, see an outside table at a small café. I sit, positioning the backpack between my legs. 'Yes, Jeanine, it's me.'

A waitress comes out and I indicate I'd like a coffee, so she disappears back inside.

'Did you talk to her? Your sister? Did she tell you to call me?' Her voice is bright, hopeful that what she did, telling a stranger about me, was the right thing.

I feel awful that I have to disappoint her again, that even though I have told Steve not to tell her because she will blame herself, I am doing it anyway. Because I have to know what's going on.

'I talked to Steve. He told me.' I pause. 'Jeanine, I don't have a sister.'

'Oh, it's just that—' She knows now why I am calling. It's not to shoot the breeze, make an appointment for a massage, ask when the next yoga class is. She knows that she was wrong to say anything about me, and she is sorry for it.

'It's OK, Jeanine, but I need to know what she looked like. I need to figure out who she really is.'

'Are you in trouble?'

I laugh. 'Jeanine, I'm a fugitive. Of course I'm in trouble.'

She gives a nervous chuckle. 'Sorry. Right. Forgot for a minute.' She pauses. 'You don't have a sister?'

'I know a Patricia Hale, but she's dead. Been dead for twenty years, so it can't possibly be the same person. Can you tell me what this woman looked like? Anything that might give me a clue as to who she is?'

'Well, she was tall and had dark hair. It was short, styled. She was pretty, built sort of like you, actually. She looked like you, in a way. But she was younger, maybe ten, fifteen years younger or so?'

She doesn't sound sure, and she's not describing anyone familiar. 'She left a card.'

'What?'

'A business card. She said maybe I could call her, when you got in touch with me. She said she misses you.'

'I don't have a sister,' I say again. 'But I need to find out who she is. She left a card?'

'Yes. Hold on, let me find it.'

It feels as though I wait forever, until finally: 'OK, here it is. Do you want the information? There's only her name and a phone number.'

'Yes, please.' The waitress is back with the coffee, and I ask for a paper and a pen. 'I need to get a pen,' I tell Jeanine.

'Where are you, Nicole?'

Uh-oh. 'I can't tell you.' But she has heard me talk to the waitress. In French.

'Why not?'

The waitress is back with the paper and pen. 'Give me the number, OK?' Jeanine does, and I recognize the Miami exchange.

'Will you tell me now where you are? Why were you speaking French? I didn't know you spoke French.'

I've made a huge mistake, but even though I think that, this phone call is worth it for two reasons: I can try to track down Patricia Hale now with the phone number, even though it's probably some sort of trick to get me to do so, and I am able to talk to Jeanine, even for a few minutes.

'I speak French,' I say softly. 'I learned it a long time ago.'

'Are you in France? Paris? I hope you're somewhere exotic, somewhere safe.' I hear the concern in her voice, and I am again moved by her friendship, even after lying to her for fifteen years.

'I'm OK, Jeanine. Please don't worry about me.'

'I'm sorry I told that woman anything. I really am. I had no idea. She looked enough like you that I believed her.'

I don't tell her that I've seen people on the street who remind me of her, too. 'I know. Don't worry. Please.'

'When are you coming home?'

I close my eyes for a second and take a deep breath. 'I don't know. I'll let you know. I have to go now. Thank you for the number. And please, can you make sure Steve is OK?'

She gives a short chuckle. 'We have dinner on Friday nights at Club Soda. Like you used to. I guess you can say we're taking care of each other.'

I envision the two of them having burgers and onion rings and beers at our old hangout, and I suddenly miss them so much that the sadness rushes through me and I feel as though I have lost all the strength to even hold the phone to my ear. 'I'm glad,' I whisper. 'I'm always thinking of you both.' And then, without saying goodbye or giving her a chance to say anything else, I hang up and turn the phone off, putting it on the table next to my cup of coffee.

TWENTY

I sit with my coffee, missing my friends, contemplating my conversations. My thoughts circle back to Patricia Hale, not my mother, but the mysterious woman who visited Jeanine. Why would she go that out of her way to ask questions? All she had to do was call the spa. Instead, she takes the hour-long ferry ride to Block Island and hunts down Jeanine. Seems like a lot of effort. Who would be that desperate?

I worry the corner of the paper on which I've written Patricia Hale's phone number. I pick the phone up off the table, but then put it back down. I don't want to do it here. I'd also like to have more information before I call.

I finish the coffee and leave some cash on the table, pick up the backpack, and start walking back to the hotel. Madame Xu again greets me as I enter. She doesn't *seem* curious about my movements; she probably sees all sorts of things in her business.

Once back in my room, I pull out the laptop and boot it up. The phone number will be easy enough to trace.

Except it's not.

I try to do a reverse directory, but nothing comes up. It's most likely a cell number; a lot of people don't have landlines anymore. Going about this the legitimate way, I could pay for a service that will tell me all the information about the owner of this phone number, but there's no guarantee that's not a scam to get a credit card number. I search for the number in social media sites, but nothing comes up. I've exhausted all the legal ways to do this. I have no other choice.

I don't for one minute believe that Patricia Hale is a real name, so the phone number is the key to who she is.

Soon I am in my zone, and my head empties of everything except what's on the screen in front of me.

I decide to start with the largest cell phone company, the one that has the most coverage. Even though price and data plans will sway customers, most of them want to make sure that their calls won't be dropped, that they can get connected anywhere. I manage to get inside more easily than I expect, although then I realize that they allow the government to monitor.

I'm close to cracking the code, to finding the list of phone numbers and their information, when I spot it. A shadow.

My shadow managed to get inside my laptop to hold it for ransom. This shadow was put there by the company's IT guys to make sure someone like me wouldn't get into the code. I smile to myself, thinking that while the company lets the government in, it might be turning the tables on it, too, by watching everything they're doing.

I slip out of the code, my fingers resting for a moment on the keys, trying to figure out how to get through the portal without being noticed. Tracker could help with this, but something – my pride? Or suspicion? – keeps me from reaching out to him.

And then I have an idea.

I hunch over the keyboard, my fingers moving swiftly, the code scrolling across the screen. I see it, the back door I can get through, and while I'm at it, I make sure it won't close so I can get through it again if I need to. Suddenly, the list of phone numbers appears, hundreds of them, and I just need to see if this one is one of them.

One of the things about what I do is that I need patience. A lot of it. Hackers spend hours looking for that one portal to get past the firewall before even more hours looking for the hole in the code that we can slip behind and then scour the information we discover. I have nothing but time here, and I can go all night if I need to.

But all of a sudden, it's there. The number I'm looking for. It doesn't take me much time to get the information I need.

Patricia Hale is not the name associated with the number, as I suspected.

But Tony DeMarco is.

I know for sure now that he is the one who managed to hack Tracker's link to me. The shadow is Tony. Even if he's not the actual shadow itself, he's pulling the strings.

I pull my hands away from the keyboard, folding them in my lap, and lean back against the pillows, staring at his name, the memories flooding back.

He and my father were the masterminds behind the bank job, but my father was one step ahead of Tony in that one of the accounts we stole from was his. They had been friends for years; Tony was my father's closest 'business associate' who brought him clients he was able to bilk out of their money. I don't know why my father felt he had to steal from his friend, but he did it. Or, rather, he made me do it. Tony testified against him, and he went to prison. I disappeared, until Tony found me last year. I got away from him a second time, which clearly did not set well with him.

I am worried even more about Jeanine and Steve. Tony is not known for being magnanimous toward anyone if he doesn't get what he wants.

And what he wants is a million bitcoins.

I close the laptop, get up, and pace in front of the bed. If Tony DeMarco has someone who can get into the chat room and hack Tracker's link, then he may have the resources to actually find me. I would give Tony as much money as he wants as long as he'll leave me and my friends alone, yet there is only one way to do it, and I vowed I would never do that again. But these are extenuating circumstances. My friends are in jeopardy. I am in jeopardy.

And since I'm up against Tony DeMarco, I definitely need an exit plan before I can do anything else.

TWENTY-ONE

I have to ask Tracker for help with documents again. I don't know who his contacts are, but he has contacts – unlike me. This, however, does leave me wide open for discovery. I have an idea, though, for delivery, and I grab the backpack and head back outside. Madame Xu is not at the front desk for once, but a young man who looks like he could be her son smiles at me and gives me the familiar nod as I push my way out the door.

I look both ways once I emerge, careful, in case Jean and Alice are watching. If they are, they are very good, because I see no one familiar as I make my way down the sidewalk.

Even though I have been living on fairly remote islands for the last several years, navigating a city has come back to me. I find the Place-d'Armes metro station and check out the map. I don't even have to change trains. I get on the next train on the orange line to Côte-Vertu. It's two stops, so when we stop at Bonaventure, I go out the doors and head upstairs. In my head, I can picture the map on the screen, not unlike how I used to picture the roads on Block Island for my bike tours. The UPS store is in the Montreal Marriott Château Champlain, close to the Starbucks.

I worry a little that my French won't be proficient enough, but the girl behind the counter doesn't seem to notice that a couple of times I slip out of Québécois and speak Parisian French. If she does notice, at least she's polite enough not to say anything.

The post office box that they rent me has an actual street address, so when I ask Tracker to send the documents here, it might be a little confusing, but that's the whole point. When he'd arranged the documents in Miami, and then last year in New York, I was supposed to meet someone at a certain time in a certain place. This time, however, it will be on my terms. A package can be delivered to this box in Montreal, and I will be able to pick it up any time I want – or not at all. Or I could send someone to fetch it and not risk getting caught. There are a lot of possibilities, and many of them are in my favor.

The box is in the name of Hélène Leblanc, the name I'm using here. By doing all this, I am laying myself wide open to Tracker. He never even knew I was on Block Island. But he does know who I am and what I've done. I could say he's as guilty as I am, since he helped me. He never even questioned it. I am not above reminding him of this, if he balks at anything I'm about to ask him to do. I need his help with the documents, but I also need his help to get those bitcoins so I can keep Tony DeMarco away from my friends.

I can sweeten the deal, too, by throwing him Alice Bessette. If he is going to send documents to Montreal, then he'll know I'm in Quebec and there is no need to keep her a secret any longer.

I realize my plans rely heavily on Tracker. I only hope he's willing.

I still don't see Jean or Alice lurking near my hotel as I approach. I've stopped off for takeout at an Indian place near the Place-d'Armes metro station on my way back. Madame Xu is back at her post, but she is busy on the phone, arguing with someone in Chinese. I slip past her and into the elevator with my takeout bag.

I try not to think about everything that's been going on while I unpack my lamb biryani and naan. I put the mango lassi on the night-stand next to the bed. On a whim, I hit the TV remote and Canadian news comes on in English. While I like speaking and hearing French, right now my native language comforts me as I eat my supper. I'm not really interested in what's happening in the world, though. When 9/11 happened, I was riveted to the television, like everyone else, but the only thing that concerns me now is the enhanced travel security. For obvious reasons.

I do consider that once I transfer the bitcoins, I could go back to the States the same way I came in. But it will be easier to get around if I have documents. I make a note that besides a passport, I need a driver's license and a birth certificate. I also need a photo for these things, so after I'm finished with my dinner, I find a bare wall and manage to take a headshot of myself with the laptop webcam. It's not the best picture, but that's not a bad thing, considering.

I wonder how long it will take Tracker to get me the documents. I don't want to stick around here too long, but I figure I can keep a low profile for a couple of days. I don't think that Madame Xu needs my room for anyone else. She hasn't indicated that she's in a hurry to see me leave.

I glance out the window, peering into the night, but I see nothing, no one on the street below. I sit on the bed and open the old laptop. I never replaced the tape that Philippe took off the webcam, but I'm not sure I want the shadow to see me with my new look. I open a drawer in the bedside table and pull out a small note pad. I fold the paper over the top of the screen, obscuring the camera, and then boot up the laptop. For a moment, I worry that those eyes will pop back up on the screen, but when nothing happens, not even a ransom note appears, I start to wonder if he's here.

I root around in the front pocket of the backpack and pull out the flash drive that Philippe gave me, the one that has the anti-malware program on it. I want to clear the laptop before I leave. I no longer want to engage with the shadow; I want to get rid of him, as soon as I get the number of the account where he wants me to transfer the bitcoins.

Before doing that, however, I check the laptop's IP address. By now, it doesn't matter if he knows what it is, because he's most likely already gotten behind the VPN and seen it. I jot down the address using the pen and pad on the nightstand, then insert the flash drive into the port on the side of the laptop. I open the folder when it installs and see another program that Philippe has downloaded as well. It makes me think that he knows a little more about computers than I've given him credit for.

While I should install the anti-malware program, I can't help myself. This other program will show all the current network and remote connections on the laptop. At first, it doesn't look like anything's out of sorts, but on closer look, something's not right. There's an IP address and a port on both the Internet and messaging applications that make me think that this is my culprit. I pull out the new laptop and when it's powered up, I find a site where I can do a search on IP addresses.

I'm not confident that what I find will be accurate. My shadow could be using a VPN, just like me, to disguise his location.

And when I see the results of the search, I know that either he's better than I am or I have a lot to worry about.

The IP address originates on Block Island.

The fact that my shadow has been able to pinpoint the location of where I lived over a year ago with his IP address is pretty ingenious. I have to admire this, despite the cold chill that's shimmied up my back. He knows where I was before I came here, which again makes me sure that it's Tony DeMarco or at least someone who works for him. Maybe the mysterious Patricia Hale. As I'm wishing I could ask who he is, the message program opens and he pops up like Aladdin's genie.

'You haven't run the program.'

At first I don't know what he means, but then I realize he's talking about the anti-malware program that's on the flash drive. He can see the drive directory, so he knows that it's here and I can run it right now if I want him to disappear.

'I haven't gotten you your money yet,' I type.

'No, you haven't. Does this mean you will?'

'Why Patricia Hale?'

'What?'

'Patricia Hale. You know what I'm talking about.'

'I don't. Who's Patricia Hale?'

I wish we were not communicating via a computer screen, because without seeing an expression, I can't tell if he truly doesn't know the name or if he's faking it.

'You know what I'm talking about,' I try next.

'When are you going to get me my money?' he asks, ignoring me.

'When you tell me about Patricia Hale.'

'I don't know a Patricia Hale.'

Again, I wish I could see his face, see his expression, to see if he's lying.

'When will you get me my money?' he asks again.

'Patricia Hale.'

'I have no idea what you're talking about. If you don't get me my money in two days, I'm coming after you.'

The message program shuts down abruptly. I don't like it that he's denying knowing Patricia Hale. How else could he have found me through the chat room, through Tracker? I have no doubt that he knows where I am or that he will do as he says. There is actually nothing keeping him from coming to get me right now, except that he does want the money. I can hope that since he hasn't shown up so far, I've got a little more time and no one will come knocking on my door tonight.

TWENTY-TWO

I have to get some air. I swing my legs over the side of the bed, stuff the new laptop into the backpack and shrug it over my shoulder. I don't bother with the elevator, instead take the stairs down. Madame Xu is on the phone; she looks up as I pass, but I don't make eye contact, just keep moving as though I don't even see her. I push the glass door outward and step into the street.

It has cooled off tonight, and I wish I'd taken my sweater, but it's upstairs, in the closet. I decide to welcome the familiar chill, goose bumps rising on my skin as I walk. I'm wearing my jade dragon pendant, and I touch it every now and then as if it will give me strength.

Even though I feel the weight of the laptop in the backpack slapping against my side, I wonder if I can stay offline. If I can resist its lure. I spot a trashcan at the corner. I could drop the backpack inside it, walk away. I pull it off my shoulder as I approach, as if I am going to actually do it. But I can't. My cash is inside. While I might be able to get away without documents, I cannot get away without money.

So I will never really know if I could do it.

I spot a small bar up ahead and decide I could do with a short one. The clientele here is younger than I am, but then again, I'm over forty so I shouldn't be surprised. Back in the day, I would have fit in with the young women in tight black dresses teetering on high heels and young men wearing tight T-shirts and designer jeans, their hair slicked back to show off chiseled jawlines. I sidle up to the bar and squeeze between two sets of girlfriends laughing and sharing stories. It takes a couple of waves to the bartender before he pays attention to me – the curse of being a middle-aged woman. But he finally takes my order and pours me a cognac. I slide a few bills across the bar and pick up my drink, moving away from the bar and to the left, where I see an open spot next to an abstract painting hanging on the wall.

I sip my drink as I examine the painting. Something about it seems familiar, and I lean closer to read the signature in the bottom right-hand corner.

I jerk back as though I've gotten too close to a fire.

This is one of Jean's paintings – Jean Bessette. I quickly glance around the bar and see similar paintings peppered along the walls. Knowing what a snob he is about paintings, I wonder if he knows the paintings are here or if they were commissioned.

I cup the glass in my hand, warming the liquid within, and think now that perhaps there is a logical reason for Jean Bessette to be in Montreal and it might have nothing at all to do with me. If he is selling paintings to bars and possibly hotels or restaurants, then it makes sense he would be here.

I am standing here, thinking about this, distracted and sipping the cognac, when I feel a hand on my arm. I look up to see the waitress cocking her head toward my drink, wondering if I want another one. Why not? She disappears back into the crowd toward the bar, and I absently finish my drink, scanning the crowd as if I am meeting someone.

That's when I see him across the room, watching me.

I think my new look has thrown him off a little, but Philippe is staring at me, knowing that he knows me but is trying to figure out from where. I have the distinct advantage of being out of context for him: he is used to seeing me in his shop, not in a club in Montreal. But my age can give me away, and that's why I am thankful that a large group has come in and is pushing its way to the bar, because I manage to slip in between them, moving in the opposite direction and out the door into the night.

I don't look back to see if he's following me, but I hear footsteps and I begin to walk faster.

And when I hear, 'Susan! Susan!' and he is suddenly right next to me, I have no choice but to stop.

Philippe frowns at me, then a wide grin crosses his face. 'It *is* you,' he says, as though I am the only person in the world he wants to see right at this very moment. 'You had your hair done. It's different. But I really like it. It suits you.' His eyes move down my body and he adds, 'The whole thing, the whole look, but it's you, right?' He sounds uncertain now, as though perhaps he has made a mistake. That I am not the Susan he thinks I am.

But his hesitation is short-lived. 'What are you doing in

Montreal? Don't tell me it was just to get your hair cut. Although I'm not surprised. It's so much more chic here.' He assumes I live in Quebec City, where he has always seen me.

I still haven't said anything and struggle with how to answer him. I glance around, worried that Alice is going to pop out from behind a building, her father close on her heels with handcuffs ready for my wrists.

'Susan?'

I force a smile. 'Yes, hello, Philippe. I wasn't sure that was you, that's why I left. It was a little uncomfortable in there. It's not exactly my crowd.'

He laughs. 'Oh, well, that.' He pauses, then asks, 'Did you ever get rid of that shadow in your laptop?'

'No, not yet. I still have the flash drive, though. I appreciate you doing that for me.'

'I put something else on there for you, too. A program.'

'I saw that. But I haven't run it yet,' I lie.

He gives me a sly smile. 'I didn't tell Alice about that one. I might not have gotten it legally, and since she's with the cyber unit, I don't want her to rat me out.'

'She's a hacker, though, isn't she?' I can't help but ask.

Philippe chuckles. 'She's really good. Which is why the police hired her. Her father is retired from the police now, but he wanted to keep her out of trouble so he got her the job. I guess he wants her to use her skills for good instead of evil.' He pauses. 'She's here, with me. Inside. Why don't you come in? I bet she'd love to see you again.'

Every muscle in my body tenses. This is what I was afraid of. Even if I don't go in, Philippe will tell her he's seen me. He will tell her how I've gotten my hair cut and colored, am wearing different clothes. He will gossip without knowing how damaging this will be.

'It would be nice to see her again, too,' I say as though I mean it. 'But I really need to get back. I've got an early start tomorrow.'

'Heading home?'

He is far too curious, and the longer we stand here, the more chance there is that Alice will emerge from the bar and discover me here.

'Yes, that's right,' I say. 'Now, go on back inside. Say hello to

Alice for me.' While I speak, I begin to back up, away from him. 'I'll see you in a couple of weeks.'

'Let me know if that program works for you,' he says, clearly not wanting to end this conversation.

'Right. I'll call you,' I say, the empty promise tripping off my tongue as easily as all the lies I've told for the last fifteen years. 'I'll give it a try when I get back home.' And then I turn away, even though I want to keep watching the bar door to make sure I'm safe, that he's not following me.

As I reach the next block, I do look over my shoulder. He is no longer on the sidewalk, and I have to assume that he's gone back inside. I hurry along the walk and, just in case, turn down a side street and then another, coming full circle back to where I can see my hotel down the road.

But something is wrong.

I see a shadow. A real shadow stepping out from an alley next to the hotel building.

TWENTY-THREE

I t's a man in a jacket, holding something.
A mugger? I begin to turn around to go back the way I came.
But there's something about the figure that strikes me as familiar.
It's not Jean Bessette; he's too tall and much fitter. This man is in
the shadows so I can't see his face.

The more I think about it, he could be the man who was with
Jean on the train, which means I need to get as far away from him
as possible.

I walk briskly in the opposite direction toward the Place d'Armes
metro station. I can hear the man's footsteps behind me, and my
heart beats with urgency as I scurry down the stairs. He does not
call out for me, as Philippe did, just keeps following. I realize I
don't have a metro ticket, and I don't have any spare time to get
one. I glance around and see a couple of tourists talking to the
attendant in the booth, who seems a little agitated. I go to the last
turnstile, put my hands on the metal barriers and swing my legs
over it, landing firmly on the other side. I can hear the footsteps
behind me, but a glance around tells me it is merely a couple of
young people staring at me, surprised at my athletics.

I make my way down the steps, and a train is arriving. I don't
care where it's going; I get on and find a seat, looking up at the map
indicating the stops above the seats on the other side of the car.

I can go two stops to Berri-Uqam. It's a large station, and it's
likely there are enough people there so if he does manage to get
on this train he won't see me get off or where I'm going. I can't
relax. The train stops at Champs-de-Mars, and panic rises in my
chest as I watch the doors open. The anxiety does not dissipate even
when the train is again on its way, even though I have not seen him.

I think about his build, his stance. It's not like when I saw Ian last
year on Block Island. Ian walked right up to me, looked me in the
eye. I recognized him right away. There is something about this man
that tickles my memory, but I cannot for the life of me place him.

Who is he? Who am I running from? I have no idea.

I don't hesitate when the subway stops at Berri-Uqam. I have been studying the metro map and see that I can get to Saint-Laurent but I have to change to the green line. From there, I can walk to the hotel.

I wonder if it's stupid for me to go back, since clearly he was waiting for me there. But I need to get the old laptop, my change of clothes. I also have a feeling that Madame Xu is no stranger to secrets, and she will not let on to anyone that I am there. Anyway, no one knows me as Hélène Leblanc, the name I'm registered under. Philippe and Alice and Jean all know me as Susan, and if this is Jean's companion, then he also knows me as Susan. Madame Xu doesn't know anyone by that name.

I'm grabbing at straws.

I transfer to the green line. I have one stop before Saint-Laurent. It will be a bit of a walk for me, but I can manage. I'm feeling a little trapped here, anyway, underground, and somehow feel that it'll be easier for me up on the sidewalk.

I put my hand up and touch the jade dragon. If there's any time for protecting, it's now, and I hope that Madame Xu was right about it.

While there are people on the street as I walk back to the hotel, no one is familiar and no one seems to be following me. Still, I zigzag up and down streets and when I am a block from the hotel, I peer around, alert to anyone stepping out of the shadows. But I see no one. That doesn't mean he won't be back. That he won't be lying in wait for me again.

I have to get my stuff and get out of here.

I am packing up, shoving my things into the backpack, when I hear a soft knock on my door, and I stiffen.

'Who's there?' I ask, as though I am indisposed.

'Excuse me?'

It's Madame Xu, from the desk downstairs. I go to the door and open it a crack. Yes, it's her. 'What can I do for you?'

'Madame LeBlanc?'

'Yes?'

'A man, he was here, looking for you.'

Panic rises in my chest. 'Who was it?' I think about the shadow outside, stepping out of the alley.

She shakes her head. 'I tell him I don't know you. That there is no one here like that.'

I am grateful for her discretion, and I begin to tell her that, but she puts her finger to her lips.

'He is going to come back. I have a place for you to go, but you have to come now. Hurry.'

I go back into the room and finish putting all my new clothes into the backpack, along with the laptops. I follow Madame Xu into the dark hallway, down the back stairs and out onto a small side street. We go to a nondescript apartment building another block down.

Somehow she knows that I cannot be found. We go inside, up a stairwell, and then she deposits me in a one-bedroom apartment with a family that speaks no English or French. She speaks very fast Chinese, pointing at me at times. The man and woman who are now my hosts seem as concerned as Madame Xu. They are introduced to me as Jin and Shu Fang, not that we will be having friendly conversation. I am given a bedroll and a corner in the bedroom in the back that I will share with the couple as well as their two little girls and a boy.

'You stay here,' Madame Xu instructs. I'm not about to argue with her. From her rudimentary description, it is not the stranger who has been asking about me, but Jean – and she knows he has connections to immigration. He did not ask for me by name, but he described me accurately, which makes me realize I did not fool him at all with my new look and he clearly saw me at either the church or in the underground and managed to follow me without my knowledge.

The children are eyeing me suspiciously from across the room, and I wonder how many people have hidden out with Jin and Shu Fang – and then wonder how many non-Chinese have been hidden here. I would be willing to bet that I am the first, from the way they seem to argue with her, but then relent after another long string of Chinese.

After Madame Xu leaves, I crawl into my corner, watched closely by the children. They don't speak, just stare, and it unnerves me a little. I am not used to children; I don't quite know how to act around them. I take my uncompromised laptop out of the backpack. It needs to be powered up, so I take out the power cord and find an outlet a few feet away. While it's powering up, I open it and boot it up. I find a couple of locked wireless networks, and I am about to hack into one of them when I notice the children have moved a little closer to me, intrigued by the machine.

I switch the keyboard to Chinese, and I hand the laptop over to the boy, who is a little older, maybe about eight or nine. The girls are maybe seven or eight. They seem to be twins. The boy does know what he's doing, because he begins to type, pointing at the screen and laughing with his sisters after every character. I am no longer necessary, and they are in their own little world. I know how they feel.

TWENTY-FOUR

I hear a door shut in the other room, and I know that Madame Xu has left when Jin and Shu Fang come into the bedroom. They hiss Chinese at the children, who give them a typical eye roll, but they hand me back my laptop before crawling to their beds, which are side by side across the room. I eye my bedroll dubiously. The hotels have been clean, but I'm not quite so sure about this place. I can't exactly do a bedbug search, though, with them staring at me. I realize that they all want to go to bed, and I shut the laptop cover but it merely goes to sleep.

I crawl into the bedroll, hoping that it's safe and I won't be making any new friends of the creepy crawly kind, my laptop still powering up. When I hear the soft sounds of sleep, I move quietly, unplug the laptop, and tiptoe softly into the front room. The light from the window casts shadows, and even though it's dark, I can see the outlines of the kitchenette in one corner and a table and chairs. I sit at the table and open the laptop, its light brightening the room so much that I'm afraid the family is going to awake.

I hack into the locked wireless network with little difficulty and then log into the chat room. I scroll through the messages left there, and one pops out at me:

'Desperately seeking Susan.'

While this is the title of a movie starring Madonna, I can't help but wonder whether it might be addressed to me. I know that this is a bit narcissistic, since there are a lot of Susans in the world. But I *am* Susan. The only one who would associate me with this chat room would be Alice Bessette or Philippe. This isn't out of the realm of possibility, since Alice knows I frequent this chat room and only knows me as Susan. Alice – and Jean – might be looking for me. I would be a little surprised, though, if it's Alice, because as far as I know, she's still out for a night on the town with Philippe. But perhaps after he told her that he saw me, she decided to go online to find me here.

The poster's screen name doesn't make sense – J!Ncks – but it probably isn't meant to, so there's no way of knowing for sure who it is. Mine won't give me away, either, so I take a chance and respond:

'What do you want Susan for?'

J!Ncks is online, so I don't have to wait long. 'Do you know Susan?'

J!Ncks should know better than to ask that. 'It depends.'

'I need to get her a message. Can you deliver?'

'Not sure. Depends if it's the person I'm thinking of. It might not be.'

'She's got a shadow.'

My heart quickens in my chest. This has to be Alice. Too many coincidences. Somehow she's going to try to trap me. I have to tread lightly around this. 'A lot of shadows out there these days.'

'Tell her she's got a friend.'

'Who?'

'Someone who is looking out for her.'

'Who?'

'Me.'

I'm not quite sure why she would want to look out for me. This has to be a trap. 'Why the desperation then?'

'Because someone's out to get her.'

'The shadow.'

'No. Not the shadow. Someone worse.'

I run a hand through my hair; the shortness of it is unfamiliar and I feel like a stranger in my own body. I think about what J!Ncks is saying, and if she really is Alice, then she knows her father, the immigration detective, is looking for me and has gotten very close to finding me. Is that what she's trying to warn me about? That Jean will arrest me, deport me? As far as I know, Alice doesn't know who I really am, so to her and Jean, I am merely an illegal alien. I know *she* isn't my shadow, because the shadow showed up before I met her. And if she doesn't know that Susan is really Tina Adler, she doesn't know anything about Tony DeMarco, who truly does scare me and most likely *is* my shadow in some form or another. My father knew about Tony's business, and since I hacked into my father's files, I know, too. Tony never hesitated to carry out his own form of justice.

'So tell me who's out to get her,' I challenge J!Ncks.

'Tracker.'

My first thought is that J!Ncks is crazy. This is posted on a public board. Tracker could be here somewhere, monitoring the chat and seeing what he's being accused of. Or is that the reason why she's saying it? Does she want Tracker to know that he's somehow connected to this mysterious Susan?

I have to assume that J!Ncks knows who I am just as I know who she is. My suspicions are confirmed when she asks me to go into a private chat.

Problem is, I know those chats aren't really private. If Tracker has seen his name here, he will be able to hack the private chat room like I did. I can't pretend that I'm the only one who's ever done that. But despite all that, I agree to meet. I want to know if she's going to show her hand.

I go behind the firewall legitimately this time, and I wait for J!Ncks to show up. I'm surprised she's not here yet, and I begin to think that this is the trap. This is what she wanted all along.

And when she finally shows up, I realize I am right.

'Susan, you have to turn yourself in.'

My instinct is to get out of here. To disengage completely. But part of me wants to hear her out, see what she has to say. I compromise with myself and don't respond, but she can see I'm still here.

'I've gotten inside Tracker's computer, Susan. He isn't who he says he is.'

Tracker has never said he's anybody. He's never presented himself as anyone other than another hacker. I still don't say anything.

'He's after you, Susan.'

Tracker isn't after Susan. He's after Tina. And anyway, she's not telling me anything I don't already know.

I am about to leave. I still have not said anything. I could be anyone here; she's laying herself out there and she could be wrong, for all she knows. I want her to think that, so I am ready to walk away without any further conversation. But her next statement stops me short.

'Tracker knows where you are.'

TWENTY-FIVE

The lights come on suddenly, surprising me. I blink a few times and turn to see Jin Fang watching me with a frown on his face.

I shut down the laptop without even leaving the chat room. I close the top and pick it up as I get up off the chair. He says something in Chinese to me, and even though I can't understand the words, I do understand the body language. I am not supposed to be here; I have to go back in the other room.

The light goes out as abruptly as it came on, and I follow him into the bedroom. Everyone else is still asleep, and I plug in the laptop again before crawling for the second time into the bedroll. The bed across the room creaks as Jin Fang gets back in next to his wife.

I stare at the ceiling in the dark, a sliver of light from a lamp post outside slicing across the wall. I think about the laptop so close to me and wonder what I would do if something happened to it. If it broke. If it didn't work anymore. Maybe that's an idea. Maybe I should get rid of both laptops, dump them somewhere after smashing them into a million little pieces so no one could ever see what was on the hard drive. I can clear a hard drive better than most people, but there might be something lurking that could be missed. No, smashing them, maybe even putting them in the road so a truck or a bus will run over them, that's what will work best.

I've lived without a computer before. For fifteen years I survived. I hardly missed it – well, no, that was wrong. There were still the dreams about source codes, firewalls, screen names, passwords. If I'd stayed away, if Ian hadn't given me the laptop last year, then maybe they would have someday faded, disappeared into the night like the ghosts they were.

I have a sickness. An obsession. An addiction. I have relapsed. This entire past year has been leading to this point, the point where I may actually be discovered only because I couldn't stay off my laptop, because I had to go back inside.

Even though I try not to believe J!Ncks about Tracker, she has planted a seed of doubt that's growing. She knew he was looking for me, that wasn't a stretch for her. She saw the messages he left for me. But the part about him knowing where I am, that's what worries me. I should never have gotten in touch with him. I was better off with no engagement at all.

He is probably in that chat room now, waiting for me to arrive. I wonder how long he will wait for me. I think about the post office box I've rented, how it will stay empty now. I can't risk giving Tracker the address. I am going to have to get out of Canada on my own somehow. Or maybe I'll stay, travel across the country to Vancouver, settle in that far west English-speaking city and adopt another name. I could find some work there. Yet I begin to wonder how I could get across the border between here and there.

I hear someone begin to snore, plunging me back into reality and where I am right now. These people may not be here legally. I wonder how they got here. They weren't crossing the border in Vermont, like me. Or were they?

I don't think I'm going to sleep at all, until I do.

I wake to see three small faces peering into mine. I jerk back, whacking my head against the wood floor, and they back off, giggling. I smell something foreign, exotic, coming from the other room.

Shu Fang comes in the bedroom and shoos the children out, pantomiming that it's time for me to get up. I glance at my watch and see it's a little after seven. I climb out of the bedroll and roll it up tightly and put it in the corner. I have slept in my T-shirt and jeans and desperately want a shower, but instead wash my face in the small bathroom and run my wet hands through my hair. I do brush my teeth, which makes me feel a little more human. When I emerge, I unplug the laptop's power cord and stuff it in the backpack. As I'm doing that, Jin Fang comes in and indicates that I must come out to the other room.

For the first time, I feel like a houseguest who might be a little bit welcome. A cup of tea is set down in front of me, a delicious aroma reaching my nose. I take a sip and savor the jasmine. A bowl of what looks like congee is poured, and while it's got a rather unpleasant, snot-like consistency, I'm hungry and I eat the whole thing. I would like a croissant or a bagel, but beggars can't be choosers, and they are harboring me so I have to be gracious. I smile, indicating that I'm pleased, and for the first time I get grins back, as though perhaps we are going to get along.

A short knock at the door, and Madame Xu appears. She glances at me and begins speaking Chinese with the Fangs. I'm getting used to hearing it and not knowing what's being said, so when she speaks to me in French, it startles me for a second.

'You need help?'

I'm not quite sure what she's asking. Clearly I need help because Jean is looking for me, but there is something else, I can tell.

'We can get you transportation.'

'Transportation to where?'

She shakes her head and puts her finger to her lips. 'How much money you have?'

I think about the backpack, the cash I have stashed there. I don't have enough for what she's suggesting, if what she's suggesting is what I suspect. Borders are ripe for human trafficking, and I shiver, thinking about the conditions I would have to endure if I choose to go along with a plan like that. And then when I look at Jin and Shu Fang, I realize that they may likely have gotten here that very way and they survived. But it still doesn't have much of an appeal. Yet I can't stay here, and I don't know how else to escape.

'Ten thousand.' Madame Xu has taken my silence as agreement that I will consider this.

And I do. I probably have about twenty thousand, so I will still have enough to get myself settled somewhere. 'Yes. OK,' I say.

She narrows her eyes at me and shrugs as she speaks rapidly to Jin and Shu Fang.

'How does it work?' I ask.

She whips her head back around to stare at me, as though I am not supposed to ask questions, but then she says, 'We have boat.'

My fingers itch to get to my laptop and look at a map. Montreal is an island, so a boat makes sense. But then what? I am not a person who enjoys spontaneity. I can't afford that. I have to know the plan thoroughly; I have to be at the ready.

'You have ten thousand?' Madame Xu is double-checking, a little dubious about my cash flow. I decide that I like this about her, her practicality, and the fact that she is going out of her way to help me, even though she doesn't know me and doesn't have to. And then she points to the dragon pendant around my neck. 'It will protect you,' she tells me again. 'Don't go out. I will come back.' She turns to Jin and Shu and even though I don't understand the Chinese, I do understand that she is telling them that they are to keep me here.

I don't have anywhere to go, so I can live with that.

TWENTY-SIX

The children shuffle off reluctantly, most likely to school, and Jin also leaves, possibly to work. I help Shu clean up the breakfast dishes, trying to make myself useful so she is not too unhappy with having me there. When we're done, she goes into the bathroom and I hear the shower start up. Again I wish I could have a shower, but I don't have a towel, none was provided to me, so I have to live with myself like this for a while. I hope that I can take a shower before I have to take my mysterious boat ride, because who knows how long it will be after that.

I pull out my laptop and again hack my way into a locked wireless network, although a different one today, in case someone is monitoring. I don't want to lay myself open to discovery.

I sign onto the chat room using a screen name that Tracker wouldn't recognize, and I see him here. I also see a message he left for me last night: 'Where are you, Elizabeth?'

It is akin to the Desperately Seeking Susan message left by Alice, and if it were another time, another place, I might feel pleased that I am so popular. Instead, it fills me with dread and worry that I won't be able to get on that boat soon enough, even without knowing where I'm going and what the end game is going to be.

If I'm leaving anyway, it shouldn't matter now if Tracker knows where I am. Once I'm gone, I'll be able to cover my tracks better so he can't trace me wherever I am. I am dubious that J!Ncks is even telling me the truth, though, about any of it. She knew about Tracker back at the computer shop. She could be making it all up to smoke me out so her father can get hold of me. She could be saying Tracker is after me and dangerous so I'll take off now and Jean, lying in wait, will nab me.

Despite her so-called warnings, I can't help myself in wanting to believe only the best of Tracker. My fingers itch to respond, and before I can talk myself out of it, I type: 'I got held up.'

Immediately, a new message pops up. 'Meet me.' And a URL. Tracker has been lurking here, waiting for me.

My curiosity gets the better of me. I double-check the URL to make sure that there is no RAT hiding within its code and when I'm satisfied, I meet him in the private room.

'What happened, Tiny?'

'Don't worry about it.'

'Did you find out about your shadow?'

'He has something to do with Tony DeMarco. That's why the ransom demand. I got Tony back some of his money last year, but he still wants me to pay for what I did.'

'How do you know it's DeMarco?'

'He sent someone to talk to my friends.'

Nothing for a couple of minutes, and then: 'How do you know?'

'I talked to them. They told me someone named Patricia Hale came to see them. Knew everything about me.' I hesitate, and then write, 'They knew about you. They told her about you.'

'So that's how they knew to put the RAT in my link to you.'

'That's right. But I'm afraid for my friends. That if I don't pay up, they will be vulnerable. I know what DeMarco is capable of.' I don't have to keep Steve and Jeanine a secret any longer. There is too much at stake.

I think about Madame Xu and the mysterious boat. I don't know the time frame of her plan, and again it irks me that I'm not privy to all the information. I need to be here long enough to do what I need to do, and then I can leave. Madame Xu does not seem like the compromising type, however, so I write: 'It has to happen soon. He's given me two days, but I'm not sure how long I'll be here. Maybe another twenty-four hours, maybe less.' I have to have Internet access long enough to do this. Once I'm gone, I don't know when I'll have access again.

If I'll have access again.

'I don't know that it can happen that fast,' he writes. 'But I know about one bitcoin marketplace that stores keys and might be vulnerable. We can get into the source code and copy the database before they even know we're there.'

Adrenaline is rushing through me as I anticipate it. I've spent the last year lurking, participating in conversations in the chat rooms about how to break through codes, find back doors into systems, but there is nothing like actually doing it, knowing how much power there is underneath your fingertips.

Shu shuffles into the room, pausing behind me. I close the laptop cover halfway, so she can't see what I'm doing, and then wonder why I'm being so careful. She seems to only understand Chinese, although I could play devil's advocate and say while she doesn't speak French, she could possibly know some English. I don't want to go out of character, though, and test her.

She says something in Chinese to me, and I shake my head, shrugging, indicating that I don't understand. She moves to the kitchen area and begins putting together some food. It's a little early for lunch, but then I see she's packing it up. I flip up the laptop cover again.

Tracker has left me the name of the bitcoin marketplace and says he'll be back.

Shu gets my attention and indicates that she is leaving me some food, but she is going somewhere. She probably has a job, too, and thinks I'm lazy because I don't have anything better to do than look at my laptop.

I give her a wave as she leaves, shutting the door quietly behind her. I hear something then, an odd click, and I push my chair away from the table and get up. I go over to the door and put my hand on the knob. It can't be. But when I try to open it, I know.

She's locked me in.

TWENTY-SEVEN

I am suddenly claustrophobic. I am on the third floor, and while there is a fire escape off the bedroom, the window won't open. It's been painted shut. For a second, I forget about myself and think about the Fang family and how if there were a fire, they would be trapped here. I get a kitchen knife and take it to the bedroom and chip away at the paint, wondering if there's lead in it and if I'm causing even more of a health hazard.

I stop what I'm doing. I'm wasting time. My hosts have made sure that I have nothing else to do except hack into that marketplace and get Tony DeMarco his bitcoins. They have also left me alone so I can organize myself without anyone watching.

First things first. I sit cross-legged on the floor and unload my backpack. I put the extra jeans and two T-shirts aside, along with the toiletries. The old laptop also comes out, and the power cord that powers up both laptops. In the bottom, at the very bottom, is the cash. I take it out and spread it out in front of me, counting and organizing it by bill denomination. When I'm done, I'm looking at piles of one hundred-, fifty-, and twenty-dollar bills in Canadian money. I've got twenty-five thousand, all told, and then I've got another five thousand in American dollars, so thirty thousand total, although with the exchange rate, I'd do better with the Canadian.

I assume that Madame Xu is talking ten thousand in Canadian currency, so I carefully count out that amount and set it aside. I'll need to have that handy. I also keep the American dollars separate. I wrap up the Canadian money in one of my T shirts and stuff it in the bottom of the backpack, then stuff the American bills into two pairs of socks and tuck them around the T-shirt with the other money in it. Now I've got to deal with the ten thousand for Madame Xu's boat.

I get up and skirt around the room, looking for an envelope or something like it, but see nothing. I don't want to go through the dresser, even though I tell myself that they've locked me in and maybe I shouldn't be so loyal. But I end up finding a paper bag in one of the kitchen drawers, and that'll do. I bring it back into the bedroom and put the money inside, but keep it out of the backpack until I get it packed up with the rest of my things. I slide the bag with the money in it in the front pocket and zip it shut.

I am beginning to think that I should have a money belt, to keep some cash closer to me than being so vulnerable with a backpack that I can be separated from. I didn't think this through, probably because my journey into Canada was so uneventful and I didn't have to worry. But now that other people are involved, circumstances are different. But I don't have a money belt and I have to hope for the best.

Now that I'm organized, I find myself back at the table in front of the laptop.

I go to the Internet and do a search on the marketplace that Tracker's suggested. I remember the news stories about bitcoins being hacked, but it was clear that in most cases insiders are the ones doing the hacking. Since I'll be on the outside, it won't be as easy, and I begin to wonder about my timeline. I don't know that I'll be able to get this done before Madame Xu comes back for me. But I have to try.

I focus on the screen in front of me and soon I am in my zone. I have to get behind the firewall and into the source code to find the password to get into the database. Normally this is not a problem, but I think the fact that I know I don't have much time makes me nervous, and it's taking me longer than it should.

I have a crick in my neck, and my legs are cramping a little. I look up at the clock over the stove and see I've been working for over two hours and have not yet gotten in. I need to take a break. I stand up, my arms over my head and feeling it in my back. I bend over and touch my toes, stretching my leg muscles. I do a few more stretches, like the ones I'd do after a good long bike ride, and I begin to feel better. My stomach growls, and I remember the food that Shu left for me.

She's put dumplings in a steamer, and I put it on the stove. I'm not quite sure how long to cook them, because I am not an adventurous cook myself and have never made dumplings. After what I feel should be a reasonable amount of time, I take the steamer off the stove and put the dumplings on a plate. I have no idea what I'm eating – maybe a couple of chicken, a couple of shrimp, both with herbs and flavors I'm not used to – but they are delicious and I am soon finished. I drink a glass of water and decide my break has been long enough, and I have to get back to the matter at hand.

I procrastinate, though, and check the chat room and see Tracker there.

'Sorry I disappeared,' I write.

'Any luck?'

'Having a little trouble getting in.'

'Not me.'

The old competitiveness rises, and I push it back down. I don't have time to worry about who gets in, only that one of us does and we are able to make the transfer.

'Send me the address for the wallet your shadow wants the bitcoin deposited in,' he adds.

'I can't let you do that,' I say. If he does it, then it will all come back to him. I have no idea who Tracker is, what his life is like outside the chat room conversations we've had, and I don't want to put him at risk any more than I want to risk Steve and Jeanine's lives. 'Tony expects me to make the transfer,' I say, as though this will make a difference.

As I suspect, it doesn't.

'He doesn't know or care as long as he gets his money,' Tracker says.

'I don't want this to come back to you, in case someone can trace it,' I tell him.

'It doesn't matter, Tiny.'

'Yes, it does. No one knows where I am. I don't exist, remember? So how could anyone know it's me?'

'Maybe you're not the only one who's hiding. Have you ever thought of that?'

His words make me take pause. This is something I've never suspected. Is Tracker a fugitive, too? Maybe the bank job came back to haunt him as well. Maybe he had to disappear, just like me. Maybe he took the money I left him and he's been living on it all this time. There was enough.

Again I've created a daydream about who Tracker is, when he is actually only who he wants me to think he is.

'It doesn't matter,' I write. 'This has to be me.'

'Tell me what you've done, why it's taking so long.'

I recount my steps, and he stops me a few times, reminding me of things that should have been – and at one time had been – instinctual. I'm kicking myself, following his instructions, falling back into our easy camaraderie, and I'm reminded what was so good about the two of us back in the day.

I am almost in. I see it, the code, and before Tracker can advise me, my second nature takes over and I have successfully gotten around the password and have even given myself a back door to get back in if I need to. I am about to download the database with the keys when I hear something.

Footsteps on the landing on the other side of the door. A loud click and the doorknob turns. Madame Xu steps into the room, a grim look on her face. No. I'm not ready to be released yet. My fingers hover over the keyboard. I'm so close. Can I hold her off? I have to hold her off.

'Just a moment, OK?' I say, not really asking for permission.

But Madame Xu is not one to wait on anyone, I'm discovering. 'It's time to go,' she says firmly. 'Get your things.'

I glance out the window and see the bright blue sky. I was convinced this wouldn't happen until night fell, and now it seems that I have to go out in plain sight.

She senses my hesitation. 'Time to go,' she says again.

'One moment,' I say.

'No,' she says, coming over to me and slamming her finger down on the power button. In an instant, the screen goes dark, and I stare at it, then up at her, anger rising in my chest.

'This was important,' I say in a low voice, pushing the anger back down but not too successfully.

'You want to get caught? OK, you get caught,' she says defiantly, folding her arms across her chest. 'I have seen him twice today, and someone else, too. They are close, and you have to leave now.'

I stand and pick up the laptop. 'Why are you helping me?' I ask, curious now.

The question throws her off a little; she doesn't expect it. But after a moment, she gives me her familiar nod and says matter-of-factly, 'Because that's what I do. I help people like you.'

As I gather up my backpack and slip my laptop inside it, swinging it over my shoulder, I wonder how many people like me she has helped through the years. Something tells me there have been a lot.

TWENTY-EIGHT

I am not expecting the car that's waiting at the curb. The driver is a woman, not Chinese, but white, like me, and introductions are not made. Madame Xu opens the door for me as though she is a proper hotel concierge, and I climb inside, shifting the backpack between my feet on the floor. The window is open, and she leans in toward me. I think I have to pay her, so I begin to unzip the backpack, but she puts her hand on mine to stop it.

'No. Later. You pay her,' she indicates the driver. She reaches up and touches the dragon pendant around my neck. 'It will protect you,' she whispers, and then backs away.

I watch her get smaller and smaller in the side-view mirror until the driver turns down a side street.

I look at her profile. She is maybe a little younger than I am, with a touch of gray at her roots. She has not turned to look at me, even though I can see her eyes flicker toward me every now and then. Her hands grip the steering wheel. I know what she's thinking. If we are stopped, if I am discovered in her car, she will be culpable. I want to tell her that Jean knows me as Susan McQueen. I honestly don't think he knows I am really Tina Adler and that I am wanted by the FBI. Alice got into my laptop, but there was nothing there. And despite what she said to me in that chat room, Tracker would not give me away any more than I would give him away.

Although I did, didn't I, by telling Steve and Jeanine about him. Who's to say that he hasn't been tempted to tell someone about me, too?

Thinking about Tracker makes me itch to get back into that site. While I am grateful for Madame Xu's swift action, it was a little too quick.

My thoughts have distracted me a little, but I notice now that the driver keeps glancing in the mirrors, and her jaw is set a little too tightly. I peek into my side-view mirror and see a car close behind us. It is small, something Japanese, I think. I can't see the driver clearly because the window is in a shadow and the visor is down against the glare of the sun.

'Are we being followed?' My voice is a little too loud, startling the driver. Her fingers grip the steering wheel, her knuckles white. I take this as her way of saying yes, we're being followed, because the car speeds up. The car behind us doesn't lose a beat, though, and stays on our tail.

The light ahead turns yellow, and my driver gives the accelerator a little more pressure, and we catapult forward as the light is turning red. The car behind us runs the light. I wish a police car would come out of nowhere and stop him, but no such luck.

The car takes a sharp turn to the right, and we're heading down an alley. I clutch the armrest to steady myself, but I'm not going to be a backseat driver. Suddenly we're taking another right turn, and then a left. The car following us keeps up.

And then we're on top of a big intersection. The light is red and the cross traffic is heavy. I wait for her to hit the brakes, but she doesn't. Instead, she maneuvers around two cars in front and rides along the sidewalk until hitting the accelerator as the light turns green. We shoot off across the street, now several cars ahead of the one that's been following us.

She takes a sharp left turn into an alley and finally turns to me and speaks.

'Out.'

I am too dangerous for her. She can't risk her own life for me. I get it. But as I pick up my backpack and open the door, I wonder what I'm supposed to do now. 'Where were we going?' I ask. 'I can get there myself.'

She blinks a couple of times, uncertain whether to say anything, then says, 'The yacht club. Ask for David.'

She doesn't wait for me to close the door before the car starts moving. The door slams shut as she takes off, leaving me in the alley, exposed. I swing the backpack over my shoulder, shrugging it on so both my hands are free, and I begin to jog in the same direction the car went. When I get to the end of the alley, I realize I'm in Old Montreal. The cobblestone streets are busy with tourists. I hear something come up past me in the alley, and I duck quickly into the entry of a chocolate shop as the small car that's been following me emerges. I sink back further into the shop, rounding

the corner so I can see out the window overlooking the street. The
car is idling there, and I see the driver. It's Jean Bessette. Someone
is in the passenger seat, but I can't see a face or even a figure, just
a hand that's gesturing, pointing out the window to the right and
then to the left.

They don't know I've gotten out of the car, otherwise they'd be on
foot. I watch the car as it slowly moves into the street, turning right.

I smell it then: the chocolate. It's as though all of my senses have
been assaulted at once, and while I don't want to stop watching that
car until it disappears, the girl behind the counter is looking at me
suspiciously. I give her a small smile and glance at the sweets on
the other side of the glass.

'Can I get three truffles?' I ask in French, pointing to the ones
with salted caramel. She puts them in a small bag, and I give her
a couple of bills out of my pocket. I pop a truffle in my mouth as
I walk to the door tentatively. What if they've turned around and
come back? Figured out that I'm no longer a passenger but a
pedestrian?

But the car is nowhere in sight.

I think about the yacht club and the mysterious David. He is
expecting me, and if I don't arrive, he will assume the worst and I
will no longer have a way out of here. I have to get there and as
soon as possible. While I don't want to pay for a taxi, it seems the
best alternative, since I'm not familiar with the bus system and I
don't know if the metro will take me where I need to go. I can also
be hidden better in a cab, just like all the other tourists.

I hurry along the sidewalk, trying to spot a taxi, when I finally
see one that's dropping someone off in front of a small auberge. I
sidle up to the driver, who has finished taking the passenger's bags
out of the trunk. The passenger pays him, and I say, 'Can you take
me to the yacht club?'

He is Middle Eastern and has a handsome, chiseled look about
him. His mouth is set in grim line. 'You need to find a taxi stand.
I am with a private company.'

'I don't have time. I'm late for an appointment. Please?' I give
him the best smile I can and hope it appeals to his compassionate
side.

He looks at me warily, and I am afraid he is going to say no,
but then: 'OK.'

I climb into the back seat as he gets into the cab. He tells me a price, and I think that it's very high, but since he's not really supposed to be taking me anywhere, I agree. I wonder then about the driver of the car that picked me up and how Madame Xu had told me to pay her, but she left so quickly, before I could.

I settle back and try to relax, but I feel like an elastic band stretched so tight that I'll snap at any second. I lean my head against the back of the seat and turn it to see a car coming up alongside us.

It's Jean.

TWENTY-NINE

I can't tell the cab driver to speed up. I'm not in a car chase on TV. I slide along the seat until I'm on the other side and sink further down, giving Jean only a view of a woman's short haircut if he looks this way. I assume since he's been knocking on doors asking about me, he knows that I've cut and colored my hair, so I'm not really fooling anyone, but I'm out of context, a woman in a cab, like so many others in this city, that I hope I'll be able to escape without notice.

And a few minutes later, when I glance back, I see that my dragon pendant seems to be protecting me as it should, because Jean is gone and the cab is now making its way west down rue Notre-Dame, along the river. I can see boats in the water, pleasure boats taking advantage of the beautiful day. I still wonder why Madame Xu had me leave during the day and not at night, but I assume there's a reason that may be discovered once I get to the yacht club.

I have no idea what this boat is going to be like that Madame Xu has procured for me. I also don't know how I'm going to find David. Do I just go in and ask for someone named David? What if there are more than one Davids? Why didn't I get a last name?

I am distracted enough so when the cab slows down, I barely notice. And when it stops altogether, pulling to the side of the road, it takes me a few seconds to register it.

'I have to leave you here,' the cabbie says. 'Entrance in there.' He points to a tree-lined road. I can see a small security gate in the distance. This should be interesting. I hand over the fee I agreed to. The cab driver gives me a nod but doesn't say anything. I take my backpack and get out, shutting the door behind me, and the taxi shoots off as though he knows he shouldn't be seen with me.

I shift my backpack and contemplate how I'm going to get past that security guard. Somehow I think Madame Xu's driver would have had a plan for this, but since I've been abandoned, I have no choice but to figure it out myself.

It's a yacht club. Probably not much unlike the yacht club my family was a member of back on Key Biscayne. I consider the way I look: no shower, greasy hair, dirty jeans, rumpled T-shirt, canvas boat shoes, backpack.

But it's all about attitude; I learned that when I was young and rich and didn't care. Maybe I'd have a better shot getting past this guard if I were twenty-something rather than forty-one, but I am not a stranger to this world, whether in Miami or Quebec.

I boldly walk toward the security booth, my head high, as though I belong here.

The guard is a little surprised to see me on foot, but I don't give him the chance to question because I immediately take a deep breath and begin my diatribe. In French, of course.

'Damn taxi left me by the side of the road. Can you imagine? I'm already late, and I'm afraid I've missed my friend. His name is David. He's waiting for me. I'm on the list. Hélène Leblanc.' I say my name as though I am someone he should know, although I am certain that I am not on this particular list. But it's worth a shot as I touch the dragon pendant around my neck, praying that I have not overdone it – or underdone it.

The guard checks a clipboard in front of him, running his finger along it, until it stops and he looks at me out of the corner of his eye. 'I don't have a Hélène Leblanc on the list.'

Of course he doesn't.

I sigh as though I am very put out by his incompetence. 'Please call up to the clubhouse and tell David that I'm waiting out here.'

'David who?'

Yes, David who?

I roll my eyes. 'I don't know who hires people around here,' I mutter loudly enough for him to hear. 'Do I have to speak to your boss?' I ask.

'My boss?' He gets a panicked look in his eye. That's the one I was waiting for, because then he pushes a button and says, 'I'll let them know you're coming.'

I don't even give him another glance as I scoot through the gate that's lifted. I have to get in before he finds out a mistake was made. A sign points in the direction of the clubhouse, and I follow a path to a fieldstone building. Why not? I think, as I straighten my shoulders and walk up a couple of steps and push the door open. Another sign inside gives me the option of the restaurant or the washrooms. I debate for a second and decide on the latter, turning to my right and going down a hall and into the women's room. I figure I've got about five minutes before someone comes looking for me and throws me out.

The washroom is more like a spa, with lockers and piles of soft towels on marble countertops. There are a couple of women wearing only towels in here, and I hear a hair dryer somewhere. I peer around a corner and see a line of showers. I don't even hesitate. I grab a couple of towels and go into a shower stall, stripping down. There are dispensers with soap and shampoo, and for the first time in a couple of days I feel really clean. The towels are small, but they do the job, and I put on the clean clothes that are in my backpack.

A couple more women have come in while I've been showering, but they don't even give me a second glance when I emerge. I find the hair dryer, leaving my curls slightly damp. I survey myself in the mirror. I put on a little mascara, adjust my glasses and throw my sweater over my shoulders in a way that might make me fit in here a little more. I don't think I look half bad, considering the last couple of days.

When I leave the women's room, I am re-energized from both the shower and the fact that no one has come in looking for me.

I'm not quite sure where I'm going to find the mysterious David, and it's probably not here, at the restaurant entrance, where I find myself after turning a corner.

A woman stands at a hostess podium and greets me. I don't have much choice now; if I don't play along like I belong here, they'll kick me out. I smile widely and say, as though there is nothing odd about it, 'I am supposed to meet someone named David here, but I'm afraid I've forgotten his last name.' I laugh as though this is the silliest thing, how could I forget, and it is infectious, because she smiles back.

'Yes, we've been expecting you.'

I try not to show my surprise that my arrival was announced, but it's clear I'm not going to be escorted out. 'Thank you,' I say.

'Mr Carrington has been waiting. Please follow me.'

I do as she asks and find myself in an elegant restaurant with chandeliers and gauzy white curtains blowing in the open floor-to-ceiling windows that look out over the water and the docks full of boats outside. There are just a few people in here, scattered about, dressed elegantly as only the rich can dress in the middle of the day, in the middle of the week. Despite my anxiety about how I had to get in here, I am more at ease than I probably should be. I have my father, Daniel Adler, and his world to thank for that.

We approach a table where a middle-aged man is seated. He has not yet looked up, so I can study him first. His head has been shaved, and it is a nice shape. He wears a button-down shirt underneath a navy cotton sweater. It is understated, yet effective. He is a powerful man, and I am not certain now that this is a good idea. There must be some mistake. The David I am supposed to meet up with is probably more like a kitchen worker who needs ten thousand dollars and will do anything for it. David Carrington does not look that desperate.

The hostess gives him a smile and says softly, 'Mr Carrington? Your guest is here.' She is speaking English, despite the French we'd spoken when I arrived. I debate switching languages, but decide to stay in character.

'Monsieur,' I say, holding out my hand. 'Hélène Leblanc.'

The only way I can tell that I am not exactly what he was expecting is the small twitch of his left eye, but he smiles broadly and gestures that I should sit. He thanks the hostess, who backs away silently, and gives me a curious look.

'Do I know you?' he asks in perfect French, Parisian French.

This is a mistake, but there's no turning back now.

'I was told to meet someone here named David,' I say.

Before he can respond, a waiter appears. 'Drinks?' he asks.

David Carrington looks at me. 'What can I get you?'

Without thinking, I say, 'Cognac.'

He turns back to the waiter and says, 'A cognac for the lady, and I'll have a scotch on the rocks.'

The waiter disappears, and I see David Carrington is waiting for me to explain. I also notice how he studies my face, and it makes me uncomfortable. I fidget in my seat, tightening my feet around the backpack between them.

'I'm not the person you were expecting to see, am I?' he asks.

'I don't think so,' I say.

'But it's my lucky day.'

I frown, uncertain what he's saying.

'It's not every day that I get to spend time with a beautiful woman like you.' He smiles widely. In another time, I would welcome his attention, the diversion. But I need to find the right David or I'm going to lose my chance.

I begin to apologize, and the drinks arrive. I take a small sip while considering how I'm going to get out of this gracefully, and the cognac moves with a white heat down my throat.

'As far as I know, there are no other Davids here today,' he tells me. 'Not even kitchen or the dock staff. I know everyone here. I'm the manager.' He pauses. 'You are very resourceful, although that has now presented more of a challenge, as you might suspect.'

And he gives me a look that tells me that perhaps he is the person I'm supposed to meet with after all.

THIRTY

Leaning across the table, he says softly, 'You shouldn't have told me your name, but I understand that you're confused. What happened to the car?'

I'm not quite sure what to say, but he fills the silence by adding, 'You're not the usual kind.' He sees my frown and continues, 'I didn't expect someone like you. You seem so—' he pauses – 'normal.'

I want to laugh. I am so far from normal, but he doesn't know me, doesn't know my story, and it has to stay that way. I don't understand how a yacht club manager could get mixed up with this, either, which makes me suspicious. But if he does this a lot and it's ten thousand a head, then he's got quite a nice little stream of undocumented income coming in.

As if he's read my mind, he lowers his voice even further and says, 'You don't have any documents?'

I think about Tracker and before I can stop myself, I shake my head.

'No problem.'

The waitress comes back, and he gives her a smile. 'Two steak frites, Isabelle.' She disappears, and he continues. 'We're going to have lunch, and then you're going for a little boat ride on the river. How does that sound?'

I have read enough crime novels to know that this might not be a good idea. I have no idea who he really is, if he is who he says he is. Jean Bessette could be lying in wait on the dock, ready to deport me to a country where I will no doubt be identified for who I really am and end up in prison for a very long time.

I could get up now and walk away. I could make my way west, find another place to hang my hat and hope that there are no other Jean Bessettes. I could go back to the States the way I came. I feel as though there are plenty of options.

But I don't get up. A salad arrives, and its vinaigrette is delicious. I still haven't said anything, and David Carrington watches me closely as though he knows I'm considering fleeing. He would have no reason to stop me, except for the cash that I'm carrying. And while he seems respectable enough, there is a glint in his eye that tells me he could sell me out at any moment. He's a respectable yacht club manager, and I'm illegal. Who would the authorities believe if it came to he said/she said? I've come too far to back out now.

I don't know if anyone notices that we don't speak, or at least I don't. Over the steak and fries, David tells me about the yacht club, its long history, how many boats sit in the slips outside. If anyone is paying attention, he would think that I am a prospective member being wooed by the club manager.

I am distracted by an urge to go online, to go to the chat room and find Tracker. I have no idea when I'll get another chance, and I need to transfer those bitcoins so Steve and Jeanine can stay safe.

'Would you excuse me for a few minutes?' I ask, the first words I've spoken since our drinks were delivered. I don't wait for permission, just get up and take my backpack.

'Certainly,' he says, but I am already halfway out of the restaurant and going toward the women's room.

There has to be wireless Internet here. I hear a shower running, but I go into one of the changing rooms and close the door. I pull the laptop out of the backpack and power it up. There is wireless here, and there is a network for guests. I use my VPN and find my way to the chat room. I scan the posts for Tracker, to see if he's online. I have to do this quickly; I can't be gone too long or David Carrington will get suspicious.

Finally, I see him. Tracker is here. I post a note asking to meet me in a private chat with the screen name I used the last time we chatted.

'Tiny?'

'I don't have much time. I got to the database, but I couldn't download it. Something came up.'

'Are you OK?'

I think about this for a moment. Am I OK? Not really, but I type, 'Yes. But I'm going to be offline for a while. I'm not sure how long.'

'What's going on?'

'Nothing, it's fine. Can you do the transfer for me?' I hate asking, because it's him who will be on the line for it if he is caught.

'I told you I would.'

That's right, he did. He's going to wonder what's going on now that I've changed my mind, but I don't have time for this. 'Thank you.'

'I need the address. The one to send them to.'

Right. 'Hold on.' I pull the old laptop out of the backpack and get that one powered up, too. I don't have anything to cover the webcam, but it doesn't matter now anyway. Enough people have seen my makeover that I cannot think I am fooling anyone. When I log in, I wait to see if my shadow has another message for me, but it's quiet. I pull up the message program, and I see our messages from before. There it is, the address.

I quickly type it into the chat for Tracker.

'I really appreciate this,' I add.

Suddenly, a new message pops up on the old laptop: 'Where have you been? I'm still waiting for my money.'

An irritation rises in my chest. 'I'm working on it,' I write. 'You should have the money soon.'

'How can I be sure of that?'

'You can't be. You have to trust me.'

'How can I trust a criminal?'

I stare at the word 'criminal'. That's right. That's what I am. I don't know what Tracker's story is, but I don't want him to sink as low as I have. I can't ask him to do this. I have to do it.

'I won't have access for a couple of days,' I write my shadow, hoping that it will only be a couple of days, but who knows. 'But I promise that I will make the transfer as soon as I can.'

'Why can't you do it now?'

'I'm not in a secure place.' I also don't have enough time. I have to get back to the database, and while I have saved the password to get in, it will still take a while to get the job done. 'This is not something I can help right now. But I will get you your money in a couple of days. I promise.'

'I don't know if I can trust you.'

'Please. There's nothing I can do right now.'

'OK. But you have one day. That's all.'

I turn off the laptop and turn back to the other one, where Tracker is waiting.

'Never mind,' I type.

'Never mind what?'

'I can't ask you to do this. I have to do it. I'll be in touch when I can again. I don't know how long.'

'What are you doing, Tiny? I want to help.'

'You can't. Sorry.' And I shut down the laptop and shove both of them back into my backpack, heading back out to whatever plan David Carrington has for me.

THIRTY-ONE

I apologize for being so long, but I make it sound like it's a 'woman's problem', and he doesn't question me. We actually have coffee, as though this is truly a real lunch, and when we are done, we push our chairs back and stand. I sling the backpack around my shoulders and follow him out of the restaurant. Instead of going outside, he leads me down a hall and to a door that reads 'Manager'. He unlocks it and we step into his office. It is as plush as the restaurant, with a long, teak desk and awards and medals adorning the walls.

He leans in and says into my ear, 'You have the money?'

I nod. 'In my backpack.'

'Leave it.'

'The money, you mean.' Panic bubbles up inside my chest. He can't expect me to leave the backpack.

'I'll take it.' He reaches around me, about to take the backpack off my shoulder, but I twist to the side and step back.

'I'll give you the money, but I have things in this backpack that I need.' I try not to raise my voice, but it quivers underneath the words.

He steps back. 'Fair enough, but I need to see.'

He wants to see inside my backpack. He'll see the laptops and the clothes and the cash at the bottom. My hands are shaking as I unzip it. I reach inside and pull out the bag with the ten thousand dollars in it and shove it at him. 'It's all there, you can count it.'

But he's not paying attention. He's got his eye on my laptops. 'Why do you need two?'

'It's a long story.'

He's holding the bag, but folds his arms across his chest. 'We've got time.'

'I've got a shadow in one of them, someone's taken over my laptop, so I got the other one so I can go online without being watched.' It's as simple as I can make it.

He frowns. 'A shadow?'

'That's right. I clicked on a link that had a virus in it. It gave him access to everything inside my laptop.'

'You can do that?'

'It's pretty easy, actually.'   ·

He quickly looks inside the paper bag, fingers its contents – he's probably counting it – then puts the bag down on the desk and cocks his head at the laptops. 'Show me.'

'What?'

'Show me how easy it is.'

While I don't want to encourage this, it gives me an idea. 'If I show you, I can keep the backpack, right? And everything in it?'

He indicates a laptop on the desk. 'I don't need a laptop. But I do like this idea. Yes, show me and you can keep everything.' He pauses. 'Except this, of course,' he adds, indicating the paper bag.

I go around the desk, sit down and open his laptop. 'OK. I'll show you.' He comes around behind me. 'First, you need a VPN.' He looks at me quizzically, and I say, 'Virtual private network. It will disguise your IP address so if anyone tries to trace you, they won't be able to.'

He likes this idea, too. I walk him through installing the VPN, then I go to the site where they sell the RATs. I tell myself that I'm not really doing anything criminal myself, even though I'm showing him what to do.

'I don't want to use my credit card,' he says when we reach that stage, but I can see the need in his eyes, the need to have it, to discover what he can do with it.

'You have to buy it somehow,' I say, 'and it's not exactly illegal to buy it. You just have to make sure you don't do anything illegal with it.'

'But isn't getting into someone else's computer and spying on them illegal?'

I shrug. 'Gray area. If you protect yourself, no one can ever find out you're even there.'

He eyes me suspiciously. 'How do you know so much about this?'

I give a short chuckle. 'You don't want to know.'

'Maybe not.'

He finds a credit card to use. I pretend not to notice that the name on it is not his own. Who am I to judge? I walk him through

the rest of the steps to download the code. He stares at the jumble
of letters and numbers.

'It's the source code,' I explain. 'You insert it into a link and
send it to someone. Once the link's opened, you'll have access.'

'Show me.'

I shake my head. 'It's easy from there. You'll see.' I don't want to
take it further. I don't know who he wants to spy on, and it's none
of my business.

He is watching me as I stand up. 'You know your way around
a computer.'

'A little.'

'How about this, Madame Leblanc? I'll give you your ten
thousand dollars back, and you stay here. I can get you documents;
you can be here legally. You can work for me. I have a feeling
that you have skills I am in desperate need of.'

For a moment I consider this. I could be sort of legitimate. I
have no doubt that David Carrington can deliver what he's prom-
ising. But then I realize it's impossible. I can't stay here. It
doesn't matter how much I change my appearance. Jean Bessette
will always be around the next corner. I could run into Philippe,
Alice.

And then I think about what David Carrington is up to, here at
his yacht club and the boats. He is smuggling people – and possibly
other things – in and out of the country. Even though I am a fugitive
and have committed my own crime, I don't want to be a part of this,
part of *his* criminal activity. I know it's ironic that I would have
standards about this, but I do.

I can't tell David Carrington any of it, though, without giving
myself away. Instead I shake my head. 'No, I think we need to stick
to the original plan.'

'Are you sure?'

He wants to give me a second chance. To change my mind. To
start my life here all over again. But the specter of Jean Bessette
hovers. 'Yes.'

'OK, but remember this later.'

I don't like the sound of that and begin to think that perhaps I
should reconsider, but he has already moved to the door, waiting
for me to follow. I do just that, and we go outside, down a long
pathway to the edge of the water and a large fence with a sign that

declares only members can go past at this point, and we walk through as though everything is perfectly legitimate.

The dock is a little unsteady under my feet and we pass several large sailboats, the kind that I remember from my days on Key Biscayne: large, ostentatious, flaunting money. Boat owners are partying on the decks, music emanating from somewhere within, drinks overflowing, glasses clinking. As we pass, David Carrington is greeted by a few people, but not everyone. 'Manager' means employee, not equal.

We are almost at the end of the dock when he stops at a power-boat. There is a flurry of activity aboard; a man and a woman are readying the boat for a trip, and I realize that this is my ride. David climbs on board and talks closely with the man. The woman is studying me as I continue to stand on the dock.

David turns and gestures for me to come aboard, so I do. He leans toward me and says softly, 'Last chance, Madame Leblanc. Stay here and work for me. Or take your chances with them.'

Again, I don't like the sound of the choice I have, yet I need to take my chances. The plus about staying here would be that I can get my shadow his money much sooner, but at what price? I will be safer getting the money far away from here.

'Thank you, Mr Carrington,' I say, 'but I really do need to leave.'

'You're not like the others,' he says then. 'It's not going to be easy.'

I force a smile. 'I haven't had it easy in a very long time, Mr Carrington. I've made it this far, and I can do it again.'

He studies my face for a second. 'I don't know what you're running from or why, but I hope you get somewhere safe soon.'

'Me, too,' I whisper. 'Me, too.'

THIRTY-TWO

I am told to go below as we cast off. No introductions are made; the silence is loud against the sound of the engine. I have no idea where we're going or where I'll end up, and the uncertainty worries at the edges of my brain. I touch my dragon pendant, but its power seems to have taken a break. I touch the backpack, wishing I could go online, to the place that always calms me down. But there is no Internet here, or at least no Internet that's going to do what I want it to. I might be able to find a weak signal, but for how long?

The boat lurches away from the dock; it vibrates under my feet. I push aside the small curtain covering the porthole and see that we are passing the other boats in the marina, the open water of the river in front of us. I hear footsteps overhead, but no one comes down here. I sit alone, perched on the small bunk. Every muscle is at attention; I cannot relax. I look around me; this boat is not meant for comfort, despite its outward appearance. The bunk has a thin blanket on it, nothing more, not even a mattress. I check the drawer that pulls out underneath, and it's empty. The small galley kitchen is bare. I get up and check out the lavatory; it seems functional, but who knows. I'm glad I had a shower at the yacht club, because I have no idea when I'll get another one.

I settle back on the bunk and pull my legs up underneath me, the backpack at my side. I keep looking at it, wanting to take out the laptop, but it would be futile. For the first time in over a year, I am left without my crutch. I can't disappear into my online world, wearing a screen name that protects me. I am more exposed than I've ever been: on a boat heading for who knows where with two strangers, a corrupt yacht manager and a Chinese woman the only two people who know where I'm heading. I am anxious to get off this vessel, despite where I might find myself, so I can at least regain control again.

Right now, though, I am helpless, so I close my eyes and concentrate on the rocking of the boat as we move along the river.

*　　*　　*

I wake when they cut the engines, the white noise disappearing, and suddenly I can hear them up on deck, talking to each other, although I can't make out the words. I again pull back the small curtain behind me and see we're coming into a private slip, a house teetering on the edge of the water. It's not in the best shape, the house. The paint is curling, peeling off the wood; the roof has been battered by weather, shingles loose and flapping in the wind. A window is broken on the second floor. This does not make me feel comfortable, but it's not as though I have had any expectations.

I feel the boat hit the side of the dock. Someone jumps off; I hear it rather than see it. I get off the bunk and swing the backpack around, settling it on my shoulders against my back.

The hatch opens and light splashes against the floor. The woman descends into my cavern. I see now that she's not tanned, as I initially thought when seeing her briefly before we set off, but she's Native American, her dark hair pulled back to show off remarkable cheekbones and chiseled features. She holds up her hand to indicate that I need to stay where I am, so I wait.

The boat shifts a little, throwing me off balance, and I stumble, grabbing for the stairway railing to steady myself. I see a small glimmer of a smile on the woman's lips, as though she finds it amusing that I don't have sea legs. I catch her eye and shake my head and give her a sheepish grin.

Our moment passes immediately, though, as a shout comes from outside, and she gestures that I should follow her up the ladder.

The sun isn't high in the sky anymore, but it's bright enough after being below. I see now that the man is also Native American, although a little lighter skinned than the woman. He has tied the boat up and is waiting on the small wooden dock. It's a private slip. There's another boat in the slip next to it, but that one is a small sunfish sailboat, the kind I used to sail when I was a kid in Miami. I hope I don't have to switch to that one, because it's been a long time since I sailed and I'm not sure I could do it now.

Fortunately, the woman steers me up a small wooden gangplank to a gravel driveway next to the dilapidated house. She takes out a key, and I don't like the look of this. She opens the door at the side of the house and crooks her finger at me, indicating I should follow.

I don't want to. I don't like the idea of being trapped in this house with strangers. The claustrophobia that I remember from being locked in the Fangs' apartment comes rushing back, and I stop just short of the steps. The woman gestures that I need to come in, but I can smell it from here. There is something rotten in that house. The scent of garbage and urine and vomit is strong enough to emanate out here, and I put my hand to my mouth, hoping I won't gag.

Without thinking, I say in English, 'Is there a car I can use?'

The woman looks behind me, and I turn slightly so I can see the man standing there. They've got me cornered, but I can't go in that house. Who knows who's been in there or who might still be inside. I can't be that desperate. I've gotten this far.

When they don't answer, I repeat in French, 'Do you have a car I can buy?'

I have no idea if they understood the English, but they understand the word 'buy', because they both start at the sound of it.

'How much?' the woman asks in English, and I know she's asking how much money I have.

I do a little quick calculation in my head. I've still got fifteen thousand in Canadian money. It might be useless once I'm in the States, since I'm not sure I can exchange it easily without a passport or license. I will need the five thousand in US dollars, so I will pretend I don't even have that.

'Five thousand,' I say, willing to part with at least that much, if not more if they try to negotiate.

But this seems to be the magic number, because their faces light up and they exchange a look that clearly indicates there might actually be a car they can sell me. The woman closes the door to the house and comes down the steps.

'Come with me,' she says.

I follow her, the man behind me as though I might try to run back and take the boat. We go through a small hedge, and we're in a driveway. A beat-up pickup truck that looks to be at least twenty years old is parked there.

But the truck isn't what they want me to see. On the other side of the truck is a small Volkswagen Bug, circa the 1970s. It's baby blue with rust creeping around the bottom of the doors. The woman skirts around me as I'm looking at it and whispers to the man, who frowns, then nods. They turn to me.

'You pay us now.'

'Yeah, sure,' I say. I stick the backpack on the back of the car so they can't see everything inside, and I reach in and fumble around for the Canadian money at the bottom. I manage to pull out enough bills, then zip the backpack shut. I go over to the couple, and the woman reaches out for the money, but I hold it back.

'Key first,' I say.

She pulls it out of her pocket. But that's not enough.

'Start it,' I instruct.

The woman and the man exchange another look, but the woman obeys, climbing into the driver's seat and starting up the Bug. It coughs once, and the engine catches and it purrs. She gives me a tense smile, then gets out.

'Border patrol?' I ask.

Both of them shake their head.

'No patrol.' The man finally speaks. 'Take this road straight out. You'll hit Route thirty-seven. East you go toward Malone. West, Ontario.'

'No border patrol?'

They both shake their heads again. I have no idea if they're telling me the truth, if I'll drive down the road and end up at a border crossing with police waiting for someone like me. But I can't go into that house, so I'm going to take my chances with the car.

I hold out the cash, and the woman snatches it out of my hand. She quickly counts it, then looks up at me.

'There really is no police. You can cross the border with no problem. But you are supposed to check in at the first checkpoint.' It's clear that she knows I'm not going to do that.

'There are no sensors or anything?' I can't let this one go. There might be someone in a room somewhere with a laptop. Like me.

'Not here.' She does not elaborate. 'Good luck.' The couple turns and walks away, leaving me out in the open next to the running car.

I'm still uneasy. I dodged a bullet and managed to get into Canada through the forest, but I'd heard about border patrol on major highways checking vehicles even a hundred miles from the border on the States' side. I can't dwell on it, though. I have to try. The couple seemed certain that there wouldn't be any patrols here – wherever *here* is – so I'm safe for a little bit.

I toss the backpack in the passenger seat as I get into the car. I close the door and contemplate this. I haven't driven a car in sixteen years, but fortunately I do know how to drive a stick.

I put the car in gear, and with a rough start, back down the driveway, hoping I don't stall it out, and head toward the border.

THIRTY-THREE

They weren't lying. There is no border patrol here. After driving down a very narrow road with myriad potholes, I see a large post office, and then a speed limit sign that's in miles, not kilometers. Somewhere I've crossed the border, but there is no indication of where it was. I'm on St Regis Road, and I have no idea where I'm going, but I finally see a sign for Route 37. If I go west, the bridge to Canada in Massena is thirteen miles; if I go east, it's twenty-two miles to Malone. I opt for Malone, since I have just spent a day getting out of Canada.

Route 37 is a bigger road than the one I've been on, but not much bigger. The scenery is dull, concrete and trees that seem to go on forever, and then all of a sudden dingy white houses with porches that seem to be held together with Scotch tape. The bright flowers and colors and tidiness of Quebec have not made it across the border, and I find myself wondering what people do for a living here.

The car runs as well as an old VW will run, but I doubt that if border police come out of nowhere and begin to chase me, it will hold up very well. I am constantly checking the rear-view and side-view mirrors, but so far my journey is uneventful. I can't count on the couple not to tell anyone, though, that I'm driving around in an old VW. Maybe they wouldn't tell border police, but they might mention it to someone who notices that the car is missing. I need to put as much distance between them and me as possible.

I do, however, need to get some gas and I soon come upon a truck stop. While I haven't seen very many vehicles on the road, there are six tractor-trailer trucks parked side by side in the parking lot here. I have to go inside to pay for the gas, since I don't have a credit card, and while I'm in here, I pause at a display showing local attractions. I don't think that Burlington, Vermont, or Lake George are that close, but I could be wrong. I do see one brochure that catches my eye that's advertising the Akwesasne Mohawk Casino Resort. I am apparently on a reservation, which I can only

see as a good thing. Reservations have their own police force;
they're not beholden to a state or a country. They probably won't
mind a fugitive like me wandering about; there could be dozens
like me. I wonder if this is also a reason why there is no border
patrol in sight.

I think for a few minutes about the casino. Where there is a
casino, there will be a place to stay that might have wireless
Internet. I probably can't get it out here in the middle of nowhere,
but I am willing to bet that a casino is going to offer its guests
what they can't get anywhere else around here. I take the brochure
up to the cash register and after I pay for the gas ask how far
away the casino is.

It's my lucky day. It's only a couple of miles from here. While
I don't like the idea of sticking around, I need to get online and
take care of the shadow as soon as possible. I also need to check
in with Tracker, tell him I'm OK, considering how I cut him off so
abruptly earlier.

I'm getting used to driving the VW, and I'm happy that I can
still handle a clutch. I turn into the road that leads to the casino,
and I come upon it in a matter of minutes. It looks like a chain
hotel with a big sign slapped on it that says 'casino'. I think about
the cash in my backpack and wonder about my luck. I've gotten
this far on my wits; do I want to take a chance at the tables? Maybe
a little blackjack. Or maybe just some slot machines.

I remember a trip to Vegas with Ian back in the day. He was
greedy and lost everything he had. I was more cautious and managed
to win a little. He spent my winnings by buying dinner for us.
Even then he used me in so many ways. I wonder what my life
would be like now if I'd said no to him when he came to me with
the plan to hack into the bank and steal the money from those
accounts.

Problem is, I know I could never have said no to him. Not only
because I loved him and would do anything for him, but because
the minute he suggested it, I wanted to do it. I wanted to show off,
prove that I could.

That's why I'm driving a ratty old Volkswagen Bug into the
parking lot on a Mohawk reservation in New York State, trying to
come up with a new name to use at the front desk. Elizabeth
McKnight won't do. That's the name I used online for Tracker to

find me. It would be a stretch if anyone looked for Elizabeth McKnight here, but I don't want to take that chance. Hélène Leblanc disappeared the minute she got on that boat at the yacht club. Nicole Jones became Susan McQueen and crossed the border in Vermont and vanished. Tina Adler transferred ten million dollars out of strangers' bank accounts and became Amelie Renaud.

I wonder how many more names I'll have before I get tired of it all and surrender.

The hotel lobby is done up in muted browns, beiges, grays and blues. It has a rustic elegance to it. I don't think there will be a problem paying cash for a room for one night, and I am right. I register as Alison Armstrong, the University of Miami roommate I had for one semester before I was kicked out for hacking into the school's system. If anyone wants to try to trace the name, maybe they'll find Tina Adler here, but I doubt it. Alison and I moved in very different circles. I was unmemorable then; the crime that resulted in my expulsion was never revealed.

The room is comfortable, plush. I put my backpack on the bed and take the laptops out. I'm not ready to have another conversation with my shadow; anyway, I've still got a day before he's expecting the money. I need to find Tracker, so my first stop is the chat room.

Z and Angel are dominating the room tonight, but I don't pay attention to what they're saying. I scan the chats but don't see Tracker anywhere. I quickly post a message for him, telling him I need to talk, giving him a URL for a private chat room, and signing it 'EMK' as we'd arranged earlier.

I'm about to head to the bitcoin depository to find the back door I left open to download the key, but a name catches my eye. It's J!Ncks. She's looking for me – or, rather, Susan – again, and she wants to meet privately. I debate this. I have no reason at all to maintain contact with her. I don't want to hear her suspicions about Tracker; she's got her own agenda, hers and her father's. I've left them miles away in Montreal. I am safely ensconced here on a neutral reservation and do not plan to be here for long. Tomorrow I will be in the wind. I will have to ditch the car at some point, since I can't rely on the discretion of my smugglers for too long. Someone will miss it; I need to dump it before they do.

I think about the sign that said Malone was twenty-two miles away. I leave the chat room and J!Ncks's request to meet and do a search for transportation out of Malone. A bus can take me to Lake George for relatively little money, and I can take a bus or train from Lake George to Manhattan, which is the most logical place to end up. It will be an easy place to hide. Not to mention that it's another island, which appeals to me somehow.

I check the chat room again but Tracker still isn't there. I begin to worry. He has always been there when I've needed him, except once. I remember that time last year when Angel told me Tracker was working on something and couldn't be reached. I quickly type up a message for Angel, asking him where I might find Tracker now.

He responds quickly: 'I'm not sure where he is. Can I help?'

'No,' I type. 'It's personal.'

I can almost hear him laughing as I read his words: 'None of us has a personal life.' He's right, but to a point. I always managed to have a personal life, at least after I met Ian. He was a distraction from my obsession, the person who pulled me away from the screen and taught me that I could have a relationship.

Too bad it was all under false pretenses.

I tell Angel if he sees Tracker that I've left a message and to make sure he see it. Angel agrees, and I switch screens.

It's time to get those bitcoins.

THIRTY-FOUR

I easily find the back door that I opened. No one has shut it. Either they haven't discovered it or they've chosen to ignore it. If they're ignoring it, then there might be a shadow watching me, ready to catch me. I have to be careful. Bitcoin depositories are set up by people like me, people who know their way around the source codes and can find the smallest mistake.

I can see the chain that contains the keys. I focus on it, the code, how to break through and download it before anyone notices.

Just as I am about to pull it out, though, I see the shadow. They're watching my every move. I can't do it. I have to stop, even though I should be shrouded by the VPN. Out here, in the middle of nowhere, the casino could be the only place for miles that could be pinpointed by an IP address. I would be easily found if they could break through my safeguard.

I thought this would be easier, but I have to be more clever about it.

I don't have time to find another depository marketplace to try. It has to be this one. But not right now. They need to think I've been scared away.

I get up and start pacing. I have to do something, get out of here for a little while, figure out what I'm going to do, how I'm going to do it. I settle back on the bed in front of the screen and go back to the chat room, but Tracker still isn't there; he hasn't responded to my message. My imagination starts going wild. Where could he be? Angel says no one here has a personal life; does that include Tracker? He is my age, or around my age, and I can't imagine that he's been isolated all this time. If I could have a relationship with Ian, Tracker could have a wife, a girlfriend, a partner and still hack. We are not all antisocial.

I think about an article I read once, about the stereotypes that are perpetuated by hackers. The 'experts' all say that we are young, male, possibly with some sort of autism spectrum disorder or other social behavior problems. I went against all the stereotypes and still do. I am forty-one, a woman who has friends – at least when I'm not running. I live alone, but so do a lot of people. I hate anyone being put in a box.

So that's why I imagine Tracker as someone unlike the textbook hacker, someone, rather, more like me. Maybe I'm fooling myself, but since I will never meet him, he can be anyone I want him to be.

I have to get out of here. I plug in the laptop to power it up since it's below fifty percent and I need to make sure it's fully powered at all times, shove some cash into my pockets, then grab the room card key and head to the casino.

Casinos are the same everywhere. Loud patterned carpet on the floor is meant to draw your eyes up to the table games, the slot machines. There are no windows that could indicate the time of day; gamblers are supposed to lose track of time and their wallets. I want to pretend that I will not be sucked into it, but getting lost in the screen of a slot machine or blackjack is not unlike being online in my hotel room.

Because we are technically in New York State, I have my American dollars, but I have also brought some Canadian money with me. I locate a currency exchange booth and brace myself for how I'm going to talk my way out of not having any official identification to prove who I am, but being a hotel guest and having cash seem to be enough, because they hand over American dollars, minus their fee. I will have to make sure to do this again before I leave, but I can't bring too much attention to myself so I will have to limit how much money I change.

I take my money and get some tokens for the slot machines. I win some, lose some, and then manage to win a little more that I decide I will use for something to eat and a drink. I am surprised at the number of people here, but then remind myself where I am and how there doesn't seem to be much else to do around here.

After a year in Quebec, it's disconcerting to hear only English and no French, but I have to get used to that since I'm back in the States. I wonder vaguely about whether I could at some point go back to France, to Paris. I push the thought aside as I head toward the casino bar. I'm not really hungry, but I could use a drink to settle my nerves before I go back upstairs and tackle the depository again.

Stone towers and Keno screens overwhelm the bar, but I sit at a table by myself and a waitress approaches. I order a cognac and attempt to clear my head while she goes to fetch it.

I scan the bar, checking out the people at the tables near me: a group of young women that has had too much to drink; an older couple who might be on an overnight tryst; and across the room, a lone man nursing a drink.

The waitress sets the cognac down in front of me, and I thank her, taking a sip. It's smooth against my throat; and I remember the drink I had with David Carrington earlier. Was that just today? It feels like a million years ago. I should be more exhausted than I am, but the adrenaline of the day's activities is still running through me.

Out of the corner of my eye, I see the lone man at the far table get up. I don't like to stare, but I find myself doing so. He has his back to me, yet a chill runs through me. He is familiar, like the man with Jean Bessette on the train, like the shadow waiting outside my hotel in Chinatown. I will him to turn around so I can see his face, but he doesn't; he leaves the bar and goes around the stone column into the casino. Without thinking, I gulp down the cognac while slapping a few dollars on the table and quickly head in the same direction.

I face the casino and scan the room as far as I can see. The flashing lights from the slot machines are like a strobe, and I blink a few times to clear my vision. Casinos used to be louder, but now it's only the bells and whistles when someone wins that echo throughout, overtaking the piped-in pop music.

I don't see him. If it's the same man, he's not wearing the suit jacket he wore both on the train and outside my hotel. He is wearing a short-sleeved shirt and jeans; he fits in with the clientele here, doesn't stand out. I look down at my own attire and get slightly distracted by thinking I might want to see if the hotel laundry could take care of my clothes before I leave.

He's gone. I skirt around the rows of slot machines, the table games, to make sure, and he's vanished.

I sigh, and suddenly I am exhausted. The day has finally caught up with me. I want to do nothing except go back to my room, see if Tracker has checked in, and fall into bed. I should see about those bitcoin keychains, maybe have some dinner, but I can hardly keep my eyes open. I stumble past the people slipping coins into the machines, their movements mechanical and mindless.

I watch the signs to make sure I'm going in the right direction toward the hotel – I don't even have to go outside – and realize I've taken a wrong turn. I force myself to focus and turn around.

He's standing right there, looking at me, but he turns so quickly and disappears around one of the ubiquitous stone columns that I feel as though I have imagined him.

I must have.

Because he's a dead man.

THIRTY-FIVE

I think I'm having a heart attack. My heart is pounding so hard it's as though it will jump right out of my chest. I hold my hand against it, willing it to calm down, taking long, deep breaths. No one around me seems to notice that I am on the brink of death, and it's only when I stumble toward one of the slot machines and sit in front of it, leaning my elbows on the edge, my head in my hands, that I realize I'm merely having a panic attack and I am not going to die.

I blame my hallucination on the fact that within the last twenty-four hours I was smuggled out of Canada and bought myself a car so I could come to the casino and hack into a bitcoin depository.

I can't possibly have seen Zeke Chapman standing in this casino in upstate New York on a Mohawk reservation.

When I left Zeke on that houseboat in Paris, I'd shot him. I close my eyes and can still see the blood. I can still hear the second shot bouncing off the edge of the Seine, the one Ian took, the one that killed the FBI agent who'd come to Paris to run away with me. He had no idea I'd been using him; he'd told his wife about me. I broke his heart and then I shot him and ran. Ian had to clean up my mess, and I left him, too, and everything we'd had together.

I glance around behind me, to make sure. Yes, he's gone. There's no one there. It was just a ghost.

'Do you want a cocktail?' A waitress sidles up next to me, a tray balanced on her hand.

I shake my head and slide off the seat, freeing it up for a real gambler, and head in the right direction for the hotel. My feet feel clumsy; I wrap my arms around my chest and hug my torso. The elevator ride seems endless yet before I know it, the doors are opening and I am in the hallway a few steps from my room. I go inside and begin shedding my clothes, turning on the shower in the bathroom, and stepping under the stream, washing away David Carrington, the boat, the car, the image of Zeke Chapman in my head.

Am I losing my mind? Have sixteen years of being on the run finally caught up with me? Should I have let Jean Bessette find me, deport me, turn me over to the FBI? The longer I stay in the shower, the more the water washes away my doubts. No, I had to leave.

I have to survive.

When I step out of the shower, I see the clothes on the floor and think about the laundry idea. I wrap myself in one of the plush terrycloth robes and call downstairs to housekeeping. If I put my clothes in one of their bags and hang it on the doorknob outside, they will pick it up and wash my clothes tonight, bringing them back in the morning.

I put all of my clothes into a bag and hope that I won't regret this, that I will have clean clothes waiting in the morning. Otherwise I will be wearing this bathrobe when I check out tomorrow.

The longer it's been since I thought I saw him, the more I realize it was merely my exhaustion. There was a time when I would see him all the time out of the corner of my eye. The casino lighting is hardly bright; he was standing in a shadow. It was a man who had similar features, but there are a lot of men who might be mistaken for Zeke if I really thought about it.

Zeke had been good-looking, but not in the same way Ian was. Ian was tall, with a chiseled jawline, bright eyes, and a sexy smile that made me feel as though I were the only girl in the room. He still has that quality, as I found out last year, but he's married now. Zeke was married back then; he was huskier, more muscular, like a football player. He was gentler, though, and kinder, belying any stereotype I may have had about FBI agents.

I didn't know what I was doing when I seduced him, all I know was that he let me. I was playing a dangerous game, trying to make Ian jealous. I should have known it would end the way it did.

I push the thoughts out of my head. I want to crawl under the covers and sleep, but first I have to check the chat room. I'm glad when I do, because he's here. Tracker is back.

'Where did you go?' he asks.

'Long story. I tried to download the key, but there was a shadow. Someone watching from inside.'

'They're hard to crack,' he concedes. 'There are a lot of safeguards. They've been hacked before, so they're on alert. I'm not surprised they're lying in wait.'

'So how do I get around them?'

'There's a way.'

As I read the words, my exhaustion slips away and the adrenaline returns. He has a way inside. I tuck my feet underneath me and sit cross-legged on the bed. I no longer think about how soft it is, how comfortable. I only see the screen and Tracker's words.

'Do you want me to help?' he asks.

'Yes.'

'There's another back door.'

'Not the one I created?'

'They've found that one. There's another one. One they haven't discovered.'

And I know then that he's been there, that he's the one who got behind their firewall and changed the code so I could get back in. It's possible that's what he's been doing all day, why I couldn't reach him.

I pull up another screen on the laptop and call up the site. I find the source code and toggle back to Tracker. 'Where?'

'See if you can find it.' He's challenging me, like he used to, back when I first met him online. 'I know you can do it.'

I'm not a kid anymore, but because of my long absence online, my skills are no longer on par with that girl I used to be. But when I start scrolling through the code, I see it. Tracker is clever. He's created a back door in the back door I'd already put there. I keep an eye out for shadows, but don't see any this time. I slip inside easily and find the list of keys I need. Within minutes, I'm downloading all of them. I hope I have enough space on the laptop for all of it. If I don't, it will stop downloading and I probably won't get anything at all.

I toggle the screen. Tracker is waiting.

'It's happening,' I say.

'It might take a while.'

'I know.'

'Do you need anything else?'

I'm not quite sure what he's asking. 'Like what?'

'What you needed before.'

He's talking about the documents. 'No. Not now.'

'Are you OK?'

'Yes.'

'What about that detective? And the police hacker?'

'I don't have to worry about them anymore.'

A few seconds, then, 'What's going on, Tiny?'

'Don't worry. I'm fine. I just need to transfer these bitcoins and everything will be OK.' At least I hope so. Tony DeMarco is unpredictable. Even if I get him his money, he might still threaten Steve and Jeanine. I wonder if this is merely his way to smoke me out of hiding. Using my mother's name certainly got my attention, although if I hadn't called Steve, I would never have known what he was up to.

I watch the files downloading and it does seem to be taking a long time. I hear something outside my door, and I climb off the bed and look through the peephole. A woman in a housekeeping uniform is carrying off my bag of dirty clothes.

When I turn around, I see a message on the screen that the download is finally complete.

THIRTY-SIX

boot up the old laptop while plugging in the new one to power it up. The download has used up a lot more power than I expected. The old laptop's screen springs to life, and I wonder where the picture of those eyes has gone, prompting me to wonder why the shadow used it once but never again. Was it that he became more confident as time went on that he might actually get the money he's demanding? Or is there something more sinister at play?

I push the thoughts aside as I call up the message program to find out where he wants me to send the bitcoins, but another message from Tracker distracts me.

'You have to make sure they don't trace where you send them,' he says.

I don't really care about that. Once I've transferred them to the shadow's account, it's his problem. He can send them himself into a bitcoin tumbler, which will mix them up with other coins and conceal their origin. I'm not the one who will be traced, it's the bitcoins. I tell this to Tracker.

'You've been doing your homework.'

I'm not a hundred percent sure, though, that Tony DeMarco's minions will be able to handle this, that *they* won't be traced. I can only hope that he realizes I kept my end of the bargain, and he has to leave my friends alone now.

I turn back to the old laptop and realize the bitcoin wallet address was not in the messages, but in the box that had appeared with the ransom request. Because the keys are long and case-sensitive and they are on a different laptop, I debate what to do. I should have downloaded the keys on the old laptop. It wouldn't have mattered if the shadow had seen me do it; he's getting them anyway. The only way to practically give him the keys is to cut and paste them into a message and send it to my message program in the old laptop.

I'm surprised that while I'm doing this, he hasn't popped up with any new messages for me. There are no eyes staring out at me. It's as though he's disappeared. Maybe this is his plan, to make me think that perhaps he's gone and then when I least expect it, he will reappear like a magician's rabbit.

I leave the keys for him but don't bother with any sort of message. There's no point.

I shut down the old laptop and push it aside. I don't have any more need for it, but worry begins to nag at me. What if he doesn't get the keys? What if he claims he never got them and then went after Steve and Jeanine anyway? No, I need to hold onto it. I'll check it in the morning, see if he's there, make sure that he's gotten what he wanted and will now leave me and my friends alone.

Tracker is still in the chat room.

'Done,' I type.

'How will you know if your friends are safe?' he asks.

'I don't know,' I say honestly.

'You don't have any contact with them?'

'No.' I think about the phone calls, the only time I've talked to them in over a year. I desperately want to call them again, hear their voices, but I can't. Even though Tony will have his money, he'll keep an eye on them, in case I ever go back. It's possible that 'Patricia Hale' will show up again, too, and I may have to keep sending Tony money. This sort of blackmail would not be beneath him. He would relish the control he has over me.

I am, even while hiding, doing his dirty work for him. My father used to talk about Tony's business, how he wasn't more than a common thief himself. That's why he thought Tony wouldn't sell him out, because Tony was just as dirty as he was. But he underestimated his business associate, and when the chips were down, Tony made sure my father ended up in prison and he was safely on the outside.

Tracker is quiet, but he is still in the chat room. I lean back on the pillows and close my eyes. Within minutes, I am asleep.

When I awake, I have no concept of time. It's like being in the casino; the curtains are drawn over the window with their light-resistant shades pulled tight. I roll over, my knees hitting something hard. Right. The laptop. The light on the power source is green, telling me that it's all set to go. The cover is still open, but the screen is dark; it probably went to sleep about the same time I did. I hit one of the keys and it jumps to life, the light startling me.

The chat room is empty. I don't know when Tracker left, but he didn't say good night. Neither did I.

I transfer the cord to the old laptop, which is still showing fifty percent, but I don't want to take the chance that it will lose power anytime soon.

The clock says that it's seven a.m. I've been asleep for four hours. I roll off the bed and go to the door, wondering if my laundry has been done. I open it and yes, there's the bag, hanging on the knob. I grab it and close the door again, securing the chain. Even though I took a shower last night, I take another one, this time to wake myself up fully. It could be another long day, and I have to be at my best.

I take care blow-drying my hair, putting some mascara on. The clean clothes make me feel human again. When I'm all put together, I sneak a peek out the window. The parking lot is half full; as I suspected, there isn't much entertainment around here so everyone comes to the casino. I spot the little Volkswagen Bug, happy at first that it's still here, but that all-too-familiar worry begins again.

I can't be sure that the owner of the car isn't missing it. That he hasn't told the authorities that his car is gone.

I spot a couple of large tour buses on the other side of the parking lot and an idea begins to form. I had planned to drive to Malone, which is about ten miles from here, and then take a bus to Lake George, and from there, head to Manhattan. But maybe there's another way to travel.

I repack my backpack. This time, I make sure my American dollars are accessible, some of the Canadian money in the front pocket so I can exchange it in the casino. The two laptops fit snugly inside, cushioned by my sweater and T-shirts. I am looking forward to getting somewhere I can stay awhile, so I don't have to live out of this backpack anymore. I may invest in a money belt, to be on the safe side.

I'm hungry, and I stop in at the restaurant for a cup of coffee and a plate of eggs and bacon. The way things are going, I never know when my next meal might be, so I need to refuel whenever possible. I eat quickly, then go to the casino, change some money, and make my way out front to one of the tour buses in the lot. People are boarding; the driver is tossing bags underneath in the luggage compartment. I approach him, thinking about what I'm going to say.

When he looks up at me, I give him a sheepish smile. 'Hi. I'm wondering if there's any way I can get on the bus.'

He stands up taller, puts his hands on his hips. 'I can't let anyone on who doesn't have a ticket.'

I give him an exasperated sigh and a worried look. 'See, I've got a little bit of a problem. I came here with my boyfriend last night, but he took off with one of the waitresses and left me here all by myself with no way to get back to the city.'

A man comes over and drops a bag next to the driver and then rejoins his wife. They climb on the bus.

The driver shifts a little on his feet as he thinks about my story. Finally, 'We only go as far as Saratoga Springs.'

'That would be fine,' I say quickly. 'I can figure it out from there.' I indicate my backpack. 'I can pay. Don't worry about that.' I smile conspiratorially. 'I won a little bit at blackjack this morning.'

The driver glances at the people who are boarding the bus, then back at me. 'Don't worry about it,' he says softly, then gives a snort. 'He left you here?'

I nod.

'Asshole,' he mutters.

'You got that right.'

He cocks his head toward the people waiting to board the bus. 'Just get on. There's room. Middle of the week, we're usually not that full. Weekends are another story.'

I smile. 'Thank you. I really appreciate it.'

'If anyone asks, tell them you missed the other bus.'

'There was another bus?'

He grins. 'There's always another bus.' He starts loading the bags again, and I am clearly dismissed, but I thank him again anyway and make my way to the line. There are a couple of people in front of me, and I shift the backpack around a little as I climb the steps into the air-conditioned coach. He's right about the bus not being full, if everyone is already aboard. It's maybe half full, and everyone seems to be in their sixties or seventies. But I'm not going to complain. I make my way along the aisle and slip into a seat about three quarters of the way down. There is a couple sitting behind me, and two women in front. No one says anything to me or even seems to notice that I'm a stowaway.

The driver gets on, closes the door, and starts up the bus. As we pull out of the parking lot, we pass the Volkswagen Bug. I paid five thousand dollars for it, and it's a shame I have to leave it behind.

THIRTY-SEVEN

I find myself on alert, constantly looking ahead at the road to make sure that there is no border patrol roadblock. Even though I am clearly an American, I do not have any form of identification, so talking my way out could prove difficult. Yet we arrive in Saratoga Springs without incident. I discover that Saratoga Springs is a cute little town. If I thought I could get away with it, I might decide to stay here. The main street is lined with a lot of restaurants and shops, and I vaguely wonder about the 'spring', and if I might have time to take the waters while I'm here. Anything to rejuvenate the spirit, but regrettably, I can't linger. At least not too long. I've got a few hours before the train leaves. My ticket is in the backpack. I find a place to have lunch, and I indulge in a glass of wine with my pasta and shrimp.

I have spent so much time alone in the last sixteen years, and most of it without a computer, that to sit and have a leisurely lunch by myself has a calming effect. For the first time in a long while, I am not tempted by the laptops in my backpack. I vaguely consider that there is wireless Internet here, and I could easily get online, but right now, that's not the world I want to be in. I want to sit here at my table on the sidewalk and watch the tourists and college students. I want to hear snippets of their conversations that make me long for my days on Block Island, the most peaceful I have ever had. There were times when I was on the island that I felt that I had successfully beaten my addiction because I could resist it, I could live without it. But when Ian gave me that laptop after so long without one, something snapped inside.

But sitting here, enjoying the afternoon like a regular person, gives me hope.

I wonder about Tracker. Is he a normal person? Is he having lunch somewhere, ignoring the call of his computer?

A tenseness works its way into my shoulders as I remember J!Ncks' warning about him. She said that he knew where I was, that he wasn't who he appeared to be. Which is who, exactly? What does she know about him that I don't? I admit that I never pushed with him, not that he'd answer any questions about himself. But I also never really tried to find out anything further about him. It's possible I could have found out something more, but maybe I've always liked the mystery around him. Sometimes knowing all the truths about someone ends badly. Look what happened with Ian. With my father. With my mother.

The shadow claims that he didn't know a Patricia Hale, but I know he was lying. Yet, why so insistent when I asked? Tony DeMarco could have several angles at play, using multiple people to get what he wants. The shadow might not know about Patricia Hale, but he knows about Steve and Jeanine, otherwise he wouldn't have shown me those photographs.

I begin to wonder how I can turn the tables on Tony DeMarco. How he could be taken down. Those bitcoins might be a key. If they go anywhere near an account associated with Tony, he can be found out. He will have to face the consequences of my crime. But then what? Will he again come after me, after my friends?

I take a sip of wine and realize I wasn't thinking when I transferred those bitcoins. Tracker encouraged me, telling me that I am not the one who will be traced, but if Tony is pulling all the strings, somehow it will come back on me.

The train ride to New York City's Penn Station takes about four hours. I have not been online since late last night, and I am starting to feel withdrawal. I take one of the laptops out of the backpack and set it on the drop-down tray in front of me, but since there is no wireless on this train, I can do nothing except look at it. J!Ncks' comments about Tracker are circling in my head, and I try to formulate how I can find out more about him without knowing anything about him.

It's easy to do a search on someone if you have his real name. Maybe he is on social media, if you're lucky. Maybe there is a professional site that tells you what he does for a living. Maybe there are videos. News stories. It's very hard for people to disappear – like me – with the technology today, because we all leave little traces of ourselves across the Internet.

I try to remember if Tracker has ever said anything to me that might give me a clue to who he is, but he's been pretty careful. He knows who I am, of course, because he helped me with the bank job, which was splashed all over the news, especially when the media found out that my father was the con man Daniel Adler, who bilked millions out of celebrities and the very wealthy. My screen name 'Tiny' was a very weak alteration of my name 'Tina'. I never kept it a secret that I was a girl hacker, and mistakes I made showed him that I was young. He didn't know about Ian, not until after.

But Tracker has always been careful about dropping anything about himself. I pushed him to meet, but he says that not meeting will always be one of the biggest regrets of his life.

Tracker must have been right, that Alice is his shadow. I gave her access to him when I let her look at my laptop. Before he saw her there, she found out something about him, maybe more than one thing. And she wanted to warn me about him. At least that's the impression she gave. But why did she show her hand and let him see that he had a shadow? That was sloppy, but maybe she's not as good as I've given her credit for.

I absently worry the edge of my dragon pendant, which, at least until now, has protected me as Madame Xu predicted it would. I touch the cover of the laptop, knowing that it conceals Tracker's secrets so tightly that even I am not able to crack them. I stare out the window at the landscape rushing past. The gray clouds are low, swirling, as raindrops splatter the glass. I wish I had my paints to capture the moment.

It's been a long time since I've been in New York City. The sidewalk is dark with the damp reminder of the storm that's passed. People move past in a hurry to get wherever they're going; no one makes eye contact. It's well past rush hour, but the bustle never stops. The city is impersonal, which makes it a logical place for me to hide. But that impersonal feel is exactly why I didn't end up here. I wanted human contact, I wanted to make friends, a new life. New York has always seemed to me to be a sort of weigh station in between where someone is from and where he's going.

The last time I was here was my twenty-first birthday. Ian brought me here to celebrate. It was long before the bank job, but looking back, I can see the signs of what was to come. We stayed in Midtown, which now seems so terribly clichéd as I navigate the streets. It's easy, with the grid and the numbers of the avenues and streets. So

unlike the rolling hills and stonewalls on Block Island that have no
definite destination, since it's all about the journey. Ile-aux-Coudres
was reminiscent of that.

Someone bumps into me, and I feel the backpack shift on
my shoulders. I've forgotten that I'm in a place where backpacks
are more vulnerable, so I pull it around my body and cradle it to
make sure that no one can reach inside. Even though Montreal is
as much a city as New York, I didn't have that menacing sense that
I feel here.

I need to find a place to stay tonight, and for who knows how
long. I don't have unlimited cash, and money doesn't go as far here.
I suddenly wonder if this was really a good idea. Until now, I've
been able to take refuge in places where I can sell my art, do my
bike tours and no one questioned paying me in cash, no one asked
me for a Social Security number or made me fill out a tax form.
Tracker asked me if I needed documents, and I said no. But perhaps
I should say yes, even though I still need to find work under the
radar somewhere, because any legitimate company might want to
do a background check and they won't be able to find me anywhere.
I have no work history, and if I'm using a different name, I can't
use Pete from the bike shop or Dominique from the gallery as refer-
ences. While it seems logical that the city is the better place to hide,
maybe that's wrong.

I am lost in my thoughts, scanning the sidewalk up ahead to see
if I can find a coffee shop with wireless or a small hotel that might
not cost too much. I am not paying attention to anything else, which
is why when he grabs my elbow and begins steering me toward a
waiting car, I am so startled that I don't resist until the door is open
and he's pushing me inside.

THIRTY-EIGHT

He shoves me to the other side of the back seat, climbs in and slams the door shut. Instinctively, I reach for the handle to open the door closest to me, but before I can open it, the car begins to move, shooting out into the line of traffic. Horns blare, taxis and cars and trucks whiz past. I contemplate how bad it would be if I jumped out.

'Don't even think about it,' he says, his voice a low timbre.

His profile is dark, and it's only when flashes of light strobe through the window that I can make out his features. I don't recognize him.

'Who are you?' I ask, hugging my backpack to my chest.

'Don't worry about that. We're getting you somewhere safe.'

I have no idea what he's talking about. 'I think perhaps you've mixed me up with someone else,' I say. 'I just got here.'

'I know. The eight-fifty train in from Saratoga Springs.'

Every muscle in my body tenses. 'How do you know that? What's going on?' No one knew I was on that train. Did they?

He gives a short, low chuckle. 'Miss Adler, you have no idea the kind of danger you're in, do you?'

Adler? He knows who I am? How is this even possible? And what kind of danger? Does this go back to last year? To Block Island?

To my shadow?

It's all starting to make a little bit of sense. My shadow knows who I am, he also knows who my friends are. Tony DeMarco and Ian found me last year, but so did the FBI.

My brain gets a little less muddled as I sort it out, but I can't figure out if this is one of Tony's minions or FBI. I am almost afraid to ask, because either is dangerous to me. He says he's taking me somewhere 'safe'. That's not possible under any scenario.

The car is veering back and forth through traffic and turns a couple of times so we're no longer on a main artery. I see that we're going uptown on First Avenue, passing Fifty-Third Street.

'Who are you?' I ask my abductor.

'Just call me Paul.'

'Well, Just Call Me Paul, that doesn't tell me anything.' I try to muster more anger up through the fear, so my voice won't shake, and I'm about half successful.

'You'll find out everything when we get there.'

'Get where?'

'Somewhere safe.'

I peer around the driver's head, out the front window. 'How do you know it's safe?'

'Trust me.'

'I don't trust anyone,' I say truthfully.

The car turns up on Eighty-First Street and slows in front of a tall apartment building, then stops.

'We're here,' Paul says. I wait, and then he adds, 'You can get out.'

I open the door and see that yes, I can get out. I'm on the sidewalk, clutching the backpack. I take a step, ready to run, but suddenly another man grips my upper arm and steers me into the building. I try to wrench my arm free, but he tightens his hold.

'Stay with me,' he instructs. 'There's no reason to run.'

I beg to differ, but keep my mouth shut. They already know my name; they've managed to catch me in a place where I thought I'd be even more hidden. Maybe that's how they did it: my guard was down, I felt confident that I'd eluded everyone. I feel incredibly stupid, since when they found me last year, I'd made a mistake. I know I haven't made any mistakes this time.

So how did they find me?

The man holding my arm and Paul flank me in the elevator, as though I'm going to try to escape from a closed box that's moving. When the doors slide open, I brace myself, but no one is on the other side, just a hallway with doors. They take me halfway down, and Paul pulls out a key and unlocks one of the doors, swinging it open and indicating that I should go inside.

It's dark, and I hear a switch being flipped. We are bathed in fluorescent light in a small foyer. Paul sidles around me and another light turns on, and we move into a small living room, with a couch on one side, a bookshelf with a TV on the other. A bank of windows is directly across, with mini-blinds that have been pulled half open.

A couple of cloth Ikea-type chairs flank the couch. There are no personal possessions in sight or any artwork on the walls. I peer around and see a galley kitchen to the right; a doorway to the left opens into a small bedroom with a bed and a dresser. Again, nothing to indicate anyone lives here.

'What is this place?' I ask no one in particular.

'It's your safe house.'

He steps out from behind me; I'm not sure exactly where he came from, but it doesn't matter.

All I can think is: I wasn't hallucinating at the casino. It really was him. Zeke.

THIRTY-NINE

I catch my breath and stumble. Arms pull me up, and I'm walked over to the couch, where I'm set down. But I can't sit. I jump back up and stare at him like the ghost he really is.

'We've got people watching your friends on Block Island,' he says calmly, as though seeing him is not like sticking a knife in my chest. 'So far, they're safe. We'll make sure they stay that way.'

I barely hear him. He's alive. He's really alive.

'What the hell happened in Paris? Why aren't you dead?' I blurt out.

Zeke looks at Paul and then the other man and gives a short head shake toward the door. The two men go outside, leaving us alone.

'I really wanted to tell you,' Zeke begins, but I don't let him finish. I rush him, raising my fists and pounding them against his chest.

'You're supposed to be dead!' I shout.

'Sssh,' he whispers, wrapping his arms around me and trying to pull me into a hug, but I'm too fast for him. I duck underneath his arms and take three steps back, so I am almost to the windows.

'No. No, no, no.' I can still see the blood when I close my eyes. 'You were dead. I heard the shot. Ian shot you.'

Zeke shakes his head. 'No. *I* shot *him*. I tried to find you, but you were gone, and then they decided that it was better that way.' He smiles, but sadness laces it. 'We had no idea how good you'd be at running and disappearing.'

I don't want compliments. I don't want to see his smile. I think about how 'they' thought it was better that I ran.

'You shot Ian?' I ask after a few minutes. 'But you were—'

'You didn't do such a good job at shooting me yourself,' Zeke says. 'Really, you only grazed me, but there was a lot of blood, so I guess I'm not surprised you thought you killed me.'

So many things are rushing through my head, bumping up against each other, that I can't figure out what to focus on.

Finally, 'But why didn't Ian tell me then, last year?'

'Because he's working for us.'

'He's working for Tony DeMarco.'

'Yes. And us.'

I remember now that Ian told me they found him in Coconut Grove. The FBI. 'So why are you showing up now? There were FBI agents on Block Island last year, looking for me. Why didn't you magically reappear then? Ian was using your name.' I shudder, remembering how it felt when I heard it that first time in such a long while. My entire world was turned upside down all over again.

'Things have changed since then,' is all he says.

'Changed how?'

'We want to take down Tony DeMarco, and we think you can help us.'

My heart has started to slow, and I am breathing a little more easily now, which clears my head somewhat. 'Don't you want to throw me in prison?'

Zeke tries to conceal a smile. 'Not right now, Tina.'

'Why not? Isn't that why you've been looking for me for all these years?'

'I didn't exactly want to find you, to be honest. You broke my heart.'

I remember then: his wife. How he said he told his wife and had left her. But if he had a wife, and there was an obituary in the paper, then what—

'You weren't really married, were you?' I demand. 'It was all a lie.'

Immediately, I can see that I am wrong. That it wasn't a lie. His jaw tightens as he looks away; he absently touches his ring finger that's empty now. But I am not willing to let him off the hook. 'So tell me, were you after my father or were you after me, or both?'

He glances toward the door. 'Do we need to go over all that now?'

I put my hands on my hips and glare at him. 'Yes. You owe me that.'

'You're the one who shot me. I'm not sure I owe you anything.' It seems for a moment that he is not going to say anything more, but then he sighs. 'I was never there for your father. You were just a job. Until you weren't. There was something about you, your

passion, in so many ways . . .' his voice drifts off for a few seconds.
'My wife played the widow willingly. She was angry, and I don't
blame her. She said she had never wanted to see me ever again
anyway. I tried to find you. I knew about Amelie Renaud, that you
were using her passport, but you were always one step ahead of
me, and by the time I got back to the States, you were gone.' He
pauses. 'You look really good, Tina.'

I fold my arms across my chest, unwilling to be swayed by his
story. 'Well, that's got nothing to do with you.'

'It does, actually. But you're right, we can't get into all of that
history now. There are other things to think about. Like Tony
DeMarco. We know about the bitcoin transfer you made into his
account.'

Damn. 'Is that how you found me?'

Zeke indicates I should sit, so I do, in one of the chairs, and he
sits in the other one across from me. My backpack is on the couch
between us.

'We knew he had someone shadowing your computer. We
managed to trace the shadow, and we saw the ransom demand.'

I forget everything about Zeke and what happened before as I
consider his words. 'How? How did you get inside?'

'We've been hacking into DeMarco's accounts for a long time
now, but until we found this shadow, we couldn't pin anything on
him. We didn't know until we started shadowing him that it was
you, that you were the one DeMarco was hacking.'

'He found my friends on Block Island,' I say, mostly to
myself. 'He used my mother's name and got them to tell him about
a friend I've got online, and that's how he hacked me. Through my
friend.'

'And we were able to trace his IP address and yours once we got
around your VPN and firewall and found out you were in Quebec.'

I cannot speak. I stare at him, my thoughts like bumper cars in
my head. He continues, as though he doesn't notice what his words
are doing to me. They got around my VPN. They got around my
firewall. They knew I was in Quebec all along.

'We've got a hacker there, a girl named Alice Bessette, and we
arranged for you to meet up with her at that computer shop. She
was very valuable to us.'

I thought I was being so careful. I thought I was so thoroughly shrouded that no one would be able to find me, and yet Zeke – Zeke Chapman, who should be dead – knew where I was with only a few keystrokes. And Alice. That innocent meeting was not so innocent, like I suspected, but not for the reasons I thought.

'So what about Jean Bessette?' I ask, knowing that he played a role in this.

'Once we found out where you were, we contacted the police. I'm not sure who connected the dots, but since you were an artist on Block Island, someone figured you might be doing the same thing in Quebec, and he was right. We found you through that gallery.' He gives me a funny look. 'I thought you made us on that train to Montreal.'

'I did.'

He gives me a curious look, but I don't say anything further, so he continues. 'But then you got your hair done different, and you changed your clothes. You look more like you did on Block Island, so it wasn't hard to recognize you.'

'You were the one outside my hotel that night. Why didn't you take me then? Throw me in a car in Montreal?'

'No jurisdiction. If we got you then, we'd have to go through all the red tape to get you out of the country—'

I hold up my hand. 'So you orchestrated my escape. That's why it was so easy.' As I say it, I realize now that it really *was* that easy. Madame Xu's explanation that she just wanted to help people like me hadn't really settled right with me, and this solidifies it. Zeke must have made it worth her while to help him. And then there was the boat, how I ended up on the Mohawk reservation, how there was no border patrol checkpoint anywhere.

I think about David Carrington's job offer. Somehow I think that was not part of the plan.

All of my actions in the last few days were not my own. The FBI was pulling all the strings so I would do exactly what they wanted me to do. Which was to end up in this room, to see Zeke is still alive and to help them somehow catch Tony DeMarco.

I decide not to address any of this right now, because I need more time to process it. But what I do ask is: 'If I help you nail Tony DeMarco, what will you give me in return?'

Zeke smiles again, but this time I can see it's a smile of relief. He thinks now that I'll play along – and I'll let him think that.

What he says, however, shocks me even more, and it throws me even further out of sync.

'You get full amnesty. No arrest. Nothing. It's as though you never committed that crime.' He pauses. 'But you have to work for me.'

FORTY

Work for him? He sees that I don't completely comprehend. 'The FBI needs people like you. Hackers. Good hackers. With the cybercrime that's going on all over the world, we can't keep up. You come work for us, and you'll never spend a day in prison, but you'll have a real job with real benefits, a pension, even.'

I can't speak. I have no words for how I'm feeling, because I don't quite know how I'm feeling.

'It's a good deal, Tina. You really need to think about it. And think fast, because the offer's only good for forty-eight hours. If you decide not to go along with it, then we will throw the book at you. We've got you, and you can't get away this time.'

I snort. 'So it's an ultimatum. All or nothing.'

'Yup.' He seems pretty proud and sure of himself, too.

I get up and go over to the window, stare down at the street below. We are on the tenth floor, and the headlights of the cars crawl like ants along the street. I feel him come up behind me, but he doesn't touch me, and I don't turn around.

'Think about it. DeMarco doesn't know we've got you. He uses that bitcoin account to launder money through a deep web site. Remember Silk Road? DeMarco's is worse, and it's mainly because we can't catch him at it. We can't shut it down.'

Against my better judgment, my head begins to spin with the possibilities. How to penetrate Tony DeMarco's site, how to get inside. I think about Tracker, how he could help me with this; he might even know about it. I can feel the pull of my laptop in the backpack on the couch, but I won't turn around to look at it, to go get it, even though I desperately want to.

'You can do it. You can help us,' Zeke whispers, and I can feel his breath on the back of my neck. It reminds me of another time, a lifetime ago.

'This is a lot to process,' I finally say, still looking out the window. 'Can I have a little space?'

He finally steps back then, and I turn. He stands there, hands at his sides. It's sixteen years later, and he's managed to look almost exactly the same. Ian had aged; he was thicker around the waist, had a little more jowl. But Zeke, well, Zeke looks like the agent who came to my house that first day with no discernible change. He is fit and maybe slimmer, actually, his brown hair cut more stylishly, no sign of gray. He is about my age, and my hair has been salt and pepper for a couple of years now. When I look more closely, I see some lines around his eyes, at the edges of his mouth, but I still resent the fact that he does not look much older.

'You look good,' I say without thinking, the same thing he said to me a little while ago.

He grins. 'I work out. You know.'

He's referring to my bike tours, how I got in shape on Block Island. He knows everything about me, and it's disconcerting.

'I didn't really break your heart, did I? I was just another job for you.'

Zeke gives me a small, sad smile, reaches up and brushes my cheek with his fingers, then briefly touches the jade dragon pendant before letting his hand drop. He cocks his head toward the bedroom. 'Why don't you get some sleep? Think about things. I'll be back in the morning. Someone will be outside your door all night.' He is all business now. It doesn't escape me that he doesn't answer my question. Instead, he goes to the front door and lets himself out without saying goodbye.

I am alone in the apartment. I can hear some murmuring in the hall, presumably Zeke and Paul and the other man. A small lamp on the end table illuminates the room with a dull yellow glow. I wonder if this place looks any less sad in the daylight or if the harsh brightness will accentuate its flaws even further.

I'm a little surprised they left me by myself in here. I go into the kitchen and open the fridge, a blast of cold air hitting me in the face. It's stocked with seltzer and milk, some fresh raspberries and blueberries in a bowl. I pick a few out and toss them in my mouth. They taste like Block Island, and the thought takes my breath away. I shut the door quickly.

Back in the living room, I sit on the couch and pull my laptops out of the backpack. I choose the new one to boot up, since I know the FBI is sneaking around behind Tony DeMarco in the other one and I'd rather not be spied on right now.

I sign on to my VPN, but before I can get into the chat room, I hear the doorknob turn. I freeze, the laptop on the coffee table, my fingers on the keyboard. Paul steps inside.

'We were wondering if you'd want something to eat,' he says apologetically, as though holding me hostage here is not his fault. It might not be, but he's an FBI agent, too, and I have enough blame to go around. 'We're thinking of calling out for Chinese.'

I had my share of Chinese in Montreal, so I shake my head. 'Thanks,' I say. 'I don't think so.'

He doesn't say anything about the laptop, but his eyes linger on it a second too long before he goes back out into the hall again. I wonder if there's a place that delivers. If they will stand sentry with their cartons and chopsticks. What would happen if Tony DeMarco sent someone over while they were lounging outside my door with their late supper? Would they drop the food and go for their guns to protect me?

I don't know if I'm being watched because of Tony or because they're afraid I'll disappear again. Maybe a little bit of both.

I wonder where Zeke is staying tonight. Is he close by as well? He made it sound like he's going elsewhere, but he could be on the other side of the door, too.

For a few minutes, I forget about the laptop as I lean back and settle against the back of the couch, my mind drifting back sixteen years. I don't let myself think about that last night in Paris, but instead remember his face, the way he used to look at me. It has been a long time. And I did shoot him, however minor his injury might have been. Perhaps that was when he realized I didn't really love him – that it was always Ian for me – and his feelings changed.

I always felt bad that I hadn't loved him like he loved me, but I doubt he'd believe me if I told him that.

I tune out their muffled voices and try to ignore the fact that I'm being babysat as I log into the chat room. I scan the site for Tracker, but I don't see him. Yet something catches my eye: J!Ncks is back. I'm using a different screen name than the one I used before when I chatted with her, so she doesn't know I'm here. She's having a rather mundane conversation with Angel about VPNs.

Now that I know she really is Alice, and that she helped Zeke and his agents find me, I am hardly interested in engaging with her again. I wonder if her 'revelations' about Tracker were more about whether she could draw me out, since she never really revealed anything at all. She said Tracker knew where I was, but it's possible she was just trying to prove something to Zeke and her father.

As I'm contemplating how I had felt an affinity for Alice, before I knew what she was up to, all of a sudden Tracker's name appears. He's here.

As usual, I feel a little thrill when I see his name pop up. I know he and I have only an online relationship, but it is the most real relationship I've ever had. Despite my earlier suspicions about him being my shadow, I still trust him beyond anyone else.

Which is why he is the only one I can turn to if I want to catch Tony DeMarco.

FORTY-ONE

I ask Tracker to meet me in a private chat, and he shows up immediately.

'What's going on, Tiny?' he asks.

'I've had a little bit of a setback.'

'Is everything OK?'

'Nothing I can't handle. But I'll need some help.'

'You know I'm here for you.'

'I appreciate that. This might be tough.' I pause for a second before I begin to type again. 'Tony DeMarco is running a money laundering scam through a deep website. I need to get inside.'

He doesn't respond for a few minutes, and I worry that for the first time he might say he won't help, but then, finally: 'Is that where you transferred the bitcoins?'

'I don't know. Maybe.'

'What sort of site?'

'I don't know.' If I were Tracker, I'd be very wary of me right now. I don't know quite a bit, but I'm still asking for help.

'How do you know he's doing this?' he asks. I am relieved that he's still with me, that he is not deterred.

'Let's just say I've got it on good authority.'

'Are you sure you want to go there?'

My fingers hover above the keyboard. I can't tell him about the FBI, because he doesn't want to be caught any more than I do and I can't risk his identity to save mine. I owe him that. 'I understand it's sort of a Silk Road.'

'There are a lot of sites like that.' He's right. If you want to buy illegal drugs or weapons online, it doesn't matter that Silk Road got shut down. It's a matter of finding the other sites. 'You're sure Tony DeMarco is part of that?'

'He'll do anything if he can make money at it,' I say confidently. 'He doesn't have a conscience.' I think about how he testified against my father, the man he claimed was his best friend. Granted, my father was a criminal, too, but Tony made money off my father.

The only reason he threw my father under the bus was to save himself.

Anger rises in my chest, and I force it back down. My problem with Tony DeMarco right now is not about my father. It's about me. And how he's managed to hack into my laptop and hold me for ransom. He hit me where he knew it would hurt; he made it personal.

'You want to shut him down?'

Tracker's words stop me short, and I realize that's exactly what I want to do. But without any input from Zeke. Maybe I can give *him* an ultimatum. I'll take Tony down, but only if he lets me go, lets me disappear again.

For a second, I wonder what Tracker would say if I told him that the FBI was offering me a job, a legitimate job as a hacker. Sixteen years ago, I'd say it was the only thing I knew how to do – and do well – but I know better now. I've supported myself as a bike tour operator, an artist. I've been able to make a living without a computer. The idea of hacking for a living – for the FBI – seems foreign to me, especially since I've been running from them so long. And who knows if Zeke is telling me the truth anyway? Maybe he's just dangling freedom and a job in front of me like the proverbial carrot to get me to do what he wants and then he'll arrest me and throw me in prison anyway. Or at the very least, expect me to pay back that ten million dollars I stole. Ten million dollars I don't have and never had.

I answer Tracker the only way I can: 'Yes. I want to shut his site down.'

'So where do we start?'

I've been thinking about this ever since Zeke told me they were trying to find the site. How could I find it, when the FBI hasn't been able to? And then I have an idea.

'The bitcoins.'

'We follow the money.'

'Exactly.' Because the blockchains are public, anyone can trace where they go.

'One problem. The bitcoins will go into a tumbler.'

He's right. If Tony's people are smart, they've transferred the bitcoins into what's known as a tumbler, or a mixer, where they'll be mixed up with other users' bitcoins. By doing that, they become associated with a new address, not the one from where they were stolen, and we might not be able to trace them. 'We need to find the tumbler that they went into,' I write, although this is harder than it sounds.

Tracker is quiet for a few minutes. I know he's thinking about what we should do, and then: 'What if he doesn't want to wait? Putting the bitcoins into a tumbler means that they have to parse them out a little bit at a time so no one notices the dirty money mixed with the clean money. What if DeMarco sent the money to a bitcoin casino?'

I contemplate this, and it hits me. 'We need to look at the account number where I transferred the money.'

'And we can try to trace it. See if it's a casino account,' Tracker writes, but I'm one step ahead of him. I reach over and pull the old laptop out of the backpack and power it up. I put the two laptops side by side on the coffee table in front of me.

But when the old laptop is up and running, I see a problem.

'He's gone,' I write.

'What do you mean?'

'The shadow. The message program has been wiped clean. The messages are gone.'

'Tiny, you know how to do this.'

I'm trying. The shadow wiped the message archive clean, and he also has deleted the history, things I would have done. I pause for a second, giving myself time to gather my thoughts. And it comes to me. If the messages had been first saved and then deleted, it could show up in the XML message log. I use one of the XML tags and do a search. Suddenly, I see the messages within the tagging. Now I have to find the right one with the right information.

I am so deep into what I'm doing that I barely hear the knock on the door. It starts to open, and I immediately shut the covers on the laptops and shove them aside, pulling the T-shirt I wear to bed out of the backpack.

Paul steps inside with an apologetic look on his face.

'I'm sorry to intrude—'

I stand up with the shirt balled up in my hand. 'I think maybe you should knock to see if I'm decent,' I say sternly.

His face flushes, which I might find endearing under other circumstances. 'I'm sorry,' he starts again. 'But I wanted you to know that we want to get an early start in the morning. About seven.'

I glance at my watch and see that it's midnight now. I could be up for hours with Tracker, working on getting into Tony DeMarco's site. 'Fine,' I say. 'But can you wait until I open the door for you?'

'Yes, certainly,' he says.

If I wasn't paying attention, I might have missed it, but I see his eyes flicker toward the laptops on the couch. I wonder if they suspect what I'm doing, if Zeke has asked him to check in on me occasionally. It's quite likely that he doesn't trust me. Why should he? I don't trust him, either.

'I'm going to bed now,' I say.

Paul takes a step backward. 'OK, fine. Yes.' He turns, opens the door and leaves, the door gently closing with a click.

I wonder if I should lock them out, but decide against it. If they want to get in, they could.

To continue the charade, just in case he decides he 'forgot' to tell me something, I get my toiletries and go into the bathroom. I shed the clothes I've been wearing and put on the oversized T-shirt. I wash my face and brush my teeth, and it's only when I'm done that I allow myself to really look at myself in the mirror. Who is it that Zeke sees? Does he see the young Tina Adler when he looks at me – or does he see the middle-aged woman she's become? He said I look good, and I suppose I do. For my age. I touch the lines at the edges of my eyes, at the corners of my mouth. I run my hand through the short auburn locks. I put my glasses back on and wonder again about contact lenses, but I'm not sure whether I could afford that now. I have the distressing thought that if I did work for Zeke – the FBI – I wouldn't have to try to figure out my finances anymore. I would be legitimate.

I shrug off the thought and go back out to the living room. I scoop the laptops up in my arms and take them into the bedroom, closing the door behind me. I turn on the bedside lamp and sit cross-legged on the bed. The screens jump to life when I open them. I am worried that Tracker is thinking I've abandoned him, so I quickly write a note.

'Got interrupted. Am close now.'

'No problem.' He's still there, waiting for me. Relief rushes through me.

I go back into the XML tagging. It's easier than I thought. There it is. The account number. I turn to the other laptop and quickly type it in a message to Tracker.

'Good work,' he says. 'Now we need to find out exactly where these bitcoins went. It could take a while.'

'No problem. I don't have anywhere to go.'

FORTY-TWO

Tracker and I work through the night. My adrenaline is pumping, and I can imagine that his is, too. This was the way it was when we did the bank job, when we were hacking into the accounts and transferring the money. Only this time, it's virtual currency and it's a little more complicated to follow its trail. We discover that Tracker is right, that some of the bitcoins went into a casino account, but not all of it. While he is working on the casino account, I am trying to follow the money through the tumbler. They were clever, parsing out little bits here and there. I wonder if the marketplace is doing what we are, to try to recover the currency that I stole.

The shades are drawn, so I have no concept of time except the faint stream of light that sneaks through the crack in the curtain. The knock startles me. It's loud enough to hear through the bedroom door.

'I have to go,' I type.

'Back later?'

'Yes. Will you still be working on it?'

'I'm on top of it,' he says.

I hate to leave it to him, but I have no choice. Tracker clearly doesn't have the FBI knocking at his door. As I shut down the laptops, I wonder about his life again. Does he have a job to go to? A family? How could he be up all night working with me?

He could wonder the same things about me, but then I remember. He knows about me. He knows I'm a fugitive, that I have been on the run. I have no family. So when I say I have to leave, I have no idea what he thinks.

I worry that there isn't enough time. Zeke told me I had forty-eight hours to make my decision, but it could take Tracker and me at least another twelve hours. Zeke will know I've been online; Paul will report that he saw me with the laptop last night, and Zeke knows my addiction. He knew exactly what he was doing when he told me about Tony's deep web site; he knew I wouldn't be able to stay away from it.

I don't want him to know *how* I'm doing it, though, and I don't want him to know about Tracker. I also don't know how much he knows about hacking. He wants to recruit me, but is it to work for him or the FBI in general? Has he spent the last sixteen years learning how to crawl around behind the source codes and peer inside to find secrets?

I have no idea what Zeke's life has been like, because I haven't asked him. I've been concentrating on what happened before, the fact that he's not dead when I've thought all along that he was.

I am the last person who can judge someone for his lies. The thought sobers me.

I've had the old laptop powering up while I've been working, on the off chance that the shadow will come back, but so far no sign of him. It's as though once I transferred the bitcoins, his job was done. That laptop is powered up completely now, so I move the power cord over to the other laptop.

The knock is louder now. I can't delay. I climb out of bed and pull on my jeans under the T-shirt and pad out to the front room, opening the door. Paul is standing there. I look around him, but I don't see Zeke.

'Agent Chapman is on his way,' Paul says, reading my mind, coming inside. He is holding a brown paper bag and a coffee, which he hands to me. 'We're not sure how you take it.'

I remember the milk in the fridge, so I take the cup and busy myself with fixing it. I open the bag and see a croissant. I find a plate and put some of the berries on it, along with the pastry, then go back out into the living room. Paul is standing stiffly at the window, looking into the windows of the building across the street.

'Berries?' I ask.

He turns and shakes his head. 'No, thanks. I had something already.'

I wonder if he has been outside my door all night or if he was able to go somewhere and get some sleep. I peer into his face but do not see exhaustion, so perhaps someone else was standing sentry. 'Are you my only babysitter this morning?'

'Until Agent Chapman arrives.'

I nibble one of the raspberries and take a bite of the croissant.

I don't know how long I have to wait for Zeke to show up, and the laptops are shouting from the other room. This is a waste of my time.

'Did you sleep well?' Paul is making small talk, which I am not very good at, but I appreciate the effort.

I have not slept at all, but he doesn't need to know that. I take a big swig of coffee and say, 'Yes, fine.'

He is younger than Zeke and me, maybe around thirty-five or so, and for the first time I notice that he's got a sort of Asian look about him. I don't quite know what to talk about, so I don't say anything. I eat my breakfast and savor the coffee, wishing I had more of it. Paul stands stiffly by the window, trying not to watch me but not being very successful.

'You don't look—' he starts.

'Like a hacker?' I smile. 'I'm a little old?'

'No, I guess, well, most of the hackers I've met are younger, and they're—'

'Guys?' I guess.

He nods.

'How long have you worked with Zeke?'

He seems a little startled that I'm using his first name, but he recovers and says, 'About two years.'

'You've been going after Tony DeMarco the whole time?'

His mouth tightens. He's not allowed to tell me what he's been working on.

'Your secret is safe with me,' I whisper conspiratorially, and his lips twitch, as though he wants to smile but he holds it at bay.

I bring my plate back into the kitchen and toss my cup into the trash. I wonder how long we're going to have to wait for Zeke. I'm a little annoyed that he's late, but it's probably some sort of head game. Again I want to go get the laptop, but I resist, instead turning on the small TV and clicking through the channels, finally landing on an old rerun of *I Love Lucy*. It's the one where she gets locked in the freezer, icicles forming on her head. Paul chuckles.

The door opens, startling us both. Zeke saunters in and nods at Paul, who doesn't even look at me before he scurries back outside. Zeke takes the TV remote and shuts it off.

'You know, we were watching that.' My tone is harsher than I intend because seeing him alive and well is still a shock.

'Were you?' His tone is playful, but I'm not in the mood. Maybe it's the lack of sleep or, more likely, the fact that I'm being held here against my will.

'You're the one who's late.' I stand up and fold my arms across my chest. It is not my best moment, but I can't help myself.

'Have you been online?' he asks, ignoring me.

I don't meet his eye, which tells him everything.

'What did you find?'

'Why are you so sure I was online?'

'Because I know you.'

I do look at him then. 'You don't know me at all.'

'You're right,' he concedes. 'It was a long time ago.'

'And I spent fifteen years without a computer. I don't have to go online.' I'm lying to him – I don't even lie about this to myself anymore. But I don't want him to think that what happened between us gives him any sort of claim on me.

'Is the shadow still in your laptop?' he asks, throwing me off a little.

'I don't know,' I say honestly. Even though there was no sign of him last night, that doesn't mean anything. He could have been spying on me when I restored the messages, but he chose not to make himself known.

'Where is it? The laptop? Can we take a look?'

I'm not quite sure what he thinks he can do, but I go into the bedroom and get it, bringing it back out to him. He's sitting now, on the couch, so I join him and put the laptop on the coffee table in front of us. I power it up, and he shifts a little closer so our knees touch. I pull away, as though I've felt an electric shock.

I barely have time to register it, however, before the screen in front of us jumps to life. It's quiet. No ransom notes, no flashing eyes. 'I haven't heard from him since I transferred the bitcoins,' I say.

'But he would still have access, right?'

'I think so. Maybe.' I never ran the anti-malware program Philippe gave me.

'Can you find him?' Zeke's tone has a dare in it, and I am vulnerable to it.

I don't say anything, just go into Philippe's program that can trace any active connections on the laptop. Most of the connections are legitimate, but one catches my eye. I point to the IP address associated with it. 'There. That's unusual.'

'So he's still in there.'

I should have looked at this last night instead of assuming the shadow was gone because he'd wiped the message program clean. But I'd had other things on my mind, and it didn't really matter anymore. 'Seems so. But he isn't engaging, so maybe he's got his computer on somewhere and he's not monitoring it constantly.'

'You were talking to him through the message program.'

I frown. 'How did you—'

'Remember, we hacked him. That's how we found you.'

I blame it on the lack of sleep that I don't remember. I mentally shake myself. I really would like another cup of coffee.

'Send him a message,' Zeke tells me.

'What?'

'Send him a message. Ask him if he got the money.' He pauses. 'We've got someone watching, tracing him. But we need him to engage.'

I don't like it that this is something I didn't know, that the shadow wasn't the only intruder inside my laptop and I didn't even notice. I give him a sidelong look before opening the message program and typing: 'Are you there?'

We wait, but no response.

'I think he's done with us,' I say. 'Like I said, there's been nothing since the transfer. Tony probably told him to monitor occasionally, but there's no real need anymore—'

As I speak, the entire screen begins to flash a bright red and the eyes return. I freeze. Zeke and I look at each other, but instead of looking upset, he's got a smile on his face.

'This is more like it.'

I'm not quite sure what to make of his reaction, but I don't have time to contemplate it. The screen suddenly goes black, but the white type appears slowly, one letter at a time until the entire sentence is scrawled across it:

'If you want your friends to live, call off the FBI.'

FORTY-THREE

My hands begin to shake, and soon my whole body follows. Zeke reaches over and closes the laptop cover. I fold my hands in my lap, trying to regain control, but it's not working. He touches my arm, and I recoil, jumping up from the couch.

'This is all your fault,' I say too loudly. 'If something happens to Steve and Jeanine, I'll never forgive you.'

'Tina, it's OK. He's lying. Your friends are safe. He can't do anything to them.'

'It's Tony DeMarco. He can do anything, get to anyone. You know that. That's why I'm here. That's why you kidnapped me. Because you can't stop him, but for some reason you think that I can help you get him.' I try to catch my breath, blinking to keep the tears at bay. 'You've got the entire FBI at your disposal and you can't catch him. Why do you think I can do something you haven't been able to do?'

'Because you can. You can help us find that website and track the money to him. We can nail him that way.'

'The man *murders* people, Zeke, and you can't pin anything on him. What is so special about this site?'

He runs a hand through his hair and shakes his head. 'It's the only thing we've got right now. You have to help us, Tina.'

'I don't have to do anything. If I help you, Steve and Jeanine will die. Tony will make sure I know that it's my fault.'

'We're protecting them, Tina. I told you that.'

'How do I know you're telling me the truth?'

I can see him thinking about it, how to prove it to me, when he finally takes his phone out of his pocket. He swipes his finger across it a couple of times and then hands it to me.

It's a picture of Steve and Jeanine. They are at Club Soda having a beer and a hamburger. They are smiling at each other. It reminds me of what Jeanine said, that they have picked up where I left off; they keep each other company. It looks like it's more than that; it's the way they're looking at each other, as though they have found a happiness that was unexpected but welcome. I feel a warmth in my chest, happy for them, happy that my absence has given them this.

'We've got someone watching them all the time,' Zeke says, interrupting my thoughts. 'We know about Patricia Hale.'

My head snaps back at the sound of her name. 'Who is she?'

'She's Tony DeMarco's daughter.'

'Adriana?' I vaguely remember a little girl trailing around after her father out by the pool. She was chubby, with pigtails. But that's about all I can remember about her.

'She spent a semester at college and flunked out, but her father set her up. She runs a couple of spas here in New York, one uptown, one downtown.'

I can't figure out why he's telling me about Adriana DeMarco, until it suddenly all makes sense.

'Is Tony laundering money through the spas?'

Zeke nods. 'We think so, but everything that has to do with Tony DeMarco always has a feel of legitimacy about it. We can't get him on anything. Except maybe the website. If we can connect him with that, then it's all over.'

'But people can hide so easily on the Internet. It's so easy to divert any kind of information, like it's easy to divert those bitcoins.'

'We need to find those bitcoins,' Zeke says, and it reminds me of Tracker, how he said we had to follow the money. Somewhere along the line, the bitcoins will be turned into cash and they will end up in Tony DeMarco's hands.

I consider telling Zeke about what I've been up all night doing, but hold back. I don't want him to find Tracker. But then I have a startling thought. Tracker had a shadow, too. I have assumed it's Alice, and now that I know she helped Zeke find me, it's quite possible that he already knows about Tracker. But I can't make up my mind if I can trust him, so I backtrack.

'You can't protect Steve and Jeanine forever.'

'Which is why we have to get DeMarco now.' He lifts the laptop cover, touches the touchpad and the shadow's message appears across the screen. 'Talk to him.'

It's the last thing I want to do.

'We're inside, too,' Zeke says softly, reminding me. 'We can try to trace him.'

Philippe's program will tell me the shadow's IP address, too, but

I won't be able to do anything without him knowing, so it's worth a shot. I sit back down and type.

'Did you get the bitcoins?'

'Are you talking to the FBI?'

I give a sideways glance at Zeke and type, 'You know who I am. Do you really think that I would talk to the FBI?'

'They could cut you a deal.'

'I stole a lot of money. I don't think they cut deals for that.'

'I need more.'

I exchange a look with Zeke. 'More what?'

'More money. It wasn't enough. If you don't give me another million, I will make sure your friends suffer for it.'

The breath catches in my throat, and Zeke covers one of my hands with his. It's warm and it takes me back for a second, remembering how gentle he'd been.

'Tell him you'll get it,' Zeke instructs, pulling me out of my memory.

'Really? I don't have it. I don't have any more.' I think about how I got it the first time. Somehow I doubt the FBI would condone that.

'You don't have to steal it this time.'

I try not to show my surprise. He knows that I stole the money from the marketplace, but for some reason he still wants me to work with him. It doesn't make any sense.

'So how do we get it?'

'We've got an account,' he says, and by 'we' I figure he means the FBI.

'That's a lot of money.'

'We'll get it back.' He sounds so sure. For a second, I consider how I can transfer it into another account, one that I can get into from anywhere. I can ditch Zeke and Paul and take off again. I did it twice already; it's not impossible. I wonder what's wrong with me. Zeke is offering me something I've never had before. But maybe that's the reason why I'm resisting. Maybe I have subconsciously relished the idea that I've been a fugitive, successfully eluding capture for so long.

Until now.

I turn back to the laptop. 'Where do you want it?' I write.

If the shadow is startled by how swiftly I agree, there is no hesitation at all in his response. 'Come back in two hours and I'll have an address for you.' The screen goes dark.

I shut the laptop cover. The exhaustion is taking over. 'I need some more coffee,' I tell Zeke. 'Can we go out and get some?'

'I'll send Paul.'

'No, I need to get out of here.' The last time I was so cooped up was last winter in Quebec. I nearly went stir crazy, and I'm starting to feel the same way now. 'You don't think you can keep an eye on me?' I ask. It is my own challenge to him, and he rises to the bait.

'All right, but while we're out, I want to show you something.' He doesn't elaborate but I don't care. I'm just happy to leave, even with a chaperone. He frowns at my jeans and oversized T-shirt. 'You might want to change.'

I go in the bedroom and put on one of my regular T-shirts and slip my feet into the canvas shoes. I put my laptop into the backpack and sling it over my shoulder.

'You don't need that,' Zeke says when he sees it.

'Yes, I do.' I am not about to leave all my money and my laptop in this apartment untended. The FBI will be crawling all over it. I can see Zeke is curious; he wants to know all my secrets.

It's bad enough he knows most of them already.

FORTY-FOUR

almost don't mind having a babysitter as I savor my coffee. Zeke wants to keep moving, so I carry the cup as we walk briskly along the sidewalk. It's warm – it's July – but not too hot, and the city is alive. I didn't realize until Montreal how much I've missed concrete, having shops and restaurants right outside the door.

Zeke makes sure that I don't lag behind even though I'd like to linger. I can feel the walking in my leg muscles, and when we pass a line of blue city bicycles lined up in a row, I stop.

'No.' Zeke shakes his head.

'Come on.'

'It's not like biking around that island of yours, Tina.'

I roll my eyes at him and don't budge. Zeke tugs on my upper arm. 'Come on.'

'We've already walked ten blocks.' We're in the upper Seventies, close to Central Park now. I can see the trees, the stone wall that runs the perimeter. But Zeke is right. Riding a bike through the park might be a bit touristy, and this outing certainly doesn't seem as though it's for leisure.

I'm not sure what Zeke wants to show me, and I consider an escape. If I could outrun him, I could duck into a storefront or a restaurant, hide in a restroom or a dressing room or a kitchen until he gives up looking for me.

The idea is ridiculous, though. From the look of him, there is no way I could outrun him in the first place, and in the second, he didn't give up looking for me when I went to Paris and clearly he has been looking for me ever since. He is tenacious, and escape is not an option for me. I might be able to hide for a little while, but he will never let me go.

I'm not sure how I feel about this, about him. There are moments when he acts as though I am merely a job, but then I catch his expression as he looks at me and I see the specter of our past relationship.

I am so caught up in my thoughts that I barely register that he's slowing down. He is concentrating on a building to our left. It's another apartment building similar to the one he's keeping me in, but this one has a doorman and a long awning reaching almost to the street. Zeke's eyes are everywhere. He's looking for something, for someone, but he's not talking, and I merely finish my coffee and clutch the paper cup in my hand.

He takes it from me and tosses it in a trashcan steps from the entrance to the building. Before I can react, he slips his arm around my waist, underneath the backpack, and pulls me close, as though we are lovers out for a morning stroll. I feel the heat from his body, and I struggle not to remember how we were together. He makes it easy, though, because he is distracted; this is clearly not personal. I am a prop.

Despite myself, I am curious about what's going on. What it is that Zeke is doing.

He nuzzles my neck, but it's not romance he's after. He whispers, 'Adriana DeMarco lives here.' I tense up, and his grip around my waist tightens.

'Why did you bring me here?' My whisper is louder than it should be.

'She's coming down the sidewalk behind me.' I feel his lips against my collarbone, and I forget Adriana DeMarco for a moment, but then I recover.

I peer around him and see a young woman with a small dog coming toward us. She is tall, dark hair pulled back in a tousled, casual way. She wears black leggings and sneakers, a tight pink nylon T-shirt. She could be coming from a yoga class, if it weren't for the dog, which is no larger than a cat. Suddenly, she leans over and scoops it up in her arm, giving it a kiss on the top of its head.

I am not a pet person, so the whole thing makes me uncomfortable. I begin to look away, but not fast enough. She stares at me, her expression one of puzzlement. Mine must mirror hers.

Because she looks like me.

Zeke runs after me when I take off in the opposite direction, my thoughts bouncing around in my head like pinballs.

Adriana looks like me. But that can't be. Can it? How can she look like me?

I feel a tug on my arm, then Zeke's hand clasps my wrist tightly, yanking me to a stop. We are a block away now. When I look behind me, I see her going into the building, the little dog trotting after her, the doorman holding the door like the obedient employee he is.

'Tina.' Zeke's tone has an urgency in it.

I stop and whirl around to face him. 'What's going on?'

His eyes fill with regret. 'I'm sorry, Tina. I didn't realize.'

'Didn't realize what? That it would shock me? That she, well, she—' I stop. I have no idea how to say it.

But he does. 'She's your half-sister.'

My brain wants to speak, but I don't even know where to start, so he tells me.

'She's the reason why Tony DeMarco ratted out your father. Your father had an affair with Tony's wife, who got pregnant. Your mother wasn't—'

I hold my hand up. I don't need him to tell me about my mother's state of mind. So this is why Jeanine was so convinced that Patricia Hale really was my sister. Because she is. Because she grew up to look like me. I quickly do the math in my head. When I left, after the bank job, I was twenty-five and Adriana was around ten, I'd guess. So since it's been sixteen years, she would be twenty-six now.

'When did Tony find out?' I manage to ask.

'Not right away. It was later, when she was a teenager—'

'And she started to look more like me.' I look like my father more than my mother. I sigh. 'So Tony got his revenge on my father, sent him to prison, and he's been after me, too. Like it's my fault.' I can't help the sarcasm. 'I didn't have anything to do with it.'

'But you stole from him, just like your father.' Zeke's voice is soft, kind. I hear his meaning behind the words: I am like my father so I have to be taken down.

'Maybe I should let him be, then,' I say sharply. 'Maybe I should give him what he wants and he'll go away. Leave me alone.'

'Tina, he'll never leave you alone. Not if you do what he wants. He'll keep coming back for more. He thinks you still owe him.'

'I paid him back last summer.'

'With money you transferred from Ian Cartwright's bank account. And it wasn't the full amount.'

'I don't know exactly how much we stole from him. I only had account numbers, no names. I figured if I gave him something, he'd lay off Ian and maybe forgive me.'

Zeke crosses his arms over his chest. 'Tony DeMarco doesn't forgive anyone.'

I am beginning to see that. 'Does she know?'

He understands my question, and he shrugs. 'I don't know.'

From the way she looked at me, I don't think she does. I think seeing me was as much a shock to her. Will she ask her father about me? *Who was that woman on the sidewalk who looks like me?* What will he tell her? And then I realize something else. If she does ask, Tony DeMarco will know that I'm here. That I'm in New York.

'So are you ready to tell me?' Zeke asks, his voice startling me out of my thoughts.

'Tell you what?'

'What you found out last night online.'

I frown, and he shakes his head. 'Come on, Tina. Do you really think you can fool me? You're a hacker. You have two laptops with you. I don't believe that you just went to bed last night and didn't bother to try to find out anything.'

I think a few seconds about how much to say. Finally, I nod. 'OK, you're right. I did go online. But I didn't find out much, except that Tony laundered some of the bitcoins through a bitcoin casino. They're pretty much in the wind, though, can't trace them there.'

'You said "some" of the bitcoins.' He makes little air quotes with his fingers. 'What about the others?'

'He put them in a tumbler. A mixer. Not easy to trace, either.'

Zeke walks in a little circle, combing his hair with his hand. He keeps his eyes on the ground. 'So we send him the next payment, but we have to somehow mark it so we can track it.' He looks up at me then. 'Can that be done?'

Against my better judgment, the adrenaline begins to swell as I consider his question. 'I'm not sure,' I say honestly. 'But I might be able to find out.' I'm thinking about Tracker, how he would know. Again, though, I don't mention him. Like Ian during the bank job, Zeke can't know that I'm not doing this alone.

'What about Alice?' Zeke asks suddenly. 'Alice Bessette? Do you think she can help?'

An unexpected surge of competitiveness rushes through me. I don't want to bring her into this; I want to do this myself – or at least only with Tracker. 'The fewer people who know about this, the better,' I say. 'Right? I mean, the shadow's already threatening Steve and Jeanine, and if he gets wind that you're involved—'

He holds a hand up to stop me. 'OK, I understand. But she could be a valuable resource at some point.'

I don't say anything, just begin walking back. Zeke falls into step beside me and lets it drop.

FORTY-FIVE

I hear him on the phone in the living room while I log into the chat room. I'm cross-legged on the bed and straining to eavesdrop. Zeke is talking to one of his hackers – he apparently has a team of them – about how to distinguish our bitcoins from others so we can trace them once they get deposited into Tony DeMarco's account. Unfortunately, Zeke lowers his voice, so my efforts are unsuccessful. I turn back to the laptop.

I look for Tracker, but he's not here. There are no messages for me, either. I tell myself that he's got a life too, or so I assume, and he probably doesn't want to spend his entire day doing my dirty work for me.

J!Ncks is here, though. I debate whether to call her out, to confront her that I know she's really Alice Bessette, but because I've told Zeke I don't want to bring her in on this, I decide against it. She might get the wrong idea and think that we're confidantes – or equals. I know I've got an ego about this, and I shouldn't. Maybe it's because she's a girl hacker, or she's young, or both, but I am threatened by her. I have the illogical thought that I'd rather work with Philippe. Maybe because I know more than he does – yet, he did give me that program that can trace IP addresses.

That program. My head begins to spin. What if there's a way to attach the bitcoin keychain to a program like that?

I am deep into the source code for Philippe's program to see if this is possible when I realize I'm being watched.

Zeke is standing in the doorway, his hands in his jeans pockets, staring at me. I am taken aback again by how little he has changed, except that he is less awkward, which is probably due to the fact that he is older and has more experience under his belt.

I take my fingers off the keys and lean back against the pillows. 'Something I can do for you?'

He opens his mouth as though he's going to say something, then shuts it again and turns and leaves. I hear water running in the kitchen, cupboards opening, closing, water turning off. I climb off the bed and go out into the front room. He's standing by the window with a glass of water.

'Maybe this isn't a good idea,' I say.

'What?' He doesn't turn to look at me.

'You. Me. Maybe Paul should—'

He takes four long strides toward me, setting the glass down on the coffee table before pulling me to him. I feel his mouth on mine, and for a moment I resist, but the familiarity of it overrides my hesitation and I kiss him back. It's not like with Ian last year, when each time felt as though it would be the last. Instead, this is familiar, yet new, holding a promise that confuses me.

I tell myself it's because the only other man I've kissed in sixteen years was Ian, and it's been over a year since that, since I found out Ian was married with children and anything we could have ever had was gone.

It's also confusing because we're not picking up where we left off, like Ian and I did last year. Neither Zeke nor I are who we were before, and we're not pretending that we are. This kiss is not to remind of us of what happened, but seems to be borne of this job, this mission that we're both on, separately and together.

We each pull away at the same time, and for a second, I see the old awkwardness in him, but then it's quickly replaced by a cocky smile.

'OK, so now we've gotten that over with,' he says. 'Did you find out anything?'

I struggle a little with the casualness of his words. Can he dismiss this so easily? He really is a different person than the one I remember. I'd kissed *him* that first time, feeling fairly confident that since he had a wife, there could be nothing real between us. Maybe he feels the same way about me now, that there can't be anything real between us because he might soon be my boss and it was only a step back into the past that we needed to take before moving forward.

That's it. That's what it is.

'I haven't had much luck,' I say once I've gotten my bearings. 'And even if I can find Tony's site, there's no guarantee that I'll be able to hack into it, much less trace it back to him.'

'Say that you do find it. And that you can hack into it. How long do you think it will take?'

'I have no idea. It could take a day or it could take a week or two weeks or a month. Or never.' I'm telling him the truth. Hacks aren't something that can be rushed.

'We don't have a lot of time.'

I'm uncertain about his deadlines. Forty-eight hours for me to decide to work for him. Wanting me to do this too fast. 'What's going on, Zeke?'

'DeMarco's leaving the country. In two days.'

'You want me to get into his site and you want to arrest him within two days? You do know that this hack isn't easy.'

Zeke's eyes meet mine, and I can see that he's dead serious. 'We have two days, Tina. No more. I can't tell you why, it's need to know, and you don't need to know. The only thing you have to do is get us into his site. We take it from there.'

I think about how Tracker isn't on the chat site, and I really could use him right now. I haven't figured out how I'm going to use anything I can find to get me out from under Zeke's watch. I can turn down his job offer, but he'll just throw me in prison. How am I going to get out of this apartment without a chaperone?

I'm distracted, and Zeke is waiting for me to say something. I merely shrug and head back to the bedroom. I shut the door behind me, getting back on the bed in front of my laptop, my head spinning with ideas. I rethink my idea about marking the bitcoins using Philippe's program. What I need to do is get into the keys' source code and mark it that way. Maybe it would even be possible to code an alert that would tell me when and where the particular key is being transferred to another account.

I read about this somewhere, but I can't remember exactly where. In an article, maybe? Or maybe in the chat room? I sit up a little straighter. That's where. I do a search in the chat room and look for the conversation. But the one I find is not the one I remember, but a different, newer one.

One between J!Ncks and Phreak.

FORTY-SIX

J!Ncks is asking Phreak exactly what I've been thinking about – how to mark bitcoins. I don't like it that she's asking about this exact thing. It makes me wonder whether she is the one Zeke was talking to on the phone. I suppose I can't fault him for trying to work all the angles on this; I'm not the only hacker he knows. But I am the only hacker for whom this is personal.

The conversation between J!Ncks and Phreak took place this morning, when Paul brought me my breakfast and we watched *I Love Lucy*. I don't want to dwell on this. Tracker's not here, but he'll show up eventually. I concentrate on my plan to mark the bitcoins that I have to give to the shadow. What I need, however, are the bitcoins themselves before I can do anything. Which means I have to talk to Zeke, since he said he's going to get them for me.

I head back out into the living room, but he's not here. I poke my head into the galley kitchen and check the bathroom, but he's nowhere. I check the front door and when the knob turns easily, I realize I'm not locked in.

'Miss Adler?' Paul is outside, standing sentry. I wonder if he ever sleeps, if he has a home, an apartment, somewhere that's not work.

'Where's Zeke?'

'Agent Chapman has stepped out.'

'To where?'

Paul's expression doesn't change, but the way he shifts from one foot to the other is an indication that he's uncomfortable.

'You don't know, do you?' I ask. 'I need to talk to him. I can't do what he wants me to do without talking to him.'

'I can get him that message.' Paul's tone is very formal, as though he doesn't remember that he'd laughed out loud while watching TV with me this morning.

'Where did he go?'

'I can get him a message.' His phone is out of his pocket now; he's punching in a number. He turns his back for a second, and it's instinct, really, what I find myself doing. I slip past him and run down the hall, not stopping at the elevator, but pushing the door to the stairs open. I hear him behind me, calling to me to stop, but I'm fast – it's all those years on the bike – and I am two stories below him when I duck back out into another hallway. Someone is getting on the elevator, and I manage to squeeze inside just as the doors are closing. I have no idea if Paul has seen where I left the stairwell.

I don't have my backpack. Everything I own is upstairs in that apartment. The laptop is open, running, the chat room on the screen. I have no money except a ten-dollar bill I'd put in my pocket in case I needed it. I probably need it now, but it won't take me very far.

I have no idea what I'm doing, except that I need to be free, even if it's just for five or ten minutes. I need to feel as though I'm in control of my own person, because ever since Paul stuffed me into that cab and Zeke walked back into my life, I haven't been. This is the reason why I'm not jumping for Zeke's proposal of working for the FBI. It makes me claustrophobic even to think about it.

I expect Paul to grab me at any second, but I'm out on the side-walk in front of the building and no one is behind me. I don't want to draw too much attention to myself, but I walk briskly in the direction I'd walked with Zeke earlier. Yellow cabs slide past; I pass a homeless person wrapped in blankets on the ground. A sign advertising a psychic is intriguing, but the ten-dollar price is all that I have. I glance behind me, but still no sign of Paul or Zeke. I pretend that I have gotten away, but I don't believe it. Still, I walk.

I see the blue bicycles, lined up and ready for riders, but I don't have a credit card so I can't take advantage of them. I think about how it would feel, the pedals beneath my feet. It wouldn't be like riding the sparse island roads, but the movement is the same, the sense of freedom. I remember riding to the small chapels on Ile-aux-Coudres just days ago and picking up a loaf of bread at the mill. The shadow changed my life, put in motion a chain of activity that caused me to end up here, on yet another island. It's as though I'm destined to land on an island somewhere, and I start thinking about where I could go next: Long Island – no, further south – the Keys, Sanibel Island. I grew up on Key Biscayne, an island off Miami. Maybe that's where I get my affinity for islands. It dawns on me that I transferred money from the bank job to the Channel Islands off the coast of England, to Grand Cayman in the Caribbean. Was this an accident – or part of my destiny? And it hits me that Alcatraz is on an island.

I push these thoughts away and concentrate on something else. The shadow has become very greedy. He's already gotten away with a million bitcoins. It doesn't sit right with me that he's asking for more. Why not ask for two million in the first place? Tracker and I haven't been able to trace the original bitcoins, so why the second request? He's risking discovery. I don't think Tony DeMarco is that stupid. Maybe he's doing it without Tony knowing. Maybe he didn't get his cut the first time around.

As I'm thinking about this, I realize I'm here. I'm at Adriana DeMarco's building.

I stop and stare at the awning. It's black with gold cursive numbers, but nothing else that distinguishes it from the other apartment buildings on the block. The doorman looks like every other doorman I've passed along here; he is pretending not to notice the woman in jeans and T-shirt who stands here. I could be a stalker. I am a stalker. I want to see Adriana, I realize. I want to see her and confront her.

The doorman is talking into a walkie-talkie. I start to move again, more slowly this time, but I force myself to leave.

I am halfway up the next block when the car pulls over and Zeke gets out. I stop, and he stands in the street, waiting for me.

When I don't go toward him, he says, 'Tina, get in the car.'

'I want to walk.'

'You can't.'

'Why not?'

'You know where you are, right?'

I look back at Adriana's building. 'Yes.'

'It's not safe.'

'Nowhere is safe.'

He takes a step toward me. 'Tina, get in the car.'

'I need the bitcoins,' I say then, surprising myself. I don't mean to bring this up here, but it seems as good a time as any.

'Let's go back to the apartment, and I'll get them for you.'

He is still hanging back, as though if he approaches me, I'll do something crazy. Maybe I will. I don't know. I've had so many shocks – Zeke is alive, I have a sister – that I'm not quite sure what to concentrate on. Except the bitcoins. I can control that, I can do something about that. Maybe I do need to go back. Maybe it's the only way to stay sane.

I start to walk toward Zeke, nodding, showing him that I'm OK, that I'll go quietly.

I don't expect the other car. The one that slams into Zeke's, pushing it into another one parked along the side of the road. As if in slow motion, Zeke ducks down; I see his gun, but he's not fast enough.

For the second time in twenty-four hours, I'm grabbed and shoved into the back of a car.

FORTY-SEVEN

Tony DeMarco is old. His dark hair has gone completely
gray; wrinkles spread across his forehead and on his cheeks.
It makes me wonder about my father. They were the same
age; my father died last year in prison. I hadn't seen him in fifteen
years, and all the newspapers ran photos of him when he was younger,
not any current pictures.

I am distracted by my thoughts, and Tony seems to know this.
He watches me, his hands folded in his lap. A driver sits in front,
another man next to him. Tony and I are alone in the back seat.
The car begins to pull away from the curb. As we pass them, I see
Zeke and Paul crouched outside by their car, which has some serious
back end damage, watching Tony take me away. They can't see us
because the windows are tinted dark.

'It's a surprise to see you, Tina.' Tony finally speaks when we are
down the end of the block, his voice deep and familiar. It is
the one thing about him that doesn't seem aged. 'Are you here to
see Adriana?'

For a second I don't know what he's talking about, but then, 'Oh,
no. I was just taking a walk.' He knows I'm lying about the walk,
but his eyebrows knit into a frown as he tries to figure out if I'm
lying about seeing Adriana.

'I didn't know you were in the city.' His tone belies his words. I
am almost certain that the shadow has traced me, and Tony knew
exactly where I was. How could he have shown up right at the moment
I arrived here? It's possible he was watching the apartment where
Zeke's been holding me and followed me when he saw me leave
alone. Maybe the doorman used the walkie-talkie to tip him off.

'I just got in,' I say casually, as though we are at a cocktail party
exchanging small talk.

'You're keeping the wrong kind of company.' With a slight movement of his head, he indicates the direction we came from.

'They're holding me hostage,' I say, as though this will appeal
to him. I'm right, too, because I see a flicker of a smile.

'Not right now,' he says.

'No. Now it's you who's taken me.' I meet his eyes, and he doesn't look away, but the small smile turns into a grin.

'You've never been afraid of me.' He says it matter-of-factly.

I don't tell him that he's wrong. I was never naïve enough to push aside those stories about him and his minions. I saw my father's business accounts when I hacked inside, and Tony DeMarco left his mark in many ways. His money came and went so fast and to so many different accounts that even I had a hard time keeping track. But I keep up the façade and don't let on that I know what he could do to me. That he could have his driver take me away now and I would never be seen again. Ever since I discovered last year that I'd stolen from Tony DeMarco, I've been hiding from him as much as from the FBI.

Yet sitting here next to him and even though I have no idea where he's taking me, I am having a hard time associating this elderly man with the robust one who strutted around our house, drinking whiskey, smoking cigars, and telling loud stories about what he would do to anyone who crossed him.

'What do you want from me?' I ask.

He leans back in his seat. His suit jacket is a little loose, as though he has lost weight recently. 'You know what I want. I'm waiting. I shouldn't have to wait so long.'

This confirms that the shadow is not working alone, that he's doing Tony's bidding. 'I'm working on it.'

'I think that perhaps you should work on it without any help.' He's referring to Zeke. To the FBI.

'They're not helping. In fact, they have no idea what I'm doing.' The lie slips off my tongue easily; it is second nature to me. But Tony knows this; he has sent his daughter to glean information about me and she has done an excellent job. He is careful, though, not to directly incriminate himself.

'Why don't I give you a place to work? We can go right now.'

I will myself to breathe normally.

'My laptops are at the apartment.' There is no use in pretending he doesn't know where I've been. 'I need them.'

'No, I don't think so. I can provide computers for you.' He pauses. 'In fact, I would like to make you an offer. I know your skills. I know what you can do. I could use someone like you.'

I resist an urge to laugh. First David Carrington offers me a job, then Zeke, and now Tony DeMarco. I have never been so sought after.

'I'm not a team player,' I say. It is an understatement. 'I don't want to work for anyone.' This is not a lie, and he sees it.

'No one?' Again he's referring to the FBI.

'Least of all them,' I say honestly. 'They're holding me hostage, but I haven't told them anything.' I think a second, then say, 'I owe you money, I know that. I can still get it to you. I don't have any allegiance to anyone, but if you take me now, they'll follow and someone might end up shot or dead.' I push aside the memory of Zeke lying on the floor of the houseboat in Paris. 'If you let me go, I'll get you your money and then I'll disappear again. You just have to do something for me.'

'What's that?'

'You have to leave my friends alone.'

He studies my face a second, and I force myself to stare back.

'How do I know that you haven't told them everything?'

He means the FBI. I give a short chuckle. 'You'll know. They'll come knocking on your door. The money is a small price to pay for my friends' well-being. I'm willing to do it for that.'

'So you admit that you have my money.'

'I don't admit anything. It's been a long time, Tony.' It's the first time I've said his name out loud, and he blinks a couple of times. 'I don't have access to any of the old accounts. I told Ian that last year, and I know neither of you believed me. But I can get my hands on money. And if your guy who's compromised my laptop is any good, he can hide it for you and no one will be able to get at it.' I pause a second, then add, 'They can't find the bitcoins I already transferred. They won't be able to find these, either. I can make sure of that.'

He sits up a little straighter, although I see a definite hunch to his shoulders. His skin has a waxy look to it, as though he's ill. Maybe he is. Maybe that's why he brought Adriana in.

'If you cross me,' he says, his voice low, 'you will pay for it.'

'I know.'

'Your friends will pay.'

'I know.'

We are stopped at a light next to the park. Movement outside the car catches my eye, and it doesn't escape Tony. Zeke and Paul are approaching, on either side of the car. I'm not sure where they've come from, but I see the gun in Zeke's hand.

'You'll have your money by tonight,' I promise, and the door locks pop up with a click. I don't wait for goodbyes, just push the door open and scramble out.

The car, which has been idling, suddenly shoots forward, skidding out into the street and up the block. Before I can follow it, Zeke grabs my arm.

'So why don't you tell us all about it on the way back?' he asks.

FORTY-EIGHT

'OK, so when did you set that up?' Zeke demands when we're in the car.

'Set what up?'

'You run out of the apartment and come here and Tony DeMarco just so happens to show up? Give me a break. What have you been doing online?'

It's none of his business what I'm doing, but his eyes are dark with anger. He really believes that I arranged this with Tony.

'I swear I didn't have anything to do with that.' I hope he believes me, enough so I can go back, he can give me the bitcoins and I can send them to Tony, like I promised. Zeke doesn't have to know that I cut a deal to keep Steve and Jeanine safe.

But he's not that stupid.

'We don't need you. We can do this without you. The girl hacker, Alice, she can do it.' He says it, but he doesn't believe it. I can see that in the flicker of his eyes.

The car begins to move. Paul is driving while Zeke glowers at me in the back seat. I glower back.

'So then why am I here? Why did you get me out of Canada? Why didn't you let me stay there, get caught by Jean Bessette, get deported, thrown into prison?' The questions fill my head, and I'm right to ask them. None of this is making sense. 'I told Tony I'd get him the money by tonight. And he'll leave Steve and Jeanine alone.'

'You shouldn't have done that.'

'But if we don't get him the marked bitcoins, how will we find his site?'

Zeke shakes his head as though I am being stupid. 'He'll get his money, don't worry about it. But do you really think he'll stop there?'

'He offered me a job,' I say softly.

Zeke whips his head around. 'What?'

'Same as you, you know. And that guy at the yacht club, the one who got me on the boat? He offered me a job, too. I'm feeling pretty popular right now.' But in reality, I'm not feeling anything but insecure. If Zeke doesn't really need me, then what about his offer? Will he arrest me now? I begin to worry about myself, my future. All those thoughts about all those islands seem futile. I will not go anywhere. Except maybe a place like Alcatraz.

I can't read Zeke's expression, but something's going on in his head. I can almost hear the proverbial wheels turning. Finally, a long, slow smile crosses his face and he looks straight into my eyes.

'Do it.'

'Excuse me?'

'Tell him you'll work for him. We can get him the money, and you can go work for him. You can be on the inside.' He is excited about this idea. Too bad I'm not.

'You're kidding, right?'

'I've never been more serious in my life.' And he is. I can see it. He thinks this is the best idea he's ever had.

'Maybe you can go undercover, but I don't know that I can,' I admit.

'What do you mean?'

'Nothing. I guess it's that you had a relationship with me when you were only supposed to catch me. But you weren't really under-cover, were you? It's not like I didn't know you were FBI. But you still had an inappropriate relationship with a suspect.'

His expression doesn't change, and I sense he wants to respond to that, but instead he merely says, 'This is huge, Tina. You can tell him that we're holding you against your will—'

'You are,' I interrupt.

He smirks. 'That's beside the point. But you're not happy with us, you think you're going to be arrested, could you take him up on his offer. You could do this, and you could get inside like no one else.' I see now that this is the sort of thing he was hoping for when he brought me back from Canada, that somehow I'd have the magic key to getting into Tony DeMarco's secret world.

I think a second. 'OK, so say I do it.' I hold my hand up to silence him when he looks as though he's about to congratulate me on our new alliance. 'You do realize that I will not be safe and there is no way you can keep me safe? I have to pretend that I'm on Tony's side, the man who sold out my father, the man who sent someone to Block Island last year to kill me?' That thought causes me to pause as I remember Ian. Ian, who is also working for Tony but is feeding information to the FBI. If I do this, I will see him again, and I'm not sure I want to do that. I find myself wondering if I can convince Tony to keep me a secret from Ian, and then I mentally slap myself. Am I seriously considering doing what Zeke is asking of me?

Zeke is talking. 'We can do what we can, but you're right. You will be on your own most of the time. But I know you. I know you can handle it.'

Again he says he knows me, and he doesn't, but I don't point it out this time. I'm too busy thinking about his proposal. He's right; I do think I can convince Tony that I'm on his side. I already set that in place by telling him I'm being held hostage. If I tell him that the money I'm transferring to him is the FBI's, he'll find that amusing. I know my father would, and they were cut from the same cloth.

'How would it work?'

The smile grows wider. 'The way I'm seeing it now is that you transfer the money, then we make it look as though you've gotten away. It's pretty clear that he's watching the apartment; he knows where we're keeping you. We can make it look like the real deal, like you've snuck out and are escaping. When he finds you, and you know he will, then you balk at first but then agree. Use your friends. Tell him you'll work for him as long as he leaves them alone. He'll cut that deal. He's not stupid. He knows what you can do.'

The speech leaves me a little breathless. He's managed to figure it all out in a matter of minutes. Would it be that easy? He makes it sound like it would. I have not completely made up my mind. I don't owe him or the FBI anything, except this could guarantee that I won't go to prison. Although I might end up doing something that would be even worse than stealing from the bank. The thought sobers me.

'What if he asks me to—'

Zeke puts his finger to my lips. 'Your job will be to get into the deep web, find out what DeMarco's doing there and report back everything you find out.'

'How do I report?' He's taken his finger away, but I can still feel its imprint.

'We set up meetings. Nothing in writing. Nothing online.'

'Meetings with who? He knows about you. About Paul.'

'I'll take care of that. We can have you meet with random members of the team who he doesn't know.'

'How will I know to trust them if I don't know them?'

'Good question. We can come up with some sort of code. How's that? Something to do with Block Island, maybe?'

I think quickly. 'They could ask if the shad is blooming.' I think about it, how it dances along the branches, and again I miss it so much it hurts.

'That's good. We can use that.' I see him making a mental note, and then I realize. Somehow I have agreed to this plan. I am going to go undercover for the FBI and see if I can't trap Tony DeMarco in the deep web.

FORTY-NINE

My laptop is as I left it, open and sleeping on the bed. Zeke doesn't hesitate this time, he follows me right in and sits on the bed as I pull the laptop toward me.

'I've got an address you can transfer the bitcoins from,' he says.

'Am I marking them?'

'Yes. And when you meet with DeMarco, you tell him they've been marked. That way he'll feel like he can trust you.'

I haven't quite figured out how to mark the bitcoins, and I wonder about Tracker, whether he could help, but Zeke doesn't look like he's going away, so I am going to have to figure this out myself.

As I concentrate, I can hear Tracker in my head, encouraging me, telling me that he knows I can do this, that I should go with my instincts. I find my way into the bitcoin key at the address Zeke gives me. I stare at the code, my head spinning. Zeke is watching me, and it makes me nervous.

'Do you think you can go in the other room?' I ask.

Instead of getting up, he pushes the laptop aside and scoots toward me. 'I really appreciate what you're doing for us,' he says. His words are all business, but his body language certainly isn't. He leans toward me and he is kissing me again. Before I can lose myself in it, he pulls back.

'I keep doing that,' he says, trying to make a joke of it. 'I'm sorry. It's just, well, sometimes you look so much like you used to, you know, back then, back when . . .' His voice trails off, and I know what he's remembering.

'It's OK,' I say, even though I'm not sure it is. I try to make a joke out of it. 'Are you supposed to fraternize with your employee?'

'No, but you're not really my employee yet, are you?' He knows I'm still questioning. He hasn't seen me in so long, and even back when we did know each other, it wasn't like it had been with Ian. He didn't know me very well in that life, either. But there's something there now that makes me feel he really does know me. Or at least he thinks he does.

'Do you need some sort of authority to sanction my undercover work?' I ask. 'Or are you going rogue?'

The way he doesn't meet my eyes gives me the answer. This is Zeke's idea. I don't know if anyone at the FBI will have any idea about my role. I begin to question how quick this has been, whether I am doing the right thing. Tony has already promised me he will leave Steve and Jeanine alone if I transfer the bitcoins. That's all I want. But what if Zeke is right, that he will never stop, that he will continue to come after me and my friends, despite this?

My eyes flicker to the screen beside me. And that's when I see it. How I can mark those bitcoins. I forget everything else. Without a word, I turn to the laptop, and I don't even notice when he leaves the room.

I take a shower and change my clothes. I've still got all my money in the backpack; Zeke asked if I had any, and I told him I did, that I didn't need any. I string the jade dragon pendant around my neck and touch it for strength. I'm going to need a lot of it to do what I'm about to do.

It's evening now; the transfer was successful. I am going to leave the laptop with the shadow here. I don't need it anymore. But I have to take the other one; it would look odd if I didn't.

Zeke's plan is for Paul to take me out to get something to eat, and I'm going to make my escape. Paul does not know about this plan, which solidifies my theory that Zeke is acting alone. I express some concern that Paul is not going to be fooled, but Zeke reminds me that I got away from him once before. I don't know that Paul will be that lax in his babysitting again, since he will not want to be shown up a second time, but Zeke insists that he's 'got it covered'.

'DeMarco will follow you. You need to be convincing in your escape, otherwise he won't buy your story.'

'I feel like the only thing that's missing is a wire.' I give a short laugh but I'm not exactly joking.

'Can't risk it,' he says seriously, as though this was a consideration at some point.

We are in the living room, waiting for Paul's call. He's gone down to get the car and will let us know when he's out front. I thought we'd be staying in the neighborhood for dinner. Zeke has a different idea. He thinks that if Paul takes me downtown, Tony will believe that they're moving me, and he can make his move. I am not feeling good about being bait, but I nod a lot and let Zeke know that I understand what's supposed to happen.

'So you've got everything,' he says, indicating the backpack that's on the sofa.

'Yes. Everything I need.'

He moves closer to me and puts his hand to my cheek. 'I won't be able to protect you when you're with him, but I'll be as close by as I can.'

'OK.' I remember something. 'You said he's leaving the country. Where's he going?'

For the first time, Zeke looks uncomfortable. 'Costa Rica.'

'Do you think he'll want to take me with him?'

'Possibly.' He stares into my eyes. 'I won't lie to you, Tina. This is a risk.'

I know all about risk. 'I'm OK,' I say, but I'm not. Not really. He is standing so close to me; the two kisses we've shared shove themselves into my memory, and before he makes the first move, I do it this time. I lean in and he meets me halfway, and again I am transported back sixteen years yet it's different – the same feeling I had before. This time, however, I feel his hands on me, and desire surges through me, and I press myself into him.

His phone rings, and rings again, and finally we cannot ignore it any longer. We separate, both of us wishing it was another time, another place, and he answers his phone. It's Paul, and he's waiting downstairs.

'It's time,' Zeke says, his voice gruff with passion, and he pulls me to him again for one last, long kiss before releasing me. 'We have a lot of unfinished business, Tina. When this is all over, maybe we can pick up where we left off.'

All of this is a bad idea, everything to do with him, but I haven't even tried to resist. I should be angry with him, for showing up when he was supposed to be dead. For telling me about Adriana DeMarco.

I say nothing, though. Just pick up my backpack and sling it over my shoulder. I am used to the weight of it, and the familiarity of it comforts me. We walk to the door, and he opens it, letting me go out first. We go down the elevator in silence, but when we get to the lobby, he takes me by the shoulders.

'Be careful, Tina. Please.'

I give him a small smile. 'You, too.'

He lets me go, and I walk out to the sidewalk, where the car is idling. I open the door and climb in, not even looking back when we pull away from the curb.

FIFTY

Paul takes me to Chinatown. I want to tell him that I'd rather go anywhere else, but he seems to have a destination in mind. We park in a lot down near Columbus Park and walk up to Bayard Street. The sidewalk is teeming with people; everyone is walking with purpose. We pass shops with Chinese dresses and umbrellas and dragon puppets hanging from the awnings. It is reminiscent of Montreal, but on a much larger scale. We have not spoken; I don't know if he's embarrassed that I escaped him earlier. Probably. I decide to make a little conversation, to put him more at ease.

'Did you grow up here?' I ask.

He gets a confused look on his face, and then recovers. 'Oh, you mean because I'm half Asian? No. I grew up in Connecticut. I like the food here.'

'Here' is a noodle restaurant. He lets me walk up the steps ahead of him, and I'm inside the smallest restaurant I have ever imagined. It is narrow and long, with the menu in pictures on the walls. I peer around the man at the cash register into the area beyond, and there are long communal tables with stools. I see no way out, but I also don't see a kitchen. Suddenly, the man behind the register turns around and slides open a door in what looked like the wall. It's a dumbwaiter, and there are steaming noodles on paper plates inside. He takes them out and calls out a number. A young couple come forward and take their plates to a couple of empty seats in the back.

The aroma is full of earthy spices, and my stomach growls. Paul tells the man that we want two plates of noodles with pork, then realizes he hasn't asked if this is what I'd like, but I nod enthusiastically. He takes two bottles of water out of the display to our left and pays. He indicates that I should follow him to two seats along the counter to our right. Again I take note that there is no escape here. I spot a door that leads to a restroom, and I wonder about it. Is there a window? A door that leads out?

This is not going to be easy.

The noodles, when they arrive, are piping hot and I realize that there is only one very long one, thick and twisted to make it look like multiple noodles on the plate. The sauce is thin but I cannot get enough of its savory seasoning. I forget about escape while I eat.

After I finish, my plate clean, I excuse myself and get the key to the restroom from the cashier. I open the door and see a long, narrow stairwell down and I take the steps carefully, the pack slapping against my back. As I suspected, however, there is no way to get out down here, so I merely do my business and go back up, trying to think of another way.

'Ready to go back?' Paul asks, not waiting for an answer.

Outside again, the air thick with summer humidity, I spot the Chinese Ice Cream Factory next door.

'I'd love one of those,' I tell Paul.

A long line has formed, and we stand at the end of it, gradually moving up the steps.

'What kind?' he asks.

I shrug. 'What do you think?'

'Green tea is always good. Cup or cone?'

'Cup.' I'm telling him this, but I have a plan, and if I can pull it off, he will be standing with two cups of green tea ice cream and I will be long gone.

Because of the number of people, it's soon clear that I may have success. Paul is standing a little taller, trying to see how long the line is up ahead, and I use that moment to fall back, letting the two people behind me go in front. I wave at them to indicate it's OK. Paul is still distracted, and I fall further behind until I am back on the sidewalk. I don't wait. I turn and don't hesitate. I'm quickly down the block to Mott Street and I go right, weaving in and out among the crowds of people. I don't look back, so I don't know if Paul is coming after me. If he is, I'll have to deal with it, but so far, I think I am in the clear. The day is fading – it's after eight p.m. – but still light enough so there is no trouble navigating.

When I reach Canal Street, I turn left and move swiftly past the carts selling fruits and vegetables that I don't recognize. I feel as though I'm moving against the tide as the sea of Asian faces comes toward me. I finally pause to look behind me, but I don't see Paul,

who is probably kicking himself and wondering how he's going to
tell Zeke about how I escaped him again. I understand why Zeke
set it up this way, but I feel bad for Paul.

I don't dwell on it. The subway station is across the street, and
I head for it. A long black car moves past me, slowing, the window
sliding down. I see him then, in the back, Tony DeMarco, beckoning
me with his finger.

He's found me in Chinatown; he must have followed us and
maybe even circled the block a few times until we finished dinner,
until I got away on my own. Adrenaline rushes through me, but not
in the same way as when I'm online. This time it's survival.

I veer left and scurry down the sidewalk, in the opposite direction
that the car is heading. They will not easily turn around, and it will
give me the time that I need. I cross the street and head down into
the subway. Granted, if Tony DeMarco sends one of his minions
down here, I'll be caught, but I don't want to waste money on a
taxi at this point. I keep looking around me as I buy a ticket and
get through the turnstile.

Best place to head is Times Square. Like in Chinatown, I can
get lost in the tourist crowds.

The subway is hot, and sweat drips down between my breasts. I
wipe my forehead as I wait for the train with a scattering of other
people. So far, I don't see anyone who's looking for someone, but
my heart is pounding with the possibility of getting caught. The
train rumbles from somewhere deep within its tunnel, until finally
I see the headlight coming toward us. The train stops in front of
me; the doors slide open, and I step inside the air conditioning.
There are no available seats, so I hold onto the pole, looking out
at the platform, but still see no one. The doors shut, and the train
lurches on its way.

I cannot relax, though. Every muscle is taut. I am ready to run
at a moment's notice. I glance around at the other passengers;
everyone is minding his own business. A woman reads a novel
across from me; a man carrying a briefcase clutches the pole on
the other side of the train. Everyone looks weary, perhaps heading
home after a long day.

Every time the train stops at a station, panic rises in my chest,
but so far so good. When we finally reach Times Square, I file out
with the other passengers and move into the station. I see a subway

map and stop to check it out. I have no definite destination; I can go anywhere.

This is what I did not tell Zeke.

I don't want to go undercover with Tony DeMarco. I've given him his money. I may have marked the bitcoins, but because I won't be looking for them in Tony's accounts like Zeke expects, Zeke's people won't know how to trace them. Maybe Tony will go back on his promise to me, but maybe he won't if I show him that I'm not working for the FBI.

If I disappear again.

FIFTY-ONE

I don't want to risk the airports, so I decide again on a train, like I did in Quebec. Trains are easier; there is no Homeland Security check. I take another subway to Penn Station. Grand Central is only a shuttle away, but I have more limited options there. I can take Amtrak out of Penn Station and go anywhere.

South is always a good choice, although it's summer. I don't know why I'm being picky about weather, but I am. I consider the opposite direction. Not where I've just come from, but Boston. Maybe Maine. There are small towns up there with art galleries that might be interested in local landscapes and seascapes. I've always painted in oils and acrylics, but maybe I'll try my hand at water-colors. I like the idea of the muted brushstrokes.

I should go further. I should go across the country, maybe find an island off the Pacific coast. Going back to New England could be too close – too close to Block Island, to Quebec. But the idea of it comforts me. It's familiar, and I feel as though I need that now. It's risky, since people in New England vacation on Block Island. Someone could recognize me. Or not. I've changed my hair color, its style. I could get contacts. I could trade the jeans and T-shirts in for a different look. I could be vaguely familiar to someone who might have crossed my path through the years, but he might not be able to place me.

I've talked myself into it, even though a nagging doubt is still lingering in the back of my head. I ignore it.

I buy a ticket to Portland, Maine, but I might get off in between. New Haven, New London – no, that's too close and too much of a temptation to get back to Block Island, a ferry runs from there – Providence, Boston. When I settle in on the train, my backpack beside me, I think about islands again – Martha's Vineyard, Nantucket. While I've chosen to go this direction because it's summer, I face the fact that these places are not inexpensive and I might run through my cash too quickly. As the train begins to glide away from the platform, I realize I've gotten by before; I can get by again.

I have had little sleep here in Manhattan, so I lean back and close my eyes. But I keep peeking, looking down the aisle, to make sure I haven't been followed. That Zeke or Paul or Tony DeMarco aren't on the train, ready to nab me again. My head spins with thoughts of Zeke, Adriana DeMarco. My thoughts linger on Adriana. Maybe in a different time, if I was a different person, we could meet again, maybe become friends. Does she know she's really my sister and not only pretending to be? I can't imagine that Tony's ego has allowed him to tell her, and my father certainly wouldn't have. Anyway, he was in prison for most of her life and now he's gone, so there's no reason to tell her anything.

Except that she's seen me. She knows there is someone out there who looks like her.

I glance out the window at the graffiti-covered buildings, the broken windows. I question my decision to leave the city, where it would be easy to hide. Yet I crave peace, quiet, water, so that's what I'm in search of.

Finally, I cannot keep my eyes open any longer and I sleep.

I get off the train at Boston's South Station. I slept through New Haven and woke up just past Providence, close to Boston. I can't stay in Boston; sometimes Steve comes here for ballgames or to meet up with old friends. The couple in the row in front of me were talking about Cape Cod, how they were going to take a bus from the station. I consider Cape Cod. It's not an island, but a peninsula, which is close enough in my mind. It will be more crowded there than on Block Island in the summer, but I can handle that. I am still a little concerned that I will run into someone I know from my Block Island days, but again I push that concern aside. The idea of the Cape appeals to me, and I seek out the bus depot, which is conveniently right here. I pick up a map and decide that I don't want to go all the way to Provincetown, which is another four-plus-hour trip. I will stop first in Falmouth, which is closest to Boston, and regroup there.

I have stopped looking for Zeke or Tony DeMarco. I focus on my new destination.

I am tired from my travels, despite my sleep, but when I get off the bus, I immediately feel at ease. I *know* this place, even though

I've never been here before. I walk up to Main Street from the depot and pass a bike rental shop. Something catches in my throat, and I move past. A coffee shop is up ahead, and I step inside the air conditioning and order an iced coffee and what looks like a home-made brownie. I had bought a sandwich for the bus, but I'm still hungry and could use the sugar rush.

There is free wireless here, so I settle in at a corner table, facing the door, and power up my laptop for the first time today. I sip my iced coffee and nibble my brownie as I log into my VPN and go into the chat room using one of my aliases that no one knows. I look for Tracker. I see him, and I send him a message: 'Le soleil brille aujourd'hui.' *The sun is shining today.* This is our old French code. Within minutes, he responds: 'Non, le ciel est nuageux.' *No, it's cloudy.*

We meet in a private chat room.

'Tiny? Are you OK? I haven't heard from you in a while. Did you mark those bitcoins?'

'Let's just say that the mission is complete. I'm disappearing again for a little while, so you won't be hearing from me.'

'But you have VPN, right? Why can't we meet here?'

I lightly run my fingers along the laptop keyboard as I think about my answer. 'I'm going offline. It's easier that way.'

A few seconds pass before his next message appears. 'Do you need anything?'

I know he's talking about a passport, a driver's license. 'I don't have enough money.' It's true. What I have is going to have to last me a little while, until I can get settled somewhere, find some art supplies and see if there are any galleries that would take my work on consignment. I might be able to work under the table at a bike shop, too. There are probably quite a few of them around here.

'I can take care of it.'

Tracker's words startle me. Again I wonder what his situation is. 'I can't let you do that.'

'But I want to.'

'No, it's not necessary.' It's not as though I'm crossing borders again. I can move fairly freely; I only need cash. 'It's time to say goodbye, Tracker.'

'I'm sorry about that. Will it be as long this time?'

'I don't know. Maybe.' A sadness rushes through me. Can I do this? Can I ditch the laptop and live offline again? This past year has shown me that while I desperately wanted to change before, I didn't – I can't. So, like an alcoholic, I need to get rid of my vice and live one day at a time. 'Will you be here when I get back?'

'I'll always be here for you, Tiny.'

Tears fill my eyes, and I don't say goodbye. I log out of the chat room, disconnect the Internet connection, and close the laptop. I put it in my backpack, finish my coffee and brownie and set back out. It's lively here along Main Street, more touristy than even Block Island, more restaurants, shops, more traffic. I walk until I see a sign indicating a motel. It's another ten minutes until I come upon the place, the ocean a block up. I step into the motel office and pay for a room. I don't even check it out before heading to the beach.

I sit as close to the water as I can on the sand in my jeans, the sun starting to edge down in the blue sky. A small plane trails an advertisement for a happy hour at a local bar. Colorful umbrellas flap in the wind. Children run past, kicking sand up. I drink in the scent of coconut sunscreen. I trail my finger in the sand beside me, and it unearths a small seashell. I pick it up and study it; it shines white and bright in the afternoon sun. I remember the stones I collected on Block Island and wonder if this isn't a sign that this might be a place I'll stay for a while.

I stick the shell in the front pocket of my backpack.

EPILOGUE

My name is Helen White, a play on my French name, Hélène Leblanc. I have been in Falmouth for two months. I am housesitting a beach house for the couple that owns the shop where I repair bicycles on weekends. They live here year round, but always take the month of September in Europe. When their regular housesitter was taken ill, I offered and they accepted. I'm less expensive.

It's a typical gray beach house with four bedrooms and a wide front porch. I sit in the evenings on the swing and watch people pass along the beach. I've got my easel set up out here, and I've been experimenting with small watercolors of brightly colored flowers and seascapes. A gallery in Woods Hole has taken some of them on and they are selling quite well. I ride my bike out there along the paths.

I still worry that someone from my old life on Block Island will discover me here, but so far I have had no such encounter. I have gotten contact lenses again and have kept up my short auburn hair, although the shade is a little less harsh here than the one the Asian ladies gave me back in Montreal. I know I am not transformed completely, and I can't stay here forever, but it's a good transition place while I figure out what my next move is. I have already been online, investigating new places that might appeal to me.

I have not gotten rid of the laptop, but I don't go on the chat room anymore. I said goodbye, and I have so far resisted. Instead, I have delved deep into the web, searching for Tony DeMarco's site, just to see if I can find it. I've found a lot of sites, but so far I haven't been able to trace any of them back to him. I followed the bitcoins I marked, but they vanished like a magic trick after the third transfer. Sometimes I wish I'd brought the shadow with me, but I did the right thing leaving him behind.

I have found Adriana on social media and am stalking her. Although we are sisters, we have little in common. There is something to the nature versus nurture concept.

I am reading her social media posts – it's so easy to hack into accounts that sometimes I think about sending her a message telling her how to secure her privacy settings – when I hear something. I am on the porch in one of the wicker chairs, my laptop balancing on my knees, and I hear it again. A whistle, someone is whistling. I tune it out, but then it's closer, and I can't ignore it. I put the laptop on the side table next to my lemonade and stand up at the railing, peering down the sidewalk.

He is coming toward me, hands in his pockets. He is sauntering as though he has no cares. He spots me, but he doesn't quicken his pace. Every muscle is tense; I don't think I could move if I tried. I don't know how he found me; I left the shadow in the laptop in the apartment in New York. I glance back at the laptop on the table, my lemonade glass sweating a dark stain on the napkin beneath it. He must have gotten inside that one, too, when I wasn't looking. There was no other way he could have traced me here.

Zeke stands at the bottom of the steps and looks up at me, a smile spreading across his face.

'How did you find me?' I ask, my voice seeming to come from somewhere outside my body.

He comes up the steps and stands next to me, leaning down and resting his elbows on the railing, his hands folded. He stares out at the water. 'It's nice here. I can see why you stayed.' He turns his head up and looks at me. 'But it was too easy to find you this time.' He cocks his head toward the laptop, and I realize I was right: they put some sort of tracking device inside it.

But it's been two months.

Somehow he knows what I'm thinking. 'We wanted to give you a little time. Think about things. Do you want to be on the run forever?'

'I'm OK with it,' I say. 'Like you said, it's nice here.'

He stands up straight then, leans against the porch post, his hands in his pockets. 'The offer still stands.'

'What offer?'

'Come work for me, Tina. Use your talents for good instead of evil. Maybe I went off half-cocked about you going undercover with DeMarco. Maybe it was too fast, but I've been talking to my people about it. We can protect you.'

I shake my head. 'I think you had your answer two months ago when I left.'

Zeke runs a hand through his hair and takes a deep breath. 'Kids are dying, Tina. He's selling some bad shit through that site.'

'How do you know it's his site?'

He's quiet for a few seconds, then, 'That's where you come in.'

'I don't want to go undercover to trap a man who sells drugs that are killing people. Can you understand that?'

'Sure. I get it. So, then, say you don't go undercover. But what about this: you could still go online and help.'

I think about how much to tell him and decide that I am going to tell the truth. 'I've tried to find his site, Zeke. I've found a lot of them, but nothing that links to him. Sorry.' And I am sorry, because this leaves the door open and I don't know how I'm going to get rid of him.

'What if I work with you? I bet we'd make a good team. Just you and me.'

I can't help but smile. 'I don't know about that, Zeke. We've got a lot of baggage. I shot you, remember?'

'You can stay here,' he says then, surprising me. 'No one needs to know where you are. DeMarco doesn't have to know, my people don't have to know.'

'Did he go to Costa Rica?' I ask, remembering.

Zeke nods. 'Yeah, but he's back. We think he was meeting with suppliers there.' He pauses. 'He got your money. The transfer. He hasn't bothered your friends. We're still keeping an eye on them, but whatever deal you cut with him, well, he's honoring it.'

Relief rushes through me.

'I wish you would reconsider. You'd be on the payroll. Sort of like a confidential informant.'

'*Your* confidential informant? So it'll just be you and me?' I laugh. 'You and me were a long time ago. We were different people back then. At least I was.'

'But we know each other a lot better than you think. I think we'd work really well together.' There's something in his expression that I can't read. He comes toward me, puts his hands on the sides of my face and forces me to look at him, his eyes staring deep into mine. For a moment, I think he's going to kiss me, but he doesn't. And when he speaks, I can't breathe and my legs give out from underneath me.

'Le soleil brille aujourd'hui.'

He's Tracker.

Lightning Source UK Ltd.
Milton Keynes UK
UKOW03f1842080217
293944UK00001B/10/P